TATUM
COMES
HOME

TATUM COMES HOME

TATUM TALKS

with **MICA STONE**

KENSINGTON
PUBLISHING CORP.

www.kensingtonbooks.com

KENSINGTON BOOKS are published by

Kensington Publishing Corp.
119 West 40th Street
New York, NY 10018

ISBN: 978-1-4967-3945-2 (ebook)

ISBN: 978-1-4967-3944-5

First Kensington Trade Paperback Printing: November 2023

10 9 8 7 6 5 4 3 2 1

For all the good dogs I've known and loved:
Snickers, Duke, Takumi, Cheyenne, Dakota, Geisha,
Tobi-Wan-Kenobi, Smith, Wesson, Cowboy, Gunnar, Tootsie,
Angel, Bow . . . and Bully, of course

To Tatum. Thank you for being a light to those in the dark,
a beacon to those who need to be found, and a voice for the
voiceless.

Dear Reader,

If you're anything like me, pets are your favorite people. Maybe photos of pets outnumber humans ten to one on your phone. Or when you meet someone new, you remember the name of their dog but forget theirs. It's also possible the cute animals you follow on social media outnumber the accounts of people you know in real life—and that's where The Dog Agency comes in!

Just as actors and professional athletes often work with talent managers, so do many of your favorite animals on social media. At The Dog Agency, we help all kinds of pets share their stories and spread joy to people worldwide. Usually those stories are shared through viral videos and photos on social media, but now you'll get to know some of the internet's most popular pets with The Dog Agency Novels!

Each novel in The Dog Agency series brings you a heartwarming new adventure starring a different real-life celebrity pet, beginning with our first novel, *Tatum Comes Home*. This feelgood novel casts Tatum from @hi.this.is.tatum in a fictional story about an irrepressible, junk food-loving dog who must find his way home after accidentally hitching a ride in a stranger's pickup truck.

The *real* Tatum, thankfully, has never undergone such an ordeal, but readers will be charmed by the novel's universally uplifting themes of friendship, second chances, and what it means to call a place—or a person—home.

To continue following his (real-life) journey, visit @hi.this.is.tatum on Instagram and TikTok. And for news of more books from your favorite internet pets, stay tuned at KensingtonBooks.com and @TheDogAgency!

Loni Edwards Lunau

Loni Edwards Lunau

Founder and CEO,
The Dog Agency and PetCon

SUNDAY

CHAPTER 1

Rides in the truck are my favorite, but scary storms are not my favorite, so I don't know whose idea it was to have them at the same time. Also, after my ride wif Dad in the truck, I went to the North Pole I fink, cuz Dad was gone but Santa was there. Maybe I'm hungwee, but dis night is cwazy, but not too cwazy cuz pot roast is a real fing.

It was a little bit crazy to think a dog could go to sleep beneath a blanket in the bed of a truck parked in front of a store in Bangor, Maine, during the scariest storm the world had ever seen, only to wake up hours later near the Canadian border. Not only that, but to find himself staring at a man who looked like Santa Claus, big and jolly and round.

But there Tatum was, hungry, scared, cold, still damp, his foreleg aching from a wound he'd licked until it had stopped bleeding. This was really not how Tatum had expected his night to go. And he didn't understand how he'd got there.

All he'd wanted was to take a ride with his dad. Family outings were more fun than playing fetch and chase in the backyard. He made sure to let his mum and dad know he was always ready for a ride. Most of the time, they let him come along. The times he couldn't weren't any fun. He didn't like staying home. It always took his parents forever to get back.

He couldn't remember exactly how he'd hurt his leg. He'd been scampering back and forth, looking for shelter, wriggling deep into bushes, crawling under cars. When he'd finally found his dad's truck again, having run away, scared by the storm, he'd jumped into the open bed, shivering because he was wet and frightened. And then he'd gone to sleep.

"Hey there, little fella," the man said, his big hands spread out on the tailgate.

His voice was gruff, and it boomed. His eyes looked like they were twinkling behind his glasses, though it was hard to see his mouth with his bushy white whiskers. Also, it was really dark in the sky, and there weren't any lights. But Tatum was pretty sure the man was smiling.

He sounded super nice. "Considering I loaded up my gear in Bangor, and I ain't been back here to check on things since, I'd say you're a long way from home."

That was the last thing Tatum wanted to hear. He tucked his tail close and lowered his ears. He gave a little whimper, but mostly because his leg hurt and he was cold. He dropped his head. He wanted his dad. He wanted his mum. He wanted to go home and see Puddles.

"Aww, what's wrong, buddy?" The man patted the tailgate and then boosted one hip to sit on the edge.

The truck bounced a bit because the man was big. He wore overalls and a shirt that looked warm. It had a lot of brown and black squares. It made Tatum think of a blanket. He really, really missed his blanket and bed. And all of his toys. Especially his squishy shark.

He thought they must be parked in front of the man's house. On the side, there was a bench in a garden with some yellow flowers he thought were called daffodils growing around it. The house was white and had black shutters. It looked like a cozy house. It didn't look like a place where bad things happened, just good things. That made him feel better.

"C'mon. Let's get a look at you and see about finding something to eat, eh? It's late, but I could use a bite myself. That was the kind of drive I don't like making. Too long and terrible weather. I think I might have some leftover pot roast and gravy in the fridge. How 'bout it?"

Eating was the other thing Tatum was ready to do. And gravy made everything in the world taste so much better. He knew that from all the times his mum would put hot water on his food and stir it up until there was gravy in the bowl. His mum made magic happen like that.

He hobbled slowly toward the man, limping on three legs, worried by the frown on the man's face. Had he done something wrong? Was the man going to be mean to him? Because Tatum was really afraid. It was going to be hard to walk back to his family if he had to run away from a mean man who had said he was a long way from home.

"Oh, boy. That looks like it might need some stitches. Think you could come inside and let me get a better look? It's too late to do anything about it tonight 'cept clean it up a bit. Looks like you're shivering pretty bad. I'll run you over to the vet in the morning just in case. She'll get you fixed right up. She's a good friend of mine."

Tatum stopped when the man said the word *vet*. He'd been to too many when his family first took him home. He'd been in pretty bad shape before getting better, but he still didn't want to go. Even if the man said she was a friend, a vet was no place for a dog.

A dog needed a big yard to run and play in. A dog needed toys to chew on and sleep with. A dog needed a soft bed and lots of cuddles from his mum and dad.

Nope. He was sure of it. A dog did not need a vet.

"It'll be all right. Now c'mon. Let me take a look at what's left of your collar. See if you've got a name or a number on there so we can let your family know you're okay."

That made Tatum feel better. It was the best idea he'd heard all night. Still, he didn't rush forward but took his time and watched the man closely. Finally he was near enough for the man to reach him. The man moved slowly and touched Tatum gently. He smelled like he'd been outdoors, or had been driving with his window down and letting in the stormy air.

"Hmm. It looks like one of your tags got torn off. This ring keeping it on is loose, but this tag tells me your name is Tatum." The man chuckled and rubbed Tatum's head. "That sounds like a great name for a young fella like you. Tatum. I like it," he said, and laughed. "Now that we've got that all figured out, let's go eat."

At that, Tatum wagged his tail and smiled.

⟶⟶◆◀⟵

Back in Bangor, four hundred miles and six hours earlier, Charles Frazier was frantic. Frantic, breathless, and worried sick. His heart was pounding to rival the thunder of the storm. He couldn't believe this was happening. Every flash of lightning lit up his truck.

His empty truck.

He'd already started it to drive home, then stepped out to better situate the plastic tubs he'd picked up. He was in the middle of organizing the garage and wanted to finish before the workweek started the following day. Nicole had told him it could wait. He could finish next weekend; they had nothing planned. He should've listened to his wife.

If he had, he wouldn't be standing there alone, his heart ripped to shreds.

He'd seen the storm coming in, but the trip should've been a quick one. For the most part, it had been. Until the wind had started whipping the trees in the parking lot and blowing the tubs in the bed of his truck, causing them to bounce around.

He'd decided to move them into the cab. He'd had his back turned for only fifteen seconds. Maybe twenty. When he reached the back seat with the first tub, Tatum was gone.

Why had he left his door open? Tatum never got out of the truck without permission. But usually the weather wasn't slamming through like a hurricane. He knew how much Tatum hated storms. He had one particular closet he crawled into at home to wait them out. Sometimes Nicole would sit with him, rubbing his head and talking softly to keep him calm.

The first time he'd run in there hadn't been long after they'd brought him home from the shelter. He and Tatum had been racing across the backyard, rolling on the grass, having a great time becoming friends. Then Charles had picked up a stick to see if Tatum knew how to play fetch.

Tatum had frozen in his tracks, then tucked his tail between his legs, and finally bolted toward the open back door. Charles and Nicole had shared a look, then gone after him. It had taken several minutes to find him huddled and shaking in the closet. Charles had been the one to sit with him then, calming him, assuring him he was safe.

Charles didn't know why he was wasting time thinking about all that now. Probably because he didn't know what to do. He was soaked to the skin, which meant Tatum would be drenched as well, wherever he'd gotten himself to. And Charles had looked for him everywhere.

Inside the store. Around the back of the store. Beneath every single car in the lot. Nothing. *Nothing.*

"Tatum! C'mon, boy! Let's go home! Mum's waiting for us!"

He was going to have to call Nicole. He would much rather have given her the bad news in person, but he needed to stay put should Tatum find his way back. He sat on the edge of his seat, his door open, and hit the Call button. She answered almost immediately.

"Where are you? I've been calling and calling. You should've been home by now."

"I'm so sorry," he said, his voice breaking. "I left my phone in the truck. I didn't hear it."

"What? Charles, tell me. What's wrong?"

He could hear her voice trembling. She didn't even know what was happening, and she was as scared as he was. He was about to make things so much worse.

"It's Tatum, Nicole. I've lost him. He's gone."

A heartbeat of silence passed before she whispered, "What?"

He closed his eyes, feeling the water from his lashes running down his face. "I was putting the storage tubs in the back seat. My door was open. There was a loud crack of thunder. He jumped out and ran before I could turn around."

"And you've called him? And looked for him?"

"Yes, yes. I ran after him but couldn't see him. The rain is blinding. I looked under every car in the lot. I asked everyone I saw. I searched inside the store. Around the perimeter. Down the block both ways. Across the street. I can't find him anywhere. I'm soaked to the skin. I can't imagine he's in any better shape." He pulled in a shaking breath after that long rush of words. "I'm sorry, Nicole. I don't want to leave in case he comes back."

She didn't hesitate but asked, her voice steady and sure, "What do you need me to do?"

CHAPTER 2

*Turns out the North Pole is not just like on TV like Mum
and Dad watch wif me, it smells like dogs used to live
here. Reindeer isn't dogs I don't fink, but also I don't know
what reindeers is. Santa makes beds so I don't know what
elfs do when it not Christmas; also him is a doctor I fink.*

Jed Allen had been without a dog for two years now. Hard to believe it had been that long since he'd lost his Rosie. She'd been
such a good girl, the best friend and companion dogs were meant
to be. An Irish setter with gorgeous deep red hair that required
more maintenance than that of most people he'd known. She'd
loved to be groomed. Just loved it. Always with a smile, that girl.
And boy could she ever run. She never wanted to stop. They'd
trekked for miles, and she'd worn out Jed long before she'd been
ready to call it a day.

He'd been a dog owner, and dog lover, since he was five years
old. That was the year his folks had given him a puppy for Christmas. He'd opened the box that was making the funniest sounds
to find a ball of black fuzz and slobber and big brown eyes.

The pup had jumped into his lap, getting his clumsy legs all
tangled up in the box flaps, and peed all over himself and Jed. He
and his parents had laughed and laughed before cleaning up.
They hadn't even been mad. They knew what it meant to take on
a dog.

As an adult, Jed knew Christmas pups didn't always work out

for kids. But he and Sam had grown up together, best friends, him and his big black Lab. He'd lost him to old age just after he'd graduated high school. It made coming home from college for holidays bittersweet, sleeping in his bed without his buddy curled up at his feet.

He still hated thinking about it. Got a big ol' knot in his gut every time. He'd never understand why man's best friend hadn't been given a longer life span. Seemed to make more sense to stick together through all the years of thick and thin than share so few.

Being without a dog was tough these days, but he was growing older and wasn't sure adding that responsibility to his life was a good idea. Some mornings, it was all he could do to walk from his bedroom to the kitchen to make his coffee. Others, he got up ready to walk for miles. He'd hate disappointing or failing a pet who expected and deserved so much more.

Inside now with Tatum, he covered the table, which he'd thoroughly disinfect later, with a clean sheet. It was an old one, white with some faded yellow flowers, one he'd used in Rosie's bed. He'd spoiled her in her later years, but he'd wanted her comfortable. She'd been his trusted sidekick through some really hard times. And it was his business, no one else's, if he babied the pups in his care.

With Tatum looking on, Jed set the small bowl of pot roast and carrots he'd fixed on one side before he reached for Tatum. He did so slowly, carefully. He didn't want Tatum to bolt.

"I know this probably isn't what you're used to. Tables are for family meals. I imagine you know that. But it's better lighting up here, and I can get a good look at this wound."

Tatum wasn't too heavy; he was a rusty-brown color, his hair short and coarse, his eyes dark gold and intense. Looked like he had some bulldog in him. Great breed. So misunderstood. Friendly and loyal and protective. He was a sharp fella, taking in his surroundings, curious and aware.

Tatum scented the food and went to town on it. Jed hadn't given him too much. Just enough to distract him while he took a look at his leg. He wet a cloth and carefully cleaned away the dried blood and dirt, clipping away matted hair. Best to get him looked at by a vet the next day. He didn't see any glass or metal shards, but the vet would do a better cleaning than he could. Little guy probably needed some antibiotics. Maybe pain meds. Man, did Jed ever hate seeing a scared animal.

Jed gave Tatum another spoonful of food, saying, "This may sting a bit, but then we'll be done here, and we can make you up a comfy bed for the night."

Just as Tatum opened his mouth, Jed sprayed the antiseptic. Tatum yelped and scampered back, but Jed had been ready with a steadying arm wrapped around him. Tatum's nails skidded on the table but couldn't take hold, and finally he stilled.

"Shh, now. All done. I'm just going to wrap this up. You finish your food there. I used to have a cone, but I donated that with most of Rosie's things. Lucky you, huh?" Jed said, chuckling when Tatum's ears perked up at the word. "Guess you'll be staying here with me till we find your folks. Hopefully they chipped you and that won't take long."

Finished licking his bowl, Tatum sat back on his haunches while Jed bandaged his wound. It was seeping a bit, but not bleeding, and only took a minute to get wrapped up. Once Jed was done, he moved all the supplies to the side so he could lift Tatum down. That's when Jed realized how still Tatum was, sitting and staring at the wall beside the pantry door.

Jed followed the direction of Tatum's gaze. He doubted the pup was actually looking at the photos framed and hung there, but it was hard for Jed to see them and not be taken back.

"That big black Lab there? That's Sam. He was my first dog. My first pet. He was my best friend for thirteen long years. He lived a good long life. Most Labs don't have that thick coat, so he might've been a mix of Labrador and another sort of retriever. Boy, did he shed. I had to brush and de-shed him and even vacuum him sometimes."

That memory had Jed chuckling. Tatum looked at him with a curious uncertainty but gave a quick tail wag.

"No need to worry. I won't be vacuuming you, though I might dig up Rosie's de-shedding tool, if I still have it, and rid you of some of that loose hair. She used to beg for that. Guess it felt good, like an itch being scratched."

Tatum dropped to his belly then, his tail wagging again. Jed pointed to another picture. "That's Rosie there. I named her that because her coat made me think of red roses. My wife, Patty, she loved red roses. Brought them home to her as often as I could."

The memory had Jed swallowing hard. He knew it would always be that way, no matter how many years passed. "Lots of men give them to their women without knowing what their favorite flower is. I knew. Patty told me early on so I wouldn't waste my money on other things. That's when you know you've got a good woman. She's not afraid to speak her mind."

Tatum hunkered down, his chin on the table, his eyes solemn as he studied Jed. "Oh, you won't have to worry about that. Just about that leg of yours and getting back home. And I'll do my best to do most of the worrying for you."

Tatum was well cared for and no doubt missed as much as he was doing the missing. Jed had never lost one of his dogs for more than a few minutes, and that really wasn't losing. They'd just decided not to listen when he called. But he remembered that panicked sensation, all of his insides dropping to his feet. He didn't want Tatum's people to have to go through more of that than they already had. He'd get him to the vet first thing in the morning.

Dogs were something else, the way they got beneath a person's skin and in no time made their way to their heart. But that was okay, and no doubt exactly how the maker had intended, Jed mused, rubbing a hand over Tatum's head, smiling as Tatum closed his eyes.

It was then Jed realized how much he'd been talking since finding this little guy in the back of his truck. Huh. Other than the visit he'd just made to the VA in Augusta, and all the talking he'd gotten in during the trip, he didn't have a lot of interest in conversing with anyone, or anyone to converse with for that matter. And now he'd be heading to the vet in the morning.

That tied a knot of another whole color in Jed's gut, one he didn't want to think about that night. He pushed away from the table, his chair's legs scraping over the worn linoleum Patty had stayed after him for years to replace, and lifted Tatum to the floor.

He should've done it for her, for the both of them, but they'd been so busy. He'd just have to do it now for himself. But he'd pick the color he knew she'd wanted. Because this had been her home for most of her life, and he owed her memory that courtesy.

"C'mon, young fella. Let me leash you up and take you out, then we'll fix you a bed. I'm way past ready to crawl into mine."

Even if he'd be doing it by himself like he had for the last fourteen years.

CHAPTER 3

If I'm at Santa's house I bet Mum and Dad will be here in the morning cuz they don't leave me alone very much and never to sleep over at Santa's house. I bet when they come get me they will be really happy cuz whenever they come home they is super happy to see me. It gonna blow Dad's mind when he finds out he's been calling me a dog all dis time and I'm a reindeer, probably cuz we bof like carrots so it's confusing.

The crowd of friends and neighbors gathering to help Charles and Nicole search for Tatum continued to grow. They all huddled beneath the hardware store's front awning, doing their best to stay out of the worst of the rain. The store was closed, as were the others that shared the center's parking lot: a mail and shipping center, a specialty bakery, a store where everything was supposed to cost a dollar but now cost more. Everyone was bundled up in rain gear and sporting flashlights. Charles was amazed at the turnout. Humbled actually.

Nicole had made the phone calls. She'd posted to their neighborhood's social media emergency message board. She'd done a group text to nearly everyone local in her phone's contact list. Charles had continued to search while waiting for help to arrive at the specified time. Quite a few people hadn't waited but had joined him immediately.

They knew how much Tatum meant to their family. And Tatum

had a lot of friends of his own. Some he shared with Charles and Nicole, but some were the owners of dogs he played with at the park. Charles recorded some of Tatum's videos there and always drew an audience, who ended up following Tatum's adventures on Instagram and TikTok.

Surely with this much interest and the sizable turnout they'd find him. Charles shoved his hand in his pocket and wrapped it around something he'd found and needed to show Nicole. But first he needed to get the searchers searching.

"Hi, everyone! Over here! Let's get started!"

He wasn't sure anyone could hear him above the rain pounding the awning, and the thunder going off like bombs as lightning cracked in volatile bursts. "Nicole has worked out a grid of the neighborhood. She'll pencil you in and give you your boundary lines, okay?"

"And for those of you who want to get out of this mess and work from home, I've compiled a list of veterinarians and animal shelters in the area," Nicole shouted, waving the pages she'd slipped into plastic sleeves. "Some of them may still be open, if anyone wants to start there. I'm sure most are closed, but they still may have an emergency contact number. And if you need to leave a message, all of our contact information is printed at the top of the sheets."

"That's assuming you can get service. Landlines will be your best bet to get through," Charles added.

"Let me have one of those." It was Evelyn Roberts. She and her husband, Bill, lived next door. She was short and wiry and talked a mile a minute in contrast to her husband, who rarely spoke a word. "I can sit in my car and make calls while Bill searches."

"Same here," said Martha Lawrence. A widow with three cats, she lived on the other side of Evelyn, and the two were lifelong best friends. "Better use of my time since my knees are shot and I'm bound to step poorly in this weather."

Nicole stepped toward them, handing both a copy of the list. "Great. Thank you. Evelyn, you take the first ten vets. Martha, you take the next ten. Who wants to start on the shelters?"

Two more friends came forward, and Nicole assigned them their call sections. She then started handing out the maps with the grids to those who'd volunteered to take up where Charles had left off. He'd head back out in a minute, this time with Nicole at his side, but he wanted to finish up the thermos of chicken noodle soup she'd brought him.

He didn't know what he'd do without her. Which made what he had to do extra hard.

"Hey," Charles said, reaching for her hand. "I need to show you something."

"What?" Her eyes were wide and frightened. He'd thought about waiting until they were home but knew that wouldn't be fair, him knowing, Nicole not. They shared everything. Even the bad. It made the bad seem less so, though he wasn't sure anything would help with this.

And he had no idea when they'd be home again. He hated thinking of being there without Tatum. He dug his hand out of his pocket and opened it, showing her what he held in his palm.

"Charles!" She pressed fingertips to her lips then lifted the two tags that had been torn off Tatum's collar. "Where did you find these?"

He pointed. "Under that thick hedge. He probably scuttled up under there to hide and got his collar caught. The ring holding these two was always kinda janky."

"But his name tag? That one wasn't there?" she asked, and Charles shook his head. "Or anything from his collar? The buckle or any fabric or threads?"

"Just these. If the collar got torn on a branch and left threads, I'm sure they've long since washed away."

She let out a mournful sob and pressed her forehead to his

chest, shaking. "How long was he there, shivering, cold, wet, scared to death? I can't even stand thinking about it."

"I know," he said, cupping the back of her head, her hair dripping wet with rain. His chest ached as if he'd been punched repeatedly, and he supposed he had. His heart pounded and pounded and pounded, bruising his ribs. "He's smart. He's a survivor. We'll find him. I mean, look at all these people searching. How can we not? We just have to be as strong as he is."

Nicole stepped away and looked up, nodding. "You're right. You're right. Let's do this."

<hr>

It took Jed a while to fall asleep. Tatum was out like a light, but the little fella had had a heck of a day. Jed listened to his soft whuffing snore and smiled. Rosie's snore had been so loud the sound had nearly shaken the walls. Sam's too. Thinking of both had been a big part of why Jed couldn't sleep. But mostly it was the thought of taking Tatum to the vet.

That meant seeing Dr. Valerie Warren. And he hadn't seen her in the two years since she'd helped him send Rosie to her final resting place. She'd held his hand while he'd held Rosie's paw. Then she'd left him alone with his girl to grieve. Val had seen him at the absolute lowest point he'd been since losing Patty. Rosie had helped him move through that loss, being at his side every single moment he'd thought he was going to break down for good.

He'd known Val for years. They'd become fast friends, breaking for the occasional cup of coffee once Rosie's checkups were done. She'd walk with him and his girl out behind the clinic, where they'd discuss everything from the state of the world to favorite ways to prepare cod. They'd tell each other about growing up and share stories of family members who had passed long ago.

The only woman he'd ever known better was the one to whom

he'd been wed. He supposed he could find another vet to look at Tatum. But Val had taken care of Rosie since she'd come into Jed's life.

Tatum's condition told Jed he shared the same closeness with his family that Jed had with Rosie. Hopefully Val would find a microchip when she scanned. He knew she'd take care of Tatum.

Especially in light of the rapport they'd developed over the years. He'd always wondered if he hadn't lost Rosie and gone into such a funk if he and Val might've become more than friends.

But the past was the past and right now all that mattered was getting Tatum home.

MONDAY

CHAPTER 4

Dear road trip diary, I don't fink I'm actually a reindeer cuz Santa said he fed me canned dog food but also carrots. Also nobuddy ever told me Santa's real name is Jed, dat is what Murray called him. Also, there is no snow at the North Pole and no elves, and Mrs. Claus is a vet, which is weird cuz Mum and Dad loves vets but all the other animals at the vet are always scared. I don't fink I'm at the North Pole.

Though he'd slept poorly when he'd slept at all, Jed was up at dawn, long before Warren Veterinary opened for the day. It had been dark when he'd arrived home the previous night, and his attention had all been for Tatum. The pup seemed in good spirits. Jed had taken him out to do his business, given him his breakfast, and was now working on his own.

That morning, Jed needed to check his property for storm damage. Cable was out, so instead of listening to the news in the living room with his coffee, he turned on the kitchen radio while scrambling a couple of eggs after frying up his remaining three strips of bacon. The last of his eggs too, actually. He needed to get to the store.

Tatum watched from Rosie's old bed between the cabinets and the door to the carport that sat in front of the garage. Jed was all out of kibble—he hadn't had need for any for a long time now—

but he'd found a can of dog food in the pantry. Must've been one of the last he'd bought for Rosie because it hadn't yet expired. He'd added a spoonful of carrots and gravy on top, and Tatum had downed his meal in what seemed like two gulps.

Nothing like an appreciative customer, Jed mused with a smile. "Sorry, fella. I don't have any eggs to spare. Barely have enough for my own breakfast. One cup of coffee. One slice of toast. Someone around here needs to get to shopping." He looked down at his plate. "Though, I suppose, I could give up a slice of this bacon if you're interested."

Tatum sat up in the bed and cocked his head to the side.

Jed could almost hear him saying, *Bacon?* He grinned and reached for the longest strip. "Good stuff, bacon. Always found it great for training dogs. Let's see what you know," he said as he snapped an inch-long piece from one end.

Tatum straightened his head and went perfectly still. A drop of saliva hung from his lower lip.

Jed held out one hand and slowly lowered it as he said, "Down."

Tatum dropped to his belly on the bed, and Jed said, "Good boy," and tossed him the treat. It disappeared as if it were vapor, and Tatum wagged his tail.

"Okay, let's try this one." Another piece of bacon at the ready, he commanded, "Sit!"

Tatum scrambled up to his haunches, most of his front weight on his good leg.

Jed held out his hand with the bacon in his palm and said, "Stay."

Tatum didn't move, then Jed said, "Come," and Tatum walked toward him, stopping and waiting for Jed to say more.

He thought for a moment, commanding Tatum, "Stay," and backed up a couple of steps before setting the bacon on the floor. Tatum moved forward, then Jed said, "Leave it."

All Tatum did was stare at Jed, his big brown eyes seeking approval. He seemed to want that almost as much as the bacon, which had Jed wondering what he'd been through in his young life.

"Good boy. Good dog. Go ahead," he added with a nod. "You earned it."

Tatum gobbled the bite, and Jed rubbed his head, then handed him the rest of the piece. Tatum carried it with him back to the bed while Jed stood at the stove to eat.

He thought back to Rosie. He thought back to Sam. They'd both taken to learning as if doing that for him was the highlight of their day. He loved that loyalty. It made for such a great relationship, man and his best friend. Tatum's owner had to be missing the pup sorely.

Jed got back to his food, and it occurred to him as he did that he was out of a whole lot more than what he ate for breakfast. He got that way, letting things slide until the last minute, when what he should've been doing was taking care of himself.

He'd been bad about doing that after losing his Patty, but instead of bouncing back as he learned to live with the grief, he'd gotten worse. He really wasn't sure why but wouldn't doubt his was an infliction other widowers shared.

"Guess I'll run in and pick up a few things after we see Valerie. Weather's good. You'll be fine in the truck. Won't take me but ten minutes to grab what we need. I tend to eat the same things over and over," he admitted. "Could be I need to get out of that rut, whaddaya say?"

Tatum wagged his tail, catching it up in the bed's sheet, then standing and turning in a circle to free himself. Jed just shook his head, scraping up the last bite of his eggs, then washing his plate, his utensils, and the pan he'd used, racking them in the drainer next to the sink.

According to the news, a whole swath of the state was dealing with power outages, and even more people were without cell service. Jed picked up his phone off the kitchen charger and sure enough: completely useless since he had no Wi-Fi signal without cable and no data available with the cell outage.

"Guess we're back to living in the dark ages," he said to himself, though Tatum wagged his tail again. "Have to resort to the landline to call the vet in a bit. Let me finish off my coffee here, and we'll go out and see what's what in the yard."

Jed's house sat on a half acre. After living through a couple of storms that brought trees down on his childhood home, he'd cleared away any within striking distance. He still had a pretty nice wooded area out back. Patty had loved their private little park, and he'd continued to keep the brush cleared away. Made for easy walking when he'd gone out with Rosie.

The sun was up just enough to give him a good view of the state of things. Didn't look too bad. Nothing he shouldn't be able to clean up on his own. He hooked Tatum's leash to a wrought iron curlicue on the arm of the bench in Patty's reflection garden. Tatum cocked his head to one side and sat, his ears perked, his nose lifted and scenting the air.

"You'll need to watch from here, little fella," Jed told him, scratching behind his ears. "I don't want you taking off after something that smells good, and there is a whole lot of that out here. Rosie told me so many a time. But she knew her way around and never went far."

The sound of a truck engine had Jed looking up in time to see Murray Tiller pull to a stop on the driveway, just short of the carport, and exit the pickup's cab.

Murray raised a hand. "Hey, Jed. How'd you fare overnight?"

"Mornin', Murray. I was on the road for most of it, but doesn't seem too bad." He gestured toward the wooded part of the yard. "One big limb, the rest small branches. How 'bout yourself?"

"Same." Murray adjusted his cap against the bright morning sun. "Not counting on too much of this today. Hear more storms are about to blow in."

Jed nodded. "That's what the weather report said. Main reason

I wanted to get out here and clean up yesterday's mess. Figure I'll have more to do tomorrow."

Murray nodded toward Tatum. "I see you've got a new friend there."

Jed looked down. Tatum was giving Murray a serious once-over but was being polite about it. That brought a big smile to Jed's face. This one came from good people. Well behaved. " 'Bout to take him to Warren's and get his leg looked at. His name's Tatum. He hopped a ride in the back of my truck, and I gotta figure out where he belongs."

Murray bobbed his head. "Val should be able to help with that if he's got a microchip."

Jed found himself frowning. Val? Since when was Murray on a first-name basis with Val? He rolled his neck to the right and popped it. "You still taking that old shepherd of yours to see her?"

"I am," Murray said with a nod as he smiled. "And I picked up a new gelding recently."

"That so?"

"Yep. I'd been thinking of getting back to riding." Murray scratched the back of his head, then resituated his cap. "Val's been coming out to check on him. Had some sort of parasite, but she got him all fixed up. Good as new now."

Jed leaned down and stroked his palm over Tatum's head a couple of times, smoothing his hair and rubbing his ears while gathering his wits. Didn't make a lick of sense that Murray's story had him getting riled. No sense at all. Even if Murray was all cleaned up like he had a reason to be. More reason than a new horse. He cleared his throat.

"She's the best vet in the area for sure," he said to Murray's laugh.

"I'm thinking maybe the entire state." A lopsided grin pulled at Murray's left cheek. "Not many docs of any sort who'll come out before work and again after closing up shop for the day."

As if sensing the tightening in Jed's gut, Tatum sidled closer. Jed kept his hand on the little fella's head, his own heart warming with memories of a sidekick having his back. He missed that. He hadn't realized how much until this moment. Until Tatum.

His chest swelled with a new emotion. A happy one. A good-feeling one. *Thank you, little fella. I needed that.* "Tatum, this is Murray. He's an old friend. No need to worry. No danger here. And I've still got enough pot roast left that I can top off your kibble tonight."

"Val might object to that diet," Murray said, his tone a bit too know-it-all for Jed's liking.

But that was okay. That was just fine. Right now, he didn't have time to worry about Murray and Val. He needed to get Tatum's leg stitched up and find a way to get him home.

CHAPTER 5

Dear road trip diary, I'm losing it I fink. I thought I saw Puddles today, but I didn't—maybe it was his way bigger bwother. I'm just hangin wif Jed now, I wonder where Mum and Dad are. Maybe they took a vacation, else they would've come to find me? Jed doesn't know I don't like to swim, or water, or rain, or puddles the watery kind. . . . Did Dad even give him a list of Tatum stuff like he does when other people hang out wif me?

The man's name was Jed. Tatum had heard the visitor Murray call him that, and he'd told someone on the phone who he was when he called. Tatum thought it was the vet. He felt a little bit better that morning. Especially since he'd been able to go outside and walk around and sniff the end of the storm to see if he could get a hint of home.

The night before, Jed had washed his wound and wrapped it up after smearing on some kind of goo that Tatum had tried to lick off through the gauze but couldn't. He'd slept pretty good on a bed in Jed's room. It smelled like another dog, even covered up with the soft sheet Jed had put on it before telling him good night. It made him think of his bed at home. But he didn't have his pillows. He missed his pillows. He missed his soft toys.

But at least Jed was giving him a ride in his truck, and this time he was sitting in the seat and not in the back, where he'd been so cold and wet. He was warm and dry now, and he really wasn't as scared as he'd been during the storm attack. He was still sad. He would always be sad without his family, but he thought the man Jed was trying to help get him home.

He'd been right about Jed being nice. And he made a really good pot roast with gravy, even if earlier that morning all he'd fed Tatum was a tiny bite with his can of food while Jed had eaten toast and eggs and bacon. At least he'd shared his bacon. That had been super nice. Tatum hadn't even minded working for it because he loved bacon like crazy.

The drive took longer than Tatum had expected. At home, the vet was really close. Too close if you asked Tatum, but out here where Jed lived there was a lot of space between the buildings. There were houses and a lot of what he thought were barns. But there weren't many stores or parks or Dunkin' like there were at home. Tatum really missed Dunkin'.

The truck stopped in front of a building that had pictures of dogs on it. Cats too. What Tatum thought were horses and goats, but he hadn't seen any for a long time to really remember. There were a lot of trees around, which was good 'cause he needed to do his business.

Jed got out and hooked the leash to Tatum's collar and helped him down. "I imagine you could manage on your own, but let's see what the vet says about that leg before you go jumping, eh?"

Tatum ignored that part about his leg and the vet and headed for the closest tree, sniffing around to find the best spot so everyone who came after would know he'd been here.

There had been a whole lot of dogs there already that day. He wondered if they'd had to get their legs looked at too. He wasn't sure how he felt about that. He wished he was with his dad instead of with Jed. Then he wouldn't be so nervous. Even if Jed was nice.

"All done?" Jed asked, because Tatum was taking his time, hoping maybe Jed would forget and they could go back to his house and have pot roast for lunch.

But Jed said, "C'mon, fella. Sooner we get inside, sooner we can go home."

Tatum couldn't argue with that, even if he wanted to go to his own home more than he wanted to go to Jed's. Inside, the building smelled like so many animals he couldn't count them all. Once Jed had sat, Tatum lay down and curled up into a ball, tucking his tail close.

"It's okay, young fella. My friend Val's the vet. Been quite a while since I've seen her. I was close to getting sweet on her once but didn't think it was a good idea. Decided it best to get myself straightened out before bringing another person into my life, you know?"

Jed cleared his throat, and his face, the part Tatum could see above his whiskers, turned a brighter color than the rest. "Anyway, she's going to take a look at your leg and scan to see if you've got a chip so we can get you back to your family. Does that sound good?"

Tatum yipped. He really, really wanted to see his family. Then they could look at his leg. His mum would probably spray it with something stinky, but that was okay. At least he'd be home—

Wait a minute! Was that Puddles over there in that fish tank? It was a really big one. Like a gazillion times bigger than the one Puddles lived in at home. And there were so many fish. Was this where lost fish came? Had the storm attack scared Puddles and he'd got lost too? Tatum sat up and walked as far as his leash would take him, then tugged and looked back at Jed.

"What's up, buddy? You want to check out the aquarium? Sure thing," Jed said, and moved to sit in a chair beside the big glass tank. "I'd be worried if you were a cat, and I suppose some dogs like to go fishing, but we're just going to watch them swim now, okay?"

Tatum's nails skated on the floor. He couldn't wait to see Puddles and say hi. It was almost as good as being at home, and he could tell him—

Oh, no. That wasn't Puddles. He was too big. He'd looked so much smaller from across the room. Tatum sat and stared, watching the fish play. At least they were having fun. And if Puddles did get lost, this would be a good place for him to come and wait.

One of the fish swam up to the edge of the glass and stayed there, staring at Tatum. He moved closer, close enough to press his nose to the glass. The fish opened and closed its mouth like it was talking. Then it darted away so fast it left bubbles. Tatum yipped again. He wanted to pop them, but then all the fish swam fast to the corner of the tank. All the fish except the one who looked like Puddles. He stayed there and blinked at Tatum.

And kept him company while he waited for the vet.

—————⋙•⋘—————

"Good morning, Jed."

At the receptionist's greeting, Jed looked up. Her name was June. She'd been working with Val as long as he'd been coming to Warren Veterinary. She was also the clinic's senior vet tech. She had as good a rapport with the animals as Val. They made one heck of a team.

"Mornin', June."

She'd been in the rear of the building and had no doubt heard the door chime when he and Tatum had come in.

"Good to see you again."

"Good to see you too." Her smile, as she leaned across the high counter to look down at Tatum, was warm and welcoming, just as friendly as could be. "And who's this with you?"

Jed glanced at his new sidekick and found June's smile contagious. Dogs did that to him. Always had. Always would. "This fella's name is Tatum."

"Hello, Tatum." She tossed him a treat, which he caught and gobbled. She tossed him one more, saying, "Good dog," then turned her attention to Jed.

He didn't think he'd ever seen her actually sit at her desk. Like Val, she spent her days on her feet.

"When you called, I thought maybe you'd found yourself a new companion. But good for you, rescuing a lost pup."

"He hopped my train in Bangor. I'm hoping to get him home."

At that, Tatum cocked his head. Jed wasn't sure if it was the word *train* or the word *home*, though he was pretty sure it was the latter. He scratched Tatum's neck, raising a cloud of red hair. It wouldn't take much for Jed to grow attached to the little guy. He gave him a chuckle at every turn. Maybe, like the Grinch at Christmas, Jed's heart was beginning to thaw.

"I'll bet someone is really missing him. He certainly looks well cared for," June said, making a note on a small yellow legal pad rather than her usual computer tablet. Clinic's network was probably down like everything else's in the area. "I'll get you back to see Dr. Warren in just a few."

"Thanks, June," Jed said, getting to his feet. "Do you think you could go ahead and scan to see if he's chipped? If so, I could call his folks now. . . ." He let the sentence trail, her apologetic expression the only answer he needed. "The service is down. I should've realized."

June looked up. "I can scan him, but a lot of chips up this way are registered to Maine Pets. They're a smaller registry, and their server took a hit last night. They're going to be offline for a couple of days until they get the data restored from their backup."

"Appreciate it," Jed said, as June came around the counter. He felt as if he was breaking his promise to Tatum, knowing the delay couldn't be helped. "The storm was a doozy. The downside of technology, I guess."

"Like I thought." June showed him the display that read *Maine Pets.* "I hear we're in for another round tonight. Hang on another minute or two. I'll be right back to get you."

"Will do." Jed knew about the weather from the morning's

forecast, and from Murray, but he still didn't like the idea of more wind, rain, and damage. Obviously, neither did Tatum. Smart as a whip, this one. Little fella dropped to the floor, his ears down, his tail close to his body.

Jed gave a firm, reassuring pat to his side. "It's okay. You'll be safe and dry with me. And I won't stop looking for your folks. No need to worry. Just might take another couple of days."

Tatum's tail swept the floor, a quick back-and-forth.

Probably worried more at the moment about seeing the vet, Jed mused while Tatum stared at the aquarium and watched the fish swim.

"Do you like to swim? I'll bet you do. Most dogs I've known take to the water like they've got gills of their own. I've always envied that. I float like a rock."

At that, Tatum sat up and yipped, and Jed laughed.

CHAPTER 6

Dear road trip diary, Val is just like all the vets where I live cuz she seems nice and gives me tweats but also none of the other animals is happy to be there. Jed looks at Val like Dad looks at Mum, which is the same as me when I look at the lady in the drive-fru window at the nuggets place. Val and Jed and me is gunna get more food, so I fink I'm on vacation like Mum and Dad.

"Jedediah." Val closed the door and opened her arms, moving toward him as if nothing could keep them apart. She was the only person in his life now to use his full name. It had been a while since he'd heard it spoken. "It is so good to see you. It's been too long. It's been ages."

Jed had to admit to a little skip in his step at his first sight of Valerie Warren in two years. He shouldn't have been surprised, but time was tricky. He'd forgotten how well they'd clicked. How perfectly her cloud of deep woodsy-brown curls suited her. Last he'd seen her, she'd been wearing a scrub cap printed with too-fat white cats on a background of black.

He supposed it was a defense mechanism, the forgetting what mattered and remembering an item as insignificant as a scrub cap's design. It kept the human heart safe from breaking into an irreparable pile of rubble. And now to feel her close, hugging him, well, he pushed away the regret over losing contact. All he wanted right now was to enjoy the moment.

She still smelled like springtime. That one thing would be with him always.

"Good to see you too. How have you been?" He waited for her to sit on the exam room's long bench before he joined her. Tatum sat between them on the floor.

"Same as always," she said, her eyes a sparkling green, her smile inviting. "I still look for you in Kepper's, you know. Every time I'm there. We used to cross paths so often."

"Most of the time in front of the ice cream case." Funny the little things that stuck with a person. "Vanilla toffee for me. Rocky road for you."

"Which is apparently in high demand since its slot, to this day," she said, lifting an index finger and her voice, "is always empty."

"I know. I don't go out much these days, but I still look for the rocky road." He wasn't even sure he'd been aware of how close he stuck to home until making the admission, though running out of eggs and other perishables should've clued him in. His life had become . . . stale. "And you know the size of my freezer. I stock up about once a month and don't even go through all of that."

"If that's the case, I'm going to send you a crate of fresh fruits and vegetables every week," she said with a laugh. "Man cannot live on frozen food alone. It never tastes as good."

Jed started to object, but Val didn't give him a chance. "Now," she said, "tell me about your little friend here." She rubbed Tatum's head, then reached for his name tag. "Hello, Tatum. I'm Dr. Valerie. I'm going to take a look at your leg, okay? Would you like a biscuit?"

Getting to her feet, she crossed the small room, her athletic shoes squeaking on the tile floor, and reached into a jar on the counter. Returning, she offered the treat to Tatum.

Not a surprise to Jed, he wolfed it down, already getting spoiled. "He's a big fan of food. That much I've learned."

"Good to see his appetite remains," Val said, bending to gather

Tatum in her arms and lift him to the exam table. "Now tell me how you came across him."

Jed told her the story of his overnight trip to Augusta and his return stop in Bangor. "I feel terrible. I had no idea he was in my truck. I'm planning on calling the store, see if anyone knows anything about him. But he could've come from anywhere, you know?"

"Don't beat yourself up," she said, opening Tatum's mouth, looking at his tongue and teeth, then checking his ears, his spine, his knees, his hips, his abdomen. "He was hiding from the storm and you were focused on getting home in all of that mess."

That didn't make Jed feel any better.

Val glanced over, smiling. "I'll bet you've enjoyed his company."

"Actually, yeah. I have," Jed admitted. He wasn't surprised. He loved dogs. He just hadn't expected Tatum to work his way under his skin so easily. That truth left him with some thinking to do. Maybe he wasn't as ready to live alone as he'd convinced himself after Rosie. "Figure I'll pick up a small bag of kibble on my way home. I found a can of Rosie's food in the back of the pantry this morning. He wasn't as excited about that as he was at smelling my eggs."

"Don't buy too much or you'll be needing him to stay to eat it all."

Jed laughed at that. "I'll keep him as long as it takes to find his people. Just kills me to think he might've come from right around the corner."

"Then think about getting him home instead. And don't worry about the kibble. I'll give you a bag to take with you. On the house."

"Thanks for that," he said, feeling lighter than he had in a long time. "I appreciate it."

"He's a great dog. And we all need good friends in our lives," she said, giving him a smile full of endless possibilities. It was a smile that took hold. A smile with roots. "Dogs are man's best friend. Or so the saying goes."

"Best when it comes to four-legged types anyway," Jed replied, earning another happy expression while Val shone a light on Tatum's wound.

"You've always been so good with your dogs, Jedediah. If you don't find this one's people, you should think about adopting him. You two seem meant for each other," Val said, before stepping into the hallway to call for June.

"Oh, I'll find them," Jed assured her once she was back standing across the exam table from him. "It might take some time, and I may need some help, but I'll find them. I owe him that much. I owe it to them too, for causing the heartache they must be suffering."

He hated thinking about it. Doing so caused the worst sort of hitch in his chest. He leaned down and nuzzled his face to Tatum's before leaving the exam room. "I promise you. I'll get you home."

———※·◆·※———

"He'll be fine," Val said, snapping off her gloves as June bustled about behind her cleaning up the counter and tossing away the trash. "The antibiotic injection will take care of any infection worries. The dose of pain meds will wear off soon, but he'll be groggy for a bit. Bring him back in ten days and I'll clip the stitches, unless you want to do that yourself."

"I'm hoping he'll be home in ten days," Jed said, lifting Tatum to the floor before either June or Val could do it. He didn't know why. Both were perfectly capable. "Any more word on when the registry might be restored?"

"No, but I'll call you. Or, if you want . . ." She paused, obviously working through some thoughts. "Wait here just a minute," she said, following June from the room.

Jed nodded, settling back onto the exam room's bench and

holding Tatum close to his knees. "That wasn't so bad, was it? All done, with extra biscuits, and now we just have to get the info from your chip to get you home."

Tatum turned his head around and rested his chin on Jed's thigh.

Tatum's eyes were soulful, and Jed could see his confusion. Of course he was confused. Twenty-four hours ago he'd been at home with his family, playing with his toys or curled up in his bed, no doubt happy as could be. Now he was safe, sure, but did he understand that? Did he know that Jed was a good guy? That Val had his best interests at heart?

Dogs were so smart, so intuitive, really good at reading people, but Jed still hated seeing this little guy look so forlorn. It wrecked his too-oft broken heart and his eyes grew misty, blurring behind his glasses. He took them off and used his sleeve to clear his vision.

"Sorry about that," Val said, coming into the room as he returned his glasses to his face and cleared his throat. "I was looking at the day's appointments. June's calling two of the patients to see if they can come in earlier, and that frees me up for the afternoon."

"Okay," Jed said, following her progress as she came to sit beside him, not sure what she was getting at but enjoying her company and curious.

"Let's take a drive." She patted his knee, then Tatum's head, her eyes bright. "There's a mobile vet in Shireton today. I just spoke with him. He works with Maine Pets and keeps an offline database, so there's a good chance he'll have Tatum's contact info. We could grab some dinner while we're there, if you'd like. Do some catching up once we call Tatum's family."

At those words, Tatum's ears perked up. Jed chuckled.

Val scratched Tatum's chin. "I guess you like that idea, huh, Tatum?"

He gave a couple of yips, and Jed laughed.

"Does that mean it's a date?" she asked, her gaze searching out Jed's. "I mean, you have Tatum's permission, so . . ."

He nodded, his heart full, and chuckled again. "It's a date."

"Excellent," she said, squeezing his arm. "Let me finish up here, and I'll swing by your place around one, one thirty. Does that work for you?"

Per the usual, Jed had nothing on his plate at that time of the day, but he'd have rearranged his schedule, along with the moon and the stars, if he'd needed to. "Absolutely."

CHAPTER 7

*I went for a ride in the truck wif Val and Jed today. Well,
kinda—I was doin' a snooze. Also it was more like a dog
bus for a vet cuz it had everyfing the pet store has.*

Jed stared out the passenger-side window while Val drove them
to Shireton. She had an oversize SUV and had decked out the
cargo area with kibble, water, bowls, collars, leashes, and basic
medical supplies. She could suture on site, administer antibiotics
or pain relievers, or knock out an animal as large as a horse.

Now, in the back seat as Val drove, Tatum whuffed softly.
Little fella had been through a lot and had some sleep to catch
up on.

"Kinda surprised he passed out. Figured he'd hang his nose
out the window all the way," Jed said.

"It's been a long twenty-four hours for him."

Jed nodded, shifting straighter in his seat and looking forward.
"I was just thinking about the time you stitched up Rosie after she
got caught in all that wire."

A smile passed over Val's face. "That time you swore you'd
never walk a dog again without a harness?"

"I stuck to that too," Jed reminded her. "Until I got Rosie
trained. This fella knows his commands."

"Did the wire leave scars? On your arms? I never asked."

"A couple of strips here and there." He pushed up one sleeve and pointed out the skin that was whiter than the rest. "No real damage."

"I remember Rosie having the same bare spots on her neck."

"Yep, but she recovered nicely. And her hair hid the scars."

They settled into a comfortable silence, the only sounds those coming from Tatum and the road clicking by under the wheels. The radio was on, but the volume was low. All Jed could hear was the sound of muted voices. He thought it was probably the news.

"Why haven't you gotten another dog?" Val's question came out of the blue and surprised him. "I've never known you to be without one."

It was a question he'd asked himself more than once during the past two years. "I've convinced myself it wouldn't be fair. I can't do long walks anymore. Knees are shot."

"You don't have to do long walks. An older dog would be fine with shorter, slower ones."

Jed snorted in response. "Because shorter and slower would fit me?"

"They fit me, for sure," Val said with a chuckle.

"I have a hard time believing that. You're fit as a fiddle."

This time it was Val who snorted. "From all outward appearances, sure. But my knees are just as bad as yours, I imagine. And arthritis is taking too much out of my hands. I'm not sure how much longer I'll keep practicing."

That surprised him. He wasn't sure why. She was younger than him, though not by much. He tended to forget that, to think of her as years away from being eligible for all the senior discounts he forgot to take advantage of. "You're thinking of retiring?"

She looked over and smiled. "It seems to suit you."

"Maybe. Though I've been thinking that I need to find something more to do than putter."

"Putter," Val said, then they both broke out laughing.

The sound woke Tatum. He sat up and stuck his head over the seat between them.

Jed reached up and scratched his chin. "Have a good nap, buddy?"

Tatum yawned and lay back down.

"Guess he wasn't quite done," Val said, glancing in her rear-view mirror. "Would you mind if we grabbed dinner once we're back home rather than searching out a place up here?"

"Sounds good."

"I was thinking Marbury's. I haven't been there in ages and could use a good lobster roll."

"Now that sounds extra good," Jed said, his stomach already tumbling. "Can't remember the last one I had. Can't really remember the last time I ate someone else's cooking. And road trip fast food doesn't count."

"Why were you eating road trip fast food?"

"I went to Augusta over the weekend."

"That's right, though . . ." She frowned, then asked, "Did you tell me why?"

"Not sure I did. I went to the VA to see an old friend. Stopped in Bangor on the way home." He glanced back at Tatum. "That's where this guy ended up in my truck, I'm sure."

Val was quiet for a long moment, her eyes on the road ahead. In the distance, the clouds were darkening, getting ready to bring more storms. "I'm a pretty good cook, you know."

Actually, he didn't. "I don't think I've had the privilege of eating a meal you prepared."

She gave a sharp burst of a laugh. "Not sure I'd call it a privilege, but I'd love to cook for you. Cooking for one isn't as much fun. And for some reason I always take shortcuts I shouldn't when it's just me eating."

"I get that. Food's more about sustenance these days. I eat a lot of eggs, a lot of sandwiches." Too many considering how full his freezer was. "I did make a pot roast the other night. Think I've eaten on it three days now. It's how I got Tatum to trust me."

"Dogs are simple, really. Treat them right and you'll have a loyal, protective friend for life," she said, then after a moment's thought, added, "Though I guess it's not much different with people."

"Nope. Not different at all. Just takes finding the right one," Jed said, thinking he may have been lucky now twice in his life.

CHAPTER 8

Dear Me, not every lady that looks like Mum is Mum. Also sometimes vets live in big trucks, so Dad may try and trick you some day when he doesn't say vet, but you see a big truck like you did today. I am learning a lot on vacation, but maybe dis is school like where Mum works, I don't know it.

Even though he was trying extra hard not to be tired, the farther Dr. Valerie drove, the harder it grew for Tatum to stay awake. Being so sleepy meant he was having trouble remembering that he was on his third ride of the day.

He never took three rides in one day. He didn't ever want to forget, so he thought carefully and reminded himself. First, he'd gone with Jed to see Dr. Valerie. Then he'd gone home with Jed and stayed in the truck and napped while Jed bought eggs.

Now he was going somewhere with Jed and Dr. Valerie both. He liked that they took him everywhere with them. He'd have to make sure his dad knew this was something fun other people did, and that he could go with him all the time, and he would never lose count of how many trips they took. And most important: he would never run off again. Ever.

His dad and his mum took him for Puppuccinos sometimes, but he wanted them to know he didn't always need a treat. That just sticking his nose out the window and smelling new things was a super fun one. An adventure really. He loved adventures.

Especially when his whole family came along. He'd have to tell them how Jed and Dr. Valerie had taken him on one to help him get home. He couldn't wait!

"A mobile vet, huh? That sounds like it would be interesting." Jed was sitting in the front seat, but Dr. Valerie was driving this time. "More of a variety of patients, I'd imagine."

Tatum had heard them talking about her truck, which made him think of a big box, being the best choice for the trip. Jed's truck was getting old. Like Jed, Tatum supposed. But now they were talking about another vet. He really hoped he didn't have to see another vet. Was that where they were going? Was that their idea of an adventure? Because it sure wasn't his. Adventures were fun. Vets were not. And seeing a vet had nothing to do with getting him home.

Did it?

"He does get to see a lot of unusual cases, and a lot of the countryside, but mostly it's vaccinations, dispensing heartworm medication and flea and tick treatment, things like that." Dr. Valerie glanced back at Tatum in her mirror and smiled. "It's easier for him to make a round through the smaller towns each month than for all of those pet owners to come to him."

Tatum hated fleas. He hadn't had them in a long time. His family made sure of that, but he remembered when he had how he'd scratch and scratch and they'd never go away.

He didn't like thinking about that, so he sniffed the air. Dr. Valerie had left open the window in the back just enough for his nose. Some of the smells were the same as at home, but there were a lot more animals out here. He thought there might be rabbits and squirrels, but there were some he didn't think he'd smelled before. They smelled big. Really big.

He sat back down in the seat.

"I was thinking," Dr. Valerie said, "that if Dr. Hinton can't help with the registry, we can start calling vets and shelters near Bangor. June can do some of that, but maybe you can help. You did say you needed more to do than putter."

Jed laughed. "Happy to do it all. You and June have enough on your plates. Just point me in the right direction."

"Great. As soon as we check with Dr. Hinton, and get that lobster roll, I'll set you up. All of a sudden, I'm starving. I feel like I haven't eaten in days."

Jed glanced back at Tatum. "What do you think, little fella? Sound like a plan?"

Tatum wagged his tail but kept his chin on the seat. Jed and Dr. Valerie had been talking about a lot of things: chips and scans and phone calls and lobster rolls. He knew about those and would be happy to eat five or ten. He didn't know about chips except for the ones that came in a bag his mum ate but wouldn't share even when he asked nicely, doing tricks and everything. And if Jed called his dad, he would answer. Tatum knew his dad had a phone he talked on all the time. He used it to take videos too.

So except for the part about seeing another vet, Tatum decided this was a good plan for sure. Jed was full of really good plans. Tatum thought he needed a dog for himself because he would be a really good dog dad. And Dr. Valerie would be a good dog mum. Tatum hoped they could find their own dogs soon. He didn't want them to be lonely after he was back home with his mum and dad and silly ol' Puddles.

He yawned and decided to take another nap. Going to see Dr. Valerie had worn him out with all the poking around and looking in his ears and mouth. The stitches hadn't hurt, but the shots had stung. At least his leg had stopped aching. He didn't like the way it was all wrapped up, but the bandage was a bright blue and that was pretty cool. Dr. Valerie had done a good job. He would get better now, and it would be easier to run and play when he got home.

He woke up later when the truck had stopped moving. Jed and Dr. Valerie weren't inside with him. Tatum sat up, worried, then moved closer to the window. It was still open enough for him to sniff around. There they were, Jed and Dr. Valerie, talking to another man.

The man had a giant truck that looked more like a house. Tatum did some more sniffing. Yep. Lots and lots of animals had been here. So many it made him sneeze. Twice.

Jed heard him and looked back. He made a gesture like showing him off to the tall man. He wasn't as old as Jed. He was more like Dad. And his beard was dark brown. He had on a hat, but he was wearing it backward. Tatum didn't know why. Maybe because now that it was getting dark and cloudy again, there wasn't any more sun to keep out of his face.

His house truck was parked in front of a store that looked like a big red barn. It had a whole bunch of tractors parked on the other side, and signs with words and pictures of animals that Tatum knew lived on farms. On the other side was a big pasture. And on the other side of that were trees. A lot of trees. Not like trees from a park, or a yard, but the woods, where animals were wild. Did wild animals come here to see the vet with the house truck?

There was also a lady walking on a trail that led into them. A lady who looked like—

Mum! It was Mum! He was sure of it! She was pretty far away, but her hair was the same color and it was swinging in a ponytail like his mum's did. He barked and stood on his back legs and clawed at the window. He had to get out before his mum got too far away. He'd already got lost from her once. He didn't want to do that again. He barked and barked and barked—

"Hang on there, little fella. I know you're excited," Jed said, coming closer to open the door. "Let me grab this leash here—"

Tatum was off. He leaped from the seat to the parking lot, stumbling a bit, but he ran and ran and ran so hard and so fast. Like the wind. Like horses. Like he'd never run before.

"Tatum! Come back! Wait!"

He heard Jed calling him. Heard Dr. Valerie too.

"Tatum! *Tatum!*"

Then Tatum heard her truck start up. He knew she was going to come get him, and that was okay, but first he had to catch up with his mum. She was right there at the edge of the trees—

No, Mum! Wait! Wait for me!

Tatum barked as loud as he could and kept running. He was almost there. He couldn't see her for the trees, but she couldn't be far away. And he couldn't smell her either, but there were so many other things getting in his nose. He kept sniffing. He kept running. Farther and farther into the trees. They were all around him, making lots of shadows, the branches waving around.

He slowed down. He knew Dr. Valerie couldn't drive her truck in there, so he didn't need to run so fast. He could look for his mum. He barked twice, calling her. *Mum! Mum!*

Where was she?

"Tatum! Tatum!" Behind him, Jed and Dr. Valerie and the other vet were calling for him. He thought the other vet might be coming into the trees after him. He started running again, faster and faster. He left the trail and ran deeper into the trees and out of sight.

Soon he couldn't hear anything but his own breathing, his own steps on the ground as he ran over sticks and leaves and a few things that poked his paws. He slowed down then, perking up his ears to listen for his mum. He couldn't hear anything but the leaves rustling.

He didn't know trees could be so loud, but it was starting to get pretty windy. It was also starting to get dark from the clouds and the shade of the trees. He blinked a few times, but he couldn't see his mum. He couldn't hear her either. She must've stopped walking.

But he smelled something that wasn't another animal. He was pretty sure it was food.

CHAPTER 9

Dear road trip diary, vacation is fine but I fink I miss home.
None of the beds I've laid on is my bed, none of the ladies
I've seen is Mum, and none of the stuff I eat is nuggets.

Charles was exhausted. He'd been up for almost thirty-six hours yet knew it wasn't the lack of sleep weighing him down. It was worry and fear and guilt and every related emotion he could think of. He'd never forgive himself if anything happened to Tatum, or if they didn't find him. Somehow, that possibility was harder to entertain. That Tatum would never make it home.

He stared at the ceiling over the bed, trying to think of nothing at all instead of imagining the worst. He wasn't sure he'd ever be able to move again. His bones felt as if they were made of concrete. He was physically numb and was doing his best to blank his mind similarly. Blank his overloaded emotions too. He almost couldn't feel his phone in his hand.

Even though most of the time he couldn't get a signal, he hadn't set it down since realizing Tatum was gone. It was his lifeline to the searchers, when they could get through to him, the shelters, when he could get through to them, and the clinics who were all keeping an eye out for Tatum. And now, as soon as he found the energy, he was going to use it to make a video and post it to Instagram and TikTok . . . as long as the connectivity gods allowed. Tatum had millions of fans and followers who would want to help if they could.

Charles wasn't sure why he hadn't done it the day before. Except for the fact that he hadn't had a free minute even to think beyond the moment, much less eat. Not that he was hungry—

"Charles?"

"Back here." On his back on the bed, he glanced toward the door, waiting for Nicole. The TV on the long dresser showed a *no signal* screen. He'd turned it on out of habit when he'd come to lie down and wait for her to get home from work.

Carrying two coffee cups, Nicole sat beside him on the edge of the bed, handing him one. He propped up enough to sip without spilling. The caffeine would give him a boost.

He drank more, unable yet to look her in the eye. Her worry made him want to try harder. It also made him feel worse for letting her down. She'd argue that he'd done no such thing,

But it was how he felt. He'd failed her. And he'd failed Tatum. "I need to do a couple videos and post them. Let Tatum's online fans know to keep an eye out."

"Oh, that's a great idea." A smile broke over her face. Her tone of voice was the lightest and most hopeful he'd heard since calling her with the bad news. "We should've thought of it yesterday," she added, patting his thigh. "The fact that we didn't proves that we both need some sleep. Which you're going to get as soon as you get that done and eat. I ordered pizza on the way home. It'll be here soon."

"And what about you?" he asked, leaning onto one elbow and challenging her with a look. "If I need sleep, you need sleep. You actually worked today."

She shrugged. "I'll get a nap later. Are you taking another personal day tomorrow?"

"You need more than a nap. And yeah," he said with a nod. "I'll take vacation if I need to."

"Good. And I'll be fine. I'll man the phones. Answer the volunteers' questions. Make sure all search areas are covered. Do a lot of pacing," she finally said, giving up a single soft laugh. "And

I'm sure the social media accounts will explode with comments, so I'll check those."

He shook his head and swallowed more coffee. "I can't sleep. And I was just thinking, too, that I need to call the woman who does the local human-interest stories on the evening news."

"Oh, yes. The feature she did when we rescued Tatum had a great response. I can't believe I didn't think about that either," she said, bringing her cup to her mouth, her dark hair brushing her shoulders as she turned to glance at the blank TV screen.

He loved her hair so much. "We were a little bit preoccupied yesterday."

She looked at him then, her eyes swollen from too many tears. "I know he's okay. He's got to be okay. He's smart. He'll find food and shelter. He's going to be fine until we get to him."

Charles reached up and threaded his fingers through the ends of her hair. It feathered and fell back against her blouse. "I'll never forgive myself if he's not."

"He will be, so don't say that," she said, her voice breaking, her eyes growing damp. "He's a survivor. You know that. Even if we've spoiled him."

At that, Charles laughed. "We have, haven't we? Crazy little goof. He deserves it."

"He does. He was worth waiting for. I can't even remember what life was like without him."

"Hmm. Quiet. Boring."

And that made Nicole laugh, a cheery uplifting sound. "I don't miss the boring, but the quiet . . . Yeah, I could use more of that."

Charles almost said he hoped they didn't go back to the way it had been but managed to keep the thought to himself. He was pretty sure Nicole was thinking similarly though. Her hand holding her cup shook, and the one on his thigh flexed. He covered it with his free one.

He took a deep breath and another drink of coffee, then said,

"Want to help me with the videos? Before the pizza gets here and I'm comatose from carb overload?"

"And that will definitely happen, since I ordered breadsticks too," she said, getting to her feet and holding out her hand. "C'mon, sleepy man. Let's go tell the world about Tatum. And then hope he comes home and we never need a signal to upload it."

⸺◦◦⸺

Jed marked through the number he'd just dialed and moved on to the next. June had printed out the list of vets and shelters near Bangor when he and Val had returned to the clinic earlier. Without Tatum. Even having that thought pained his midsection sorely.

She'd printed off all the ones near Mayville, Shireton, and Floyd as well. Those were the three towns closest to the trailhead of the local Appalachian loop Tatum had followed. If he kept to the path, he'd come out in Mayville, which wasn't terribly far from Val's clinic. A couple of teens who worked for Val part-time had set up a camera and were monitoring the feed as able.

When they'd returned, Val had an emergency case come in, and Jed had needed to do something productive. If he'd gone home alone, he'd have sat and brooded himself into a fury. After all his promises to get Tatum home to his family, he'd failed the pup.

He couldn't get over his mistake. He'd been so used to Rosie waiting for her leash, and Tatum had been equally patient, that it didn't cross his mind that Tatum would run.

Little fella had seen something or scented something that must've been familiar. He'd bolted away, barking like mad. Jed and Val had gone after him in her SUV. Dr. Hinton had taken off on foot. The man was young, with the long legs and stamina Jed didn't have.

Now Jed was making calls from Val's kitchen table while she

toasted some bread for a late BLT lunch, grumbling about missing out on lobster rolls. Jed wasn't sure he'd ever be able to eat again. He propped an elbow on the table and leaned into his hand, rubbing his forehead as if doing so would get rid of the ache there.

He'd never been to Val's home before. She lived fairly close to the clinic, a nice cottage that fit her, efficient and tidy. The kitchen opened up into an eating nook where he sat. One side of the table had a cushioned bench. The other had two chairs with curved spindle backs.

It was pretty homey, done up in red and yellow. Made him think of summer flowers. Even the half curtain hanging over the single window matched, a sort of a checkerboard pattern with potted plants in the squares. He knew she had two grown daughters in Boston and had lived alone since losing her husband even before he'd lost his Patty so long ago.

"No luck yet?" Val asked.

He looked up. She still wore her sneakers and jeans, but before they'd made the drive to meet Dr. Hinton, she'd changed from her scrub top printed with dog bones into a pullover sweater. It was a light yellow, and it suited her. She'd pushed up the sleeves while fixing their meal. Being near while she did was comfortable. Comforting. It helped.

"I'm only five calls in." Jed sat back, the bench creaking. "Not sure where these places are located in relation to the hardware store. The kid I spoke to there had just clocked in so took my number and said he'd call back after asking around. Who knows how far Tatum was from home or since that parking lot is where he hopped into my truck, he could've been out there a while."

"I imagine the storm is what sent him running. Lots of dogs break out of their yards if left out when the lightning and thunder start. Or he could've jumped from an open car door just like he did today. There's no telling. And he's a lot healthier than Rosie was. He hadn't missed any meals, or no more than a couple, and other than his leg, he was in great shape."

"Guess that's in his favor now, being out there alone in the wild." Jed couldn't get over his carelessness. He knew better. He'd been caught up in Tatum's excitement. But he knew better.

Val walked over and laid a hand on his forearm as she sat beside him. "Have faith, Jedediah. Dr. Hinton's still looking. He talked to one of the young cashiers at the farm supply store, and they gathered up several friends to search. They've still got a few hours before it gets completely dark." She squeezed his arm. "We'll find him."

"I should've stayed and helped." Except he wouldn't have been any help, would he? He'd have had to bring up the rear of any search party and hope Tatum backtracked.

"You're helping here," Val said as she got to her feet. "Food's just about ready."

"Appreciate you fixing it. I didn't think I was going to be able to eat, but the smell of that bacon's changing my mind," he said, the memory of Tatum showing off what he could do at breakfast gouging Jed's midsection. Val's laugh helped ease the pain.

"Bacon does that. And these tomatoes are some early ones I picked up from a greenhouse. Here," she said, and walked back with half a tomato in hand. "Smell that."

"Mmm. Okay. I'll take two sandwiches."

"Lucky for you, I've got two headed your way."

"Thanks, Val," he said, and dialed the next number on the list.

"Best Friends Veterinary Clinic. How may I help you?"

Jed cleared his throat of the emotion sitting there on top of his heavy heart. "Evening. My name's Jed Allen, and I'm calling to see if you might have a patient who's gone missing from his home there. He appears to be a bully mix, about forty-five pounds, a rusty-brown coat, golden-brown eyes, good disposition, wearing a black collar. Tag says his name is Tatum."

CHAPTER 10

I keep finkin about all the stuff that is home and is not here. . . . Dad better not be doin' constwuction wifout me.

"Hi, everyone. Charles here. Tatum's dad," he said, and waved. "Nicole's behind the camera today. Say hi, Nicole."

Nicole turned the phone around and gave a thumbs-up and a smile. "Hi, everyone. Back to Charles."

Charles cleared his throat and put his hands on his hips. He and Nicole were in their backyard, surrounded by Tatum's toys still scattered everywhere. This wasn't going to be easy to do. He looked down at the grass, nodding his head rapidly to settle his thoughts.

"Okay, friends. We've got a problem. You've probably noticed: Tatum's not here."

He waved his arm around the yard, and Nicole followed his movements before returning to him. Just saying those words was killing him. He was never going to get through this.

"So last night before the storm blew through, Tatum and I ran up to the hardware store. I needed a couple things for a project, and Tatum wanted to go. I said yes as I always do. I wasn't thinking about the weather. But who knew it was going to blow in so fast, right?"

He took another deep breath, hoping to settle his nerves before he got to the hard part. Nicole gave him a thumbs-up and whispered, "I love you. You got this."

He wanted to laugh because he knew the camera's audio would've picked up her voice. And that was okay. Her emotions were as genuine as his. They were in this together.

"Well, things didn't go so well. We were about to head home when the storm really hit. And I stepped out to move some plastic tubs from the truck's bed into the back seat. But I made a big mistake." Another breath. His throat was tight and aching. Man, he missed that dog.

He shuddered and went on. "I left my door open. And Tatum jumped out and ran. He was scared. He hates storms. I called and called, but I couldn't find him. I stayed out there for hours. And Nicole and some of our friends came to search too."

He paused again, and Nicole made a rolling-keep-going motion. He was almost done, but he couldn't stop himself from reaching down to pick up one of Tatum's toys. It was a plastic bone, red and rubbery, that stood up to his teeth and his tossing it around.

Charles looked straight into the camera then. "You all know what Tatum looks like. You know where we live. You know the big hardware store in town. If you're in the area, please keep an eye out for him. We miss him. Things around here are too quiet without him. And I know he wants to come home. He loves his yard and his toys and his bed. Please help us find him."

He tossed the bone into the air and let it fall. Nicole followed it with the camera, focusing on where it landed in the grass. Then she stopped filming.

"That was great. So great." She wrapped her arms around him and held him so tight he didn't think he could breathe. "I'll bet his friends will make the trip just to look for him."

"I need to post it first," he said with a rough laugh. It was more a release of pent-up nerves than finding anything funny in the situation. He wasn't sure he had energy to do anything but collapse onto the ground and watch the clouds scuttle by. They were still heavy, and he feared more rain would make the search harder.

He wanted to know how Tatum had fared the rest of the night. He almost couldn't deal with the idea that he'd have to go through another storm, scared, alone . . .

Just then came the sound of the doorbell.

"Here. Give me the phone. Let me get this loaded while you grab the pizza."

"As long as you make a giant pot of coffee once you're finished, you've got a deal."

"That I can do," he said as they walked into the house.

He sat at the kitchen table while the coffee dripped, the aroma a warmly comforting scent, the sound of the pot steaming familiar. The only thing missing was Tatum lying in his bed and snoring, snuffling, twitching, and running in his sleep. Every once in a while he'd give a little yip, as if excited by what he'd run across. Charles couldn't count how many videos he'd taken of Tatum in action while he slept, wondering what was happening in Tatum's dream world.

Before he could pull up the video, Nicole set the pizza on the table. He was just setting down the phone to eat when it rang, startling them both. Caller ID read: JED ALLEN.

He didn't know anyone by that name. A searcher maybe? A shelter? He put the phone on speaker. "Hello?"

"Mr. Frazier?"

"Yes?" Charles said, his heart racing. *Don't be bad news. Please don't be bad news.*

"My name is Jed Allen. I live up near Mayville and Shireton."

Charles frowned, curious and wondering, but lost. He shook his head at Nicole's inquiring gaze. "I'm not sure I know where that is."

"It's about six hours north of you. Five with good weather."

That length of a drive put the town near Canada. He couldn't even imagine a reason for this man to be calling. He didn't want to be rude, but he did need to keep his phone clear for anyone trying to reach him about Tatum.

"Okay. How can I help you, Mr. Allen?"

"Call me Jed," the man said, his voice gruff and gravelly. "I'm calling—well, I have some news about your dog. I have some news about Tatum."

Once home from Val's following dinner, Jed headed out to the garage. He wasn't sure what took him out there other than a need to keep busy and stop thinking so much about Tatum. Especially after reaching his family just hours after he'd lost their dog again.

Charles had been full of questions. His biggest one was how Jed had located him since he knew Tatum had lost his tags. Knew too, from speaking to several shelters that the Maine Pets server, where Tatum's chip was registered, was still offline. Jed had explained how June had given him a list of vets and shelters in Bangor to call since that had been the only place Jed had stopped on his drive home. Jed had been using a landline, but he'd reached Charles on his cell, and Charles had verified how the service was intermittent. He'd had local searchers who'd had to reach him on the landline. Jed getting through on his cell surprised the both of them.

That had been a heartbreaking call to make, a heartbreaking confession as well, admitting to losing Tatum. It had been just as heartbreaking for Charles and Nicole to hear, but at least they now had a solid lead on Tatum's whereabouts. They could call off the local search and focus their energies up north.

He didn't think he'd ever be able to stop worrying completely. If the little fella came to harm or was never found, he wasn't sure he'd forgive himself. The Fraziers had been gracious, amazingly so, considering the circumstances. They placed no blame on Jed for taking Tatum away from Bangor, or for the part he'd played in their dog running off again.

All he could hope was that someone kind would find him and take him in and do their best to locate his family. He shook his head, hating what the Fraziers were going through. Tatum wasn't even his dog, and he was absolutely sick with sorrow of his own.

All the calls he'd made inquiring about Tatum had stirred something inside him though. A need to volunteer. He didn't know why he'd never done so before. It would be a fulfilling use of his free time. And who was he kidding? These days, all of his time was free. It was the great thing about retirement. He could do most anything he wanted.

How Tatum had wiggled his way into Jed's heart so quickly he'd never know. Maybe it said more about the state of Jed's heart than anything. That it was empty and had a dog-shaped spot waiting to be filled with a pup just Tatum's size.

CHAPTER 11

*Dear road trip diary, vacation is busy and you never eat
any food that you eat at home. Mum and Dad don't go on
a lot of vacations cuz they say my maintenance is high.
They should do more vacation, diffwent food is
incredibow.*

Cheryl Stratton was being followed. She wasn't particularly worried, and she wasn't frightened at all. The steps were those of an
animal, but a small one. Still, she reached into her pocket for her
knife. She'd spent enough time hiking and camping to know to be
prepared for, and expect, the worst—even though the worst was
rarely the outcome.

Her father, an absent-minded professor at heart, was the one
who'd provided her camping education. Her mother, who'd had
a lifelong affair with numbers, had made certain she was ready for
any disaster. It was how her mother had coped, looking anxiously
into the future and creating images of what might come. Her father, on the other hand, had made the most of every moment of
every single day. Cheryl had grown up with whiplash trying to
keep up.

She walked on, and the animal continued to follow. She was
pretty sure it was a dog. For a dog to be this far out and following
at a distance, it wouldn't be afraid of humans, just generally wary.
And most likely lost. Which she couldn't stop thinking about the
farther she went.

She'd traveled this loop often and had decided where she wanted to camp. But with this new wrinkle, she thought it best to stop sooner. Her attention kept wandering to her shadow, when she was out here to clear her mind for her upcoming visit with her mother—her first in years.

She gave a little snort at that. Why was this particular human relationship so fraught with emotional traps? It wasn't like it was unique to her; she'd read plenty of novels with mother-and-daughter conflict as the central theme. She had friends whose mothers were their best friends. Others whose mothers had walked out when they were teens. Even younger.

Her situation fell somewhere in between. She and her mother's problems hadn't begun until she left for college on the heels of her father moving out. That had conveniently happened days after her high school graduation. To this day, she struggled with his abandonment.

Shaking off the past, she took note of her surroundings. She'd camped farther north the night before, and judging by the clutter of debris growing more dense along the way, she'd missed the worst of the storm. Hopefully her apartment hadn't lost electricity for long, though she didn't have much in the way of perishables in her fridge. She laughed at that; did she ever?

She continued for another quarter mile, listening all the while for her shadow's steps, hearing it snuffle a bit when scenting something on the ground. Soon, she reached a spot perfect for the night. And as she stepped off the trail and moved farther into the woods, she saw the dog. He was reddish brown, his coat short, his eyes bright and golden.

He was limping, which made sense with the bright blue tape binding his leg. He'd been walking quite a while on that. Someone was missing their dog. Looked like she had a job to do.

Priority number one was not to spook him. And she figured food would help.

Tatum sat next to a tree. There was another one on his other side. Both were really tall, but there were others around that were shorter. There were also logs and branches and bushes around the trees, with leaves and crunchy sticks all over the ground.

A lot of the plants had brown bark, and he thought it all might help him hide while he smelled the food the lady was cooking on the fire. It smelled really, really good.

After sniffing his way farther and farther away from the road where he'd left Jed and Dr. Valerie, he'd finally found the lady. He'd followed her while she'd hiked through the woods.

He knew she was hiking because his mum liked to do the same thing. She'd hike for a long time, and Tatum would hike beside her and want her to slow down so he could smell everything that crossed the path of his nose. But she called hiking exercise, so she liked to go fast.

The lady by the fire hadn't been hiking quite so fast the last little while as she had when he first saw her at the edge of the woods, so Tatum had been able to do a lot of sniffing. He decided this trail was used by a lot of people because he could smell them and smell their dogs. Knowing other dogs had been safe made him feel a lot better about being out here by himself, without his mum or dad. Without Jed or Dr. Valerie. He hoped they were all okay.

He really wished the lady by the fire had been his mum. Maybe she could show him the way back to Jed and Dr. Valerie so they could get him home. He should've stayed in the box truck, since he knew that's what they were trying to do, but he just knew the lady had been his mum.

It was starting to get dark, and Tatum had been sniffing the air often enough to know there was going to be more rain. He didn't want to be outside in the rain again. He wanted to be in the soft bed in Jed's room, sleeping and staying warm and dry. And eating leftover pot roast again.

Whatever food the lady was cooking did not smell like pot roast, but Tatum was hungry enough to find out if she might have extra bites to share. He was also interested in the little house she'd built nearby. It looked like it was made out of a blanket or a sheet. It was bright yellow, and it had a door that zipped up, which he wanted to look at more closely. From the inside.

He took a couple of steps. He didn't want to scare the lady or make her think he was one of the big animals living out here. Those might be dangerous. The lady needed to stay far away.

Then he took another step, limping a bit because his leg was really tired and sore, and stopped because that's when she looked up from her fire and saw him looking back.

⟶⊷⊶⟵

"Well, hello there," said the lady who looked like his mum when Tatum slowly walked closer.

He stopped out of her reach but stayed where he could see her and she could see him. He wanted to be able to run if he needed to. He hoped he didn't need to. He hoped she was nice.

She looked nice.

"I was wondering who had been following me," she said, poking a stick into her fire and stirring the coals.

They looked really warm, glowing bright. He took a few steps closer. He waited to see if he could feel the heat, then took a few more.

"I'm glad to see you're not a bear."

He cocked his head to one side and considered her, his ears perked up halfway. Were ladies afraid of bears too? Tatum had never seen one, but he'd heard his dad and mum talking about them living in the woods. And he definitely could smell an animal he didn't know that he thought was a bear. They were stinky.

"You're welcome to share my dinner," the lady told him, swirling something in a little pot and tasting it on a little spoon.

Tatum's ears perked up all the way. Then his nose.

"But I'm not sure I've got anything here that a dog might like. Oh, I do have some jerky. I'll bet you'd like that."

Tatum wasn't sure what jerky was, but he was hungry so he would give it a try. The food she was cooking smelled good, but he thought it was vegetables. Or maybe noodles like his mum ate in soup. He liked vegetables when they had gravy on them, but mostly he liked pot roast.

Maybe the lady knew Jed and Dr. Valerie and could take him to Jed's house to eat. But she didn't have a car, so they would have to walk. Tatum was pretty tired after getting his leg fixed and Dr. Valerie giving him shots. Running to catch up with the lady who wasn't his mum had really tired him out. He did want to eat, but he also wanted a nice long nap.

He wondered if the lady's funny little house had a bed, or blankets and pillows at least. Maybe a squishy toy. He didn't need much. He was a simple dog.

She found the jerky in her pack and tossed him a piece. It was pretty small. "Here you go. If you like that, I've got some more. And I've got some peanut butter I can smear on."

Tatum inched forward and sniffed at the jerky and decided it smelled a little bit like pot roast. He gobbled it up, and it tasted pretty good, though he would've liked some gravy too. He wanted another piece, so he went closer to the lady, trying his very best to be a good dog.

"Not too bad, huh? That's venison jerky. A friend of mine is a hunter and makes it. I don't eat meat very often, but it's easy protein to pack for hiking." She reached for another small piece. "I mean, it's hard to fry up fresh bacon and eggs, you know?"

Tatum snatched up the second piece she tossed him before it

hit the ground. It tasted better without dirt on it. But all too soon his mouth was empty again and there was still a lot of room in his stomach. He wondered if she had enough to fill him up. What had she said about peanut butter? He really did like peanut butter. His mum stuffed it into toys and made him lick it out.

"I've got some dried apple slices," she told him, smiling. "How about a few of those?"

Tatum thought he liked apples, so he gave a quick yip.

"I'll take that as a yes," she said, and found the apples in her bag. And what looked like a tube of peanut butter. She didn't throw him any right away. She just looked at the ones in her hand, then looked at him. It was kinda like the way his mum looked at him when she wanted him to do something. "You're going to have to come get these."

Okay. He could do that. He dropped to his belly and crawled forward. The dirt was soft and pretty cold, and it smelled clean even though it smelled like a lot of animals. And the sticks were kinda scratchy, and the leaves crinkled as he smashed them.

But then he was next to her. The fire was in front of her. Her food smelled good and warm, and that's how the fire felt. He yawned.

"What happened to your leg there? That bandage is pretty clean, so I imagine whatever happened was recent."

She held out her hand with an apple slice, and Tatum sat up and cocked his head.

"I'll bet you've got people looking for you, huh?"

He yipped again, then he sniffed the apple and finally took it from her hand.

"I suppose I'll need to find a cell signal tomorrow. I ran across another hiker this morning who told me service was down everywhere. I might have to hike out of here to see about getting you home." She ate a piece of apple too, frowning as she chewed it up. "I suppose I can call a couple of vets in the area. My car's parked at the trailhead near Mayville. That's where I live. Hopefully we'll have a clear day tomorrow. Makes for faster hiking."

Just as she said the words, a loud boom of thunder exploded in the sky. Tatum bolted toward her funny little house and ran inside. She had a blanket in there, and he buried himself up to his nose. He didn't want to get lost again. He didn't want to get wet again. He didn't want to be scared. He wanted to go home and never be away from his family again.

Outside, the lady moved around, though he couldn't see what she was doing.

"Guess we're going to have to spend the night indoors, huh?" A few minutes later, she came inside with him.

He peeked out as she closed the front door and sat down on the other end of the blanket. She had a lamp that she turned up so he could see. That was a nice thing to do, though he could see pretty good in the dark.

"What's your name?" she asked him, reaching for his collar to read his tag. "Tatum, huh? Well, Tatum, just to set your mind at ease, I'm a big fan of dogs. And I think we're going to be great friends."

Tatum liked making friends and wagged his tail to tell her so.

CHAPTER 12

*Dear road trip diary, I left the road cuz I thought I saw
Mum, and it wasn't Mum but she smiles and feeds me food
so she's gotta be sumbuddy's mum. Her name is Cheryl.
Everyone on vacation likes dogs and tells me they like
dogs and why they like dogs. I don't fink I am a reindeer,
so I won't tell that to Dad.*

"You remind me of a dog I had in high school," Cheryl said,
reaching down to smooth the coarse hair on Tatum's head. "She
was a beagle-pointer mix, and she'd send her tail flying and cock
her front paw every time she saw a squirrel. She never caught any,
of course." Cheryl laughed, remembering. "She hated storms.
Hated them. She'd know one was coming before we did and hide
in the smallest place she could find and shake like a leaf."

Sitting on the top half of her sleeping bag, Cheryl cringed with
each clap of thunder. Tatum was huddled in the foot of the bag,
shuddering. Poor guy. Getting lost in a storm had to be the worst.
Not knowing where he was, missing his people. She blew out a
heavy sigh.

He was well cared for, groomed and fed. She'd bet he was
microchipped. Dog owners who took the care his did would
take that step too. Meaning she needed to find a clinic or shelter
to scan him. Then she could locate his family and get him home.
With this weather? They had to be frantically missing him.

She scratched behind his ears. "I'll bet this weather sent you running, huh? Candy, she was my dog, would've been buried in there as far as you are. The only thing she hated worse than storms were fireworks. We lived in a place where our neighbors spent hours shooting them off on holidays. I hated it as much as she did. It's such a nerve-racking noise. Like thunder."

And just as she said it, a flash of lightning lit the sky outside the tent, and a booming rumble of thunder followed seconds later. The rain was on its way. "I guess I'll read, since it's too loud and too early to sleep. And since you've taken over my bed anyway."

She'd packed two slim paperbacks, and it hadn't been easy to decide what to bring. She read widely, and what she read depended on her mood. She'd known this hike was going to be mentally difficult and emotionally challenging. The physical toll was never an issue.

While other kids on their way to school rode bikes, and later drove cars, and while some took buses or had their parents drive them, Cheryl had walked. She'd done so most often alone, and was pretty sure the joy she found in hiking had been born on those sidewalks and streets.

She would talk to herself about friends at school, about a book she'd been reading, even about finding a way to make her parents get along better. She'd gotten so tired of their arguing.

She hadn't kept track of the number of miles she'd covered as a child, how many she'd hiked over the years, but it had to be thousands. She'd walked gorgeous trails bathed in sunlight and the green of spring. She'd walked in the middle of winter when the world around her was a ghost town, silent and white and dead, animals in hibernation, trees nothing but skeletons.

Hiking was her therapy. Reading too. The latter was one of the greatest gifts she'd ever received from her mother. That and their shared love of dogs.

She had no idea how things between them had soured. It wasn't like her mother hadn't been fully aware of her college plans. She'd helped her research schools, helped her fill out financial aid forms, helped her with everything but choosing her major. On that, they'd parted ways.

For as long as she could remember, Cheryl had wanted to study psychology. It wasn't hard, considering her childhood, to understand her interest in what drove human behavior. But her mother had wanted her only daughter to follow in her footsteps. Probably because her mother would consider that a win in the battle with her father that had yet to end.

Once Cheryl left home, they'd lost touch, or not made the effort to stay in touch beyond the few holidays Cheryl had come home for, and then it seemed every effort she made, her mother rebuffed. She had let her. She shouldn't have. But she'd been so tired of fighting.

Shaking off the memories, she settled closer to Tatum and opened her book. But she didn't read it. She stared at the animal she found in her care and thought about another from her past.

"I was on a road trip with my mother once. I don't even remember where we were going or what we were doing. But I was too young to be responsible for a dog. We had a shepherd mix then. His name was Bear," she said to Tatum, hoping the tone of her voice would calm him.

"We stopped at a rest area, and the second I opened the door, he jumped out of the car without a leash. He ran and ran and ran. He was so happy. I could see him smiling. But I was terrified that he wasn't going to come back. That he'd run forever and I'd never see him again. That he'd lose his way and not remember where we were. But he finally did."

Next to their love of reading, she and her mother had bonded the best over their dogs. Her mother seemed to relate to animals better than she did to people. As a child, Cheryl hadn't understood, but now she got it. Her mother would love Tatum. And she wondered . . .

How would her mother feel about bringing a new dog into her

life? Not Tatum. He had a family, but if Cheryl couldn't find them, maybe her mother could foster him until they were located. Or maybe a new dog, one who needed a loving companion, would be the ticket to salvaging Cheryl and her mother's relationship.

"Thank you, Tatum," she said, hopeful for the first time in ages. "You've just given me a wonderful idea."

———⊶•⊷———

It was late, nearly dark, when Charles reached the farm supply store where Jed Allen had told him he'd last seen Tatum. The mobile vet's RV was parked at the side of the lot. Jed had told him that too. Jed wasn't there. He lived a couple of towns away, but he'd told Charles to call him and he'd make the trip back the next day. He wasn't sure what he could offer beyond moral support, but he was happy to do so. Jed was a really good man. Charles could tell.

He should've waited until the next day himself. It was almost too late to search that night. Too dark. Too stormy. He was going to do it anyway. He had flashlights. He had weatherproof boots, a hat, and a jacket. If Tatum was out in this weather, he wasn't going to let the weather keep him from finding him. He'd let down his dog once already. He was not going to do it again.

A knock on his window startled him, and he exited the truck.

"You must be Tatum's dad."

The man was tall and gangly, younger than Charles had expected. He wore jeans, sneakers, a backward ball cap, and a long-sleeved T-shirt beneath an unbuttoned plaid flannel. His hair was short, his smile warm and at the same time somber.

Nodding, Charles held out his hand. "Charles Frazier."

"Chris Hinton. You got here a lot faster than I'd expected."

The response Charles made seemed obvious. "He's my dog."

The veterinarian reached out and squeezed his shoulder. "Well, it's late, and the kids who were searching earlier called it a night an hour ago. But I can point out where he went into the woods if you want to walk down there."

"Lead the way," Charles said, pocketing his keys and his phone and his extra flashlight.

"Let me grab my light and rain gear in case it starts up again," he said, turning for the RV. "We may have a bit of a break. You lucked out."

Charles figured it was less luck and more all the prayers being sent up for Tatum's safe return home. "Hopefully it pays off."

He was still reeling from Jed's phone call and the story he'd told of finding Tatum in his truck six hours after leaving Bangor. Most worried about the wound Jed's vet had stitched up, Charles had tried the entire drive not to imagine what would've happened if someone less compassionate had been the one to find Tatum stowed away.

The thought had gnawed at him for hours. He knew it was unproductive, but it was hard to let it go—especially with all Tatum had been through in the past.

He wondered what Tatum was thinking about being outdoors with no fence and no yard, with so many unfamiliar scents, with forest animals probably just as afraid of him as he'd be of them. It was the bigger animals Charles worried about. Hopefully Tatum's instincts would send him running in the other direction should he cross paths with anything dangerous.

The dog did know how to run, Charles mused, a sad smile tugging at his mouth as behind him the door to the RV opened and closed. He turned as Dr. Hinton joined him.

"Okay, so, I was here talking to Dr. Warren and Mr. Allen. Tatum was in her SUV. We're pretty sure he saw someone he thought he knew. There was a hiker down the road a bit. That made more sense than smelling food or another animal. Mr. Allen went to let him out, thinking he needed to do his thing. But he opened the door before leashing him up. It hadn't been an issue before, he said. Tatum was great about waiting. But this time he didn't."

"He can be impetuous, for sure," Charles said. "But he's really pretty well-behaved."

"I didn't have a chance to do more than see him take off. They'd brought him to me to scan since Maine Pets is having technical issues and I've got an offline database."

That really sucked because he and Nicole had made sure Tatum was chipped before they brought him home from the shelter. But he wasn't going to blame Jed for anything. He'd gone out of his way in his efforts to get Tatum home. "So you think he followed a hiker?"

"Most likely, but then again . . ." The veterinarian shrugged. "Dogs will be dogs."

"You can just point me in the right direction. You don't have to go looking."

"No way. Animals are my life. Let's go," Chris said, gesturing down the road. They walked for several minutes, then the vet pointed out a trail. "This is where we last saw him."

He'd headed south. Charles decided that was better than heading north. He was already too close to the Canadian border as it was. Away from the road, the woods grew more dense. That would make the trek darker for Tatum, especially with the thick cloud layer rolling in.

He readied his flashlight. "Let's do this."

CHAPTER 13

Dear diary not on the road. Cheryl doesn't know I don't like rain or water either, but I don't fink she likes it, so I guess she can be my fwend. Jed didn't come wif me to meet the nice lady and I don't know why, I guess he doesn't like the stuff she cooks. It not pizza but also it not dog food, oh man why did I fink about pizza?

Tatum laid next to the nice lady with his eyes closed but his ears were open. He could hear her breathing. She made soft noises, so he knew she was still awake. Not like his dad's sleeping noises that were really loud. Jed had been loud too. Tatum thought sometimes he was loud because he would wake himself up and forget he'd been sleeping and yawn.

Mostly though he listened to all the sounds on the other side of the funny house. It was pretty noisy out there in the woods. A lot of the sounds were because of the rain.

He could hear the water drops falling on leaves, and then the leaves got heavy and the water fell to the ground and plopped in puddles. That made him miss Puddles. More rain fell on smaller bushes, making their branches rustle like some little animal was shaking them. Other rain fell closer to the trail where the ground was hard from so many people walking on it. It was louder there. Like balls.

That made Tatum think about how the rain sounded at home.

It fell in the grass and it fell on the street and it fell on the roof of the house. But when he was at home, he never thought he might get wet. Unless the rain kept going forever and he had to do his business in it.

Here in the funny house it was different. He thought the roof might cave in or the water come up into the floor. But nothing like that happened. He stayed dry. The nice lady stayed dry. She looked at her book. She looked at him. She smiled and rubbed his head.

He thought the nice lady would be a good dog mum. If he didn't already have his own, the best in the world, he might like her to be his. She'd need to buy more food than jerky and dried apples and peanut butter though. Mostly he hoped she'd get him home.

He closed his eyes again. He wasn't even sure when he'd opened them. And this time he closed his ears a little bit more. He could still hear the rain, but it wasn't as loud as before. And it wasn't as loud as the previous night had been. He couldn't believe everything that had happened since he'd jumped out of his dad's truck. He should've just waited. He knew his dad always took care of him. But for a minute there, he'd thought the entire truck was going to explode.

His dad probably got all wet looking for him, but this night he was probably warm and dry at home with Mum. Maybe they cooked spaghetti for dinner. Or maybe they were too tired after looking for him and called for a pizza to come to the front door.

If he was a person instead of a dog, he'd call for front-door pizza every day. It always smelled so good. He imagined it tasted good too. He'd snuck a piece once, but his dad had grabbed it away before he got more than a little bit on his tongue. He remembered it was warm and cheesy. He really did like cheese, so he was sure pizza would be great.

Maybe the nice lady could cook a pizza on her campfire. He wasn't sure how that would work, and she might not have any cheese in her backpack. He hadn't smelled any, that was for sure. All he'd smelled was jerky and peanut butter and apples and her vegetable soup.

This time he closed his ears all the way, and after a big yawn he closed his mouth too. His eyes were already shut, and he told his nose just to breathe the air in the funny house and stop trying to smell all the things that were outside. The nice lady had zipped up the door, though he wasn't sure that was as safe as a lock like the one his dad always checked before going to bed.

The next day would be better. He would dream it so. There would be adventures in the woods. He would smell everything and listen for more rain and birds. He would eat the nice lady's apples and peanut butter and jerky and pretend it was chewy pizza. Or pot roast with gravy. And then he would sleep in his own bed after telling Puddles good night.

A very good day and a very good night indeed.

TUESDAY

CHAPTER 14

Dear just diary now. Cheryl is on vacation too but she calls it "camping" cuz I don't know why. Jed had a dog, but it was like a hooman cuz he fed me carrots and pot roast, Cheryl puts me on a leash, so I fink Mum and Dad gave her my list. I hope I remember to ask Dad to put no fank you to rain on my list.

Charles had spent the night in Dr. Hinton's RV. It was outfitted like a clinic but still had a small upper bunk in the rear. It had been a cramped night, and the second storm had kept him from getting much sleep. He couldn't help but think about Tatum out in the woods in the rain.

There had to be any number of places for him to shelter: downed logs, thick vegetation, crawl spaces between fallen boulders. He'd get wet, sure, but he might feel safer and be a bit warmer tucked away. Charles hoped he'd find something to eat.

That was his biggest worry. Where was he going to find food and water?

"I can't offer you much in the way of breakfast," Chris said as he brewed himself a K-Cup. The aroma filled the RV. "I've got coffee and some cereal bars. That's about it."

Charles shook his head. "Coffee's fine. I can grab something to eat down the road."

The veterinarian found a second mug and handed it to him. "Couple varieties here. Bottled water under the sink. Go for it."

"Thanks." Charles set about making a cup for himself, asking Chris, "Where's the next access to the trail? I feel like I might have better luck going in from the other side. Maybe meeting him halfway."

Chris scrunched up his face and scratched the back of his head, as if trying to figure out how to give Charles the bad news. "The trailhead's in Mayville. The road here is the only break in the loop. Not sure how long it is, I don't camp, but it's a two- or three-day hike at least. It goes north out of Mayville for several miles before coming back down this way." Chris gestured one way, then the other before taking a big swig from his mug. "Does the same thing going south."

That was not what Charles had wanted to hear. He didn't have days to search. He didn't have a place to stay except for his truck. He didn't have food or water. He'd left home in a white-hot rush without asking Jed more about what he was getting into.

He needed camping gear if he was going to walk from the trailhead all the way back to the spot of Tatum's last sighting. Even if he didn't have to walk that far, if he found him halfway, he couldn't go in and come out in a single day. Not based on what Chris had said.

"I don't know whether I should go all the way home for supplies, or get what I need in Mayville. I can't just not look for him when this is where he was last seen."

"I get it. Tough call. The kids who were helping out set up a camera at the trailhead. They're monitoring that, but most of them are still in school. I know they're going out again this afternoon, some from here, some walking in from the trailhead. There's a good chance if he keeps to the trail they'll find him."

Charles rubbed his forehead. "I can't imagine he'd keep to the trail. He's going to sniff out every curious thing."

"Well, the trail does smell like people." Chris shrugged and set his mug in the sink. "So it'll smell like food."

Charles thought for a minute. "I'll call Nicole. I can take the time off work. She can't. I'll see what she thinks."

"The kids put up flyers. I'm sure they'll post an update to social media, networking, you know, as soon as they can get online again."

That triggered a thought. "How's their camera working without being connected?"

"It's a motion-detection system. Snaps a photo when something crosses its path. Someone will check it after school if it's not broadcasting by then."

Charles nodded, then finished off his coffee. "I appreciate the hospitality. And the help."

"Wish I could do more. I'll keep an eye out as long as I'm here. He may come back this way. Who knows. Just keep me in the loop."

"Sure. Will do," Charles said, leaving the RV and heading for his truck. He reached for his keys, dug for his phone, not sure he felt any better this morning than he had last night when he'd arrived. He stared into the woods, the air still and cool and foggy from the rain.

Everything smelled damp. Everything felt drowned. "Where are you, Tatum? Where's my good boy?"

———————

It didn't take Cheryl long at all to pack up her campsite. She'd been camping since she was five years old. Her dad had loved the woods and taken her as often as they could get away. He'd read to her by firelight while she toasted marshmallows—*Robinson Crusoe*, *Gulliver's Travels*, *The Swiss Family Robinson*, all the great adventures that made theirs so exciting.

She'd lain in her sleeping bag and listened to the night, the leaves rustling overhead, the insects singing their songs, owls hooting, and the predators howling. The sound of her dad snoring beside her made those not quite as scary as they might've been if she'd been alone.

She'd had less time, and to be honest, less interest, in camping as a teen. Her dad had always asked, but most of the time, he'd gone alone. His love of the great outdoors was one her mother had never shared. Cheryl didn't think it had ever caused issues, and he'd always invited Cheryl and her mother both. Maybe it had. They'd been very private people when it came to their relationship, old-fashioned about their roles, and what children should be told.

As Cheryl finished packing up, Tatum appeared. She'd heard him nosing around while out doing his business, and he'd returned each time she'd called. He'd become her priority, putting a whole lot of kinks in her agenda. She had to find him something to eat besides jerky and dried fruit. And replenish her supplies because she hadn't packed enough to share with a very hungry dog. Bottom line, her hike was now about getting back to the trailhead and civilization.

She also wanted to make sure Tatum was with her then, so she dug into her pack for the nylon rope in the bottom. She was pretty sure he'd stick close, but someone was missing their dog. She didn't want to let him get lost in the woods when she had the means to keep him close.

"Ready to hit the trails?"

He cocked his head at her as she hefted her pack onto her back, adjusting the weight evenly.

"We've got quite a ways to go today. We'll need to camp another night, but hopefully I can find a spot where I can get a cell signal and make some calls."

She fashioned a loop and slipped the rope around his neck. "Somebody's got to be looking for you. They need to know you're okay and on your way home."

CHAPTER 15

Dear vacation diary. I didn't know everybuddy goes on vacation at the same time, who does all the stuff when everyone is gone? Cheryl called me harmless today, I have a lot of nicknames but dis one is new.

They hiked for a really long time, but Tatum didn't mind that much. There were so many things to see and to smell. The nice lady talked to him while hiking. She kept him on a rope so he wouldn't wander off, she said. He didn't really like that, but he didn't want to lose her, so it was okay. Especially since she was going to help him get home.

The previous night was the first time since he was pretty little that he hadn't slept in his own bed, in his own house, with his dad and his mum and silly ol' Puddles close. Well, the previous night and the night before that, when he stayed at Jed's house. He liked Jed's house. He liked the nice lady's funny yellow zip-up house. He hadn't liked it during the rain, but she'd talked to him and told him that tents wouldn't let the water in. And if the storm got dangerous, they'd move away from the big trees.

Her funny house was called a tent. He had learned something.

He guessed the storm had stayed pretty small because he'd gone to sleep and been really warm and cozy on her sleeping bag. He'd wanted to stay inside, but she said there wasn't room.

He knew there was, but he supposed she just didn't like being squashed by a dog.

Most of the time at home he slept by himself. He had a bed in the kitchen, a bed in his mum and dad's room, and another bed in the living room, where they watched TV. He liked all of them, and he didn't mind sleeping by himself. He just liked to be where they were.

Sometimes he snuck up onto the couch, or onto the end of their bed. He was pretty sure they didn't like being squashed either. They would let him stay for a while, but he always ended up back in his own bed. And that was okay.

At least he had his squishy shark to sleep with. And really warm blankets.

Maybe by the end of the day he'd be back in his own bed. He really hoped so. Though he guessed if he had to sleep in the outdoors one more night it would be okay to do in the lady's tent.

He thought he liked tents. Maybe his dad could build one when he got home.

A yellow one. With a zipper.

⟶⟶•◆•⟵⟵

Cheryl thought they could probably reach the trailhead near Mayville by noon the next day. She supposed she could go back the way she'd come, but there was no guarantee she'd find Tatum's family there. And even with Tatum in her care, she didn't want to lose time.

She'd allotted only so much away from work, and most of her time off she was planning to spend with her mother. She wondered what her mother would think if Cheryl showed up on her doorstep with Tatum at her side. He might make for a great icebreaker. She imagined she would need one. There was something about a shared love for an animal that bridged gaps.

She truly believed that. Believed, too, that such love could heal broken people. She glanced over to where Tatum was following a trail of some scent, tugging at the rope to move deeper into the woods. She smiled. He really was a good dog, well behaved, charming.

"Not right now, Tatum. We need to stay on track." The trail they were on was a bit muddy after the storms, but they hadn't hit any spots requiring a detour. Just a bit of trudging through puddles. Her boots were made for that, and Tatum didn't seem to mind the water.

She figured he was used to being outside. If such was the case, she was glad his family was able to provide that for him. Sure, dogs had great lives indoors, but she was a firm believer that they needed regular doses of nature as much as human beings did. How anyone survived without time spent beneath blue skies and sunshine on a regular basis was beyond her. Then again, she only had to look as far as her mother for someone who thrived indoors.

She hopped across a series of puddles. Tatum was just far enough off the trail to miss them. The hard-packed earth always had low spots that held water and—

Suddenly, Tatum stopped, his ears going up before he bolted forward, jerking her arm when he hit the end of the rope.

"Tatum! Stop!"

She picked up her pace, reeling in the rope as she gained slack, and finally reached him. He'd stopped at an intersection of the main loop with an offshoot she knew was almost as long. It was also a lot more primitive. She didn't walk it as often.

This wasn't the first time she'd seen the man. They seemed to enjoy the same trails, long days spent walking, nights spent in tents beneath the stars. He was a bit older than she was, but she didn't think by much. "Sorry about that. I'm pretty sure he's harmless."

He waved off her concern. "I don't remember seeing you traveling with company before."

"I never have," she said, returning his smile. His hair was

dark, longish and unkempt, and it suited him perfectly. Sadly, she doubted her tent hair looked as good. "He's only been with me since yesterday. I'm pretty sure he wandered too far from home and found me."

"There was a mobile vet back at the county crossroad. Maybe he ran off from there."

Cheryl nodded, taking a few more steps along the trail. "I thought about that but didn't want to backtrack in case he'd moved on. Especially since I'm having to share supplies now."

"Right. Yeah. Makes sense." He pulled off his cap and cupped it in both hands, using it to scoop back his hair. "I'm Frank, by the way. Frank Ouelette."

"Cheryl Stratton," she said, switching the rope to her other hand to shake his.

His grip was strong, his hand large and swallowing hers.

"This is Tatum."

"Tatum, huh?"

Frank bent enough to give Tatum a proper hello. It wasn't an easy thing to do with the weight of the pack he carried. Cheryl was pretty sure it was heavier than hers. It would be if he was walking the Michaud Circle.

"Do you walk the circle often? I know I've seen you on the main loop, but the circle's not a challenge I'm always up to. Not on my own."

"I walk it as often as I can," he said, scratching Tatum's ears. "Which isn't often enough."

"I hear you," she said, and started walking again.

He fell into step beside her.

"How did you manage during that first storm?"

"That one was brutal," he said, shaking his head. "And I was far enough west to take the brunt of it. I'd set up in a clearing but still got hit by a couple of branches. Tent stayed up and in one piece at least. No damage."

"That's good to hear," she said, giving Tatum more slack. "Last night wasn't as bad for us, but yeah. I didn't get a whole lot of sleep the night before. And I hate having to replace equipment."

"Right? Get it just perfect, then something happens. Or I lose whatever it is because I used it for something else and didn't put it back with my gear." He crossed behind her to stay out of the way of the rope. "How'd Tatum do?"

"He buried himself in my sleeping bag. Until I made him get out," she said with a laugh. "I'm pretty sure the storm's why he's out here. Every dog who's ever owned me has hated them. He really didn't like the wind or the lightning, and it was so much worse the night before."

"I'll bet he was pretty miserable. Any idea what happened to his leg there?"

Cheryl shook her head. "The bandage was pretty clean when I first saw him, so a recent injury, I imagine. He seems to be doing okay with it."

They kept walking, the sun rising to burn off the morning fog, to filter through the branches and cast leafy shadows on the trail. The wind was cool, and Cheryl wished she'd kept out her windbreaker but knew she'd warm up soon enough. And every few steps she crossed through a ray of sunlight that reminded her how hot it was going to get.

"This may sound dumb," Frank said, laughing to himself, "but I actually love sleeping out in storms. I mean, as long as I take precautions and am not in danger."

Cheryl smiled at that. Her father had loved having the rain beat their tent. "I like my camping quiet. Or as quiet as camping gets. I grew up camping with my dad. He made me listen."

"It's crazy how loud it can get in the middle of nowhere," Frank said, echoing her thoughts. "I mean, you'd think it would be dead silent, but sometimes I need earplugs."

That was funny. "You pack earplugs?"

Frank gave her a sheepish grin. "No. I just need them. But then something about it all lulls me to sleep. That's got to sound weird, I know."

It didn't. And it made her heart flutter a little bit. "I do wish the birds didn't get started so early in the morning. That's probably my only complaint. Then again, it gets me going when I'd probably sleep till noon. And then it's almost too hot to pack up."

"Yeah, but it's a lot easier now than it was when I was a kid. We did the whole family thing. The huge tent that took forever to stake. And my dad wouldn't let me go to the bathroom until it was done. Even though we'd been in the car for hours."

"Ouch. That's kinda harsh."

"Maybe so, but it worked."

CHAPTER 16

Dear vacation diary. Cheryl is taking me for the longest walk I have ever been on, and there is more smells than I can count, pwobably like ten. Fwank is walkin' wif us; he knows the new-food-on-vacation rule, so he done dis before.

They continued to walk, covering another mile, then another, Tatum staying close to Cheryl's side, stepping off the trail to sniff the ground every so often. Once in a while, his ears shot up and he darted forward. The rope brought him back. She wished she could let him go. She couldn't even imagine how much fun he'd have out here—and how much trouble he'd find.

"Want me to hold on to him for a while?" Frank asked the next time she had to urge Tatum back in line. "He seems comfortable enough with me."

"That would be great, thanks." She passed him the rope and moved behind him to the far side of the trail. "I think he'd be okay if I let him go, but I'd feel terrible if I lost him. I mean, he could be missing medication. Or be on a special diet. Who knows?" And there she went, imagining the worst, just like her mother. She filed that away and said, "I just want to get him to a vet ASAP and hope he's chipped so he can get home."

"I suppose he's on his own, uh, incredible journey," Frank said, then after that had settled, he added, "I guess everyone out here is on a journey of some sort. Especially those of us hiking solo. Nowhere to go but forward, driven by our thoughts."

That was pretty deep, Cheryl mused, thinking how she'd considered going back but had kept pressing on. "Is that what you're doing?" she asked after a silent moment passed. She thought about the book, *The Incredible Journey,* recalled the original movie of the same title. "Trying to find your way home?"

"In a manner of speaking, yeah. I guess." He shrugged. "Hard to explain."

She was curious but didn't push. She just let him and Tatum get used to walking together. They continued on, a trio of well-matched hikers, returning to their lives. She looked at Tatum, wondering what went through a dog's mind, if he lived in the moment or remembered the past. If he looked forward to the future. Or if he was just focused on survival.

She wondered, too, if that's what Frank had meant. That hiking and camping weren't just about surviving life in the wild but getting to the other side of whatever brought them out here.

They covered another half mile in comfortable silence. Most of the morning dew had burned off, and the trees provided a much-welcomed shade when they moved out of the trail's open sections.

"How long does it take you to make the loop?" Frank asked.

"Most of the time I spend the whole weekend. I only work half days on Fridays, so I'll trek in as far as I can and camp Friday and Saturday nights. Then I'll head home late Sunday. It's a great way to spend my free time." Frank glanced over, his expression amused. "What?"

"Not sure I've ever run across anyone who felt that way. Most of my friends can't wait to go out. Clubs, movies, dinner that costs more than I spend in a week on groceries."

"I like doing all of those things. Except the spending money part," she said, ducking beneath a low-hanging branch. "But I prefer the quiet and the solitude. I like to think. And to read."

"Now you're singing my song."

"It's funny, but I rarely have anyone to talk to about what I'm reading unless the book's been made into a streaming series. Or hits one of the celebrity book clubs."

"You don't belong to a local one? Glass of wine and appetizers before the host's home-cooked meal and a dissection of the main character's choices?"

Cheryl laughed. "I should find one of those. I need more home-cooked meals."

"I can probably help with that," Frank said, and intrigued, Cheryl glanced over. "The book club part. Not the cooking. I don't really cook. But I do own a bookstore."

"Are you kidding me? That's like my dream career," she said, then grimaced with the reality. "Or it would be if I could make a living at it. Every time I turn around, one of my favorites is closing. Browsing virtual shelves isn't half as much fun."

"I'm lucky. It belonged to my parents, and they left me set. I do turn a profit, but it's not a livable one. Fortunately, I don't need it to be."

"Where's your store? I need to visit," Cheryl said, keeping an eye on Tatum as they continued to walk. He was having what looked like the time of his life, pushing the boundaries of his rope as far as he could. He had to be anxious to get home.

Frank's store was in the township just east of Mayville. "It's on the corner of Coastal and Spruce."

"I know exactly where that is. Don't be surprised if I show up one day."

"Let me know when you're coming and I'll pay someone to cook for us both."

———※◈※———

Tatum liked Frank, the really tall man who was talking to the nice lady. Her name, he now knew, was Cheryl. He had a kind voice, and he laughed a lot like Tatum's dad. Tatum did wish they'd let him run off into the trees because he smelled so many new things he needed to check into. It was hard to know if they were friends or enemies from so far away.

He wanted to find out where they came from, all those smells. When Cheryl and Frank got him back home, he was going to make sure his mum went on more hikes. He wished she knew about this place so she could bring him back here. Maybe he could find it again and bring her.

Hiking was fun, but he was getting pretty tired. And he was thirsty. His leg was bothering him too. It didn't really hurt, but he thought resting it sounded like a good idea. His dad and mum had taught him about resting. It was one of his favorite things to do after playing in the backyard. And after breakfast. And almost all the time he wasn't playing or eating or asleep.

He moved closer to the trail, listening to Frank and Cheryl talk. They really liked to talk a lot. More than his mum and dad talked, he thought, but he probably slept through a lot of that.

Finally, Frank noticed that Tatum wasn't walking as fast as he had been, mostly because of his leg but really it was time to rest. "Do you think we should give Tatum a break? He may be ready for some water."

"Yeah. I could use a bit of lunch myself."

"What've you been feeding him?"

"Jerky, peanut butter, dried fruit. I've got enough to get us through tonight, but I don't want to stop for too long, since I'm going to run out of food after we eat in the morning."

"I can help with that," Frank said. "I was going to take the Michaud back, so I packed enough for that, but the circle can wait."

"You don't have to cancel your plans for us," Cheryl said, but Tatum wanted Frank to stay with them. He wanted to know what kind of food Frank had in his pack. "I'd be happy to pay you for anything you can spare to see us through."

"Not a chance. It's just another twenty-four hours, but you might need help."

"Well, I appreciate it. We both do. And yeah. I'd feel a lot better having the backup."

"Then it's settled," Frank said, and Tatum yipped, causing both human friends to laugh.

Maybe Frank had pot roast and gravy. Tatum had decided that was his new favorite thing to eat. He would have to tell his mum to cook it all the time. He knew his dad would agree.

They always agreed about food, even if his dad didn't share his pizzas.

CHAPTER 17

*Hey diary guy, please remind me to tell Dad every time
you stop walkin' on campin' vacation you eat food. Dis is
vewy important cuz I fink I can start livin' my life like
campin' vacation but only cuz of stuff I like, not the no-
nap-all-day stuff.*

After lunch, and a whole lot more walking than Tatum had
signed on for, and after way too much talking while on the trail,
Tatum realized the sun was going down and he was going to have
to sleep in the woods again. About the same time, Frank pointed
toward a place with almost no trees. "Looks like a good place to
spend the night."

Tatum lifted his nose. He could smell the ashes from where
other people had built fires to stay warm and cook food. He
could smell some of the food, but mostly it all smelled burned.

His mum and dad never burned his food, but sometimes they
burned toast or leftover pizza. Once, when he grabbed the pizza
out of the trash, his dad had caught him and thrown it back.

It would be so nice to eat food that wasn't jerky or fruit or
peanut butter or burned.

It would be so nice to eat pizza.

Cheryl walked over to where Tatum and Frank were looking at
the ground. There weren't any bushes or any weeds or any grass
at all. Just dirt and ashes and rocks in a circle shape to keep all the

burned things in one place. That made it a lot easier to smell them.

"I'll pitch on this side, and you can set up opposite," Frank said, pointing again. "Okay?"

"Sure," Cheryl said, and nodded. "Are we going to share custody of Tatum?"

Tatum cocked his head. He didn't know what *custody* meant. He knew about sharing. Were Frank and Cheryl going to share him so he could eat supper two times?

Laughing, Frank swung his pack to the ground. "We can do that," he said, pointing one more time toward a small tree that was a little ways away. It looked so sad and lonely there all by itself. "Seems a good place to secure him while we get situated."

Frank held out his hand, and Cheryl gave him Tatum's rope. She'd been the one to keep him from running into the woods and having fun since lunch, and that had been more jerky. "I'd thought about trying to rig a harness, but this seems to be working."

"Yeah, I'm a fan of harnesses. I've seen too many dogs slip their collar." He tested Tatum's rope, then got back to his pack. He got back to talking to Cheryl too.

Tatum sat and watched Frank and Cheryl fix up their funny little houses. Cheryl's was yellow and Frank's was blue. Tatum wondered if Frank had more to eat than jerky and peanut butter and apples. He was pretty sure it was past time to eat supper. And then it would be time to sleep. His leg was really tired and his stomach was extra empty after so much hiking.

But they were doing a whole lot of talking again while they worked. He finally lay down on his belly, looking from one to the other, listening to all the sounds in the woods.

The wind was blowing the trees, and they made whooshing, crackling sounds. The trees at his house didn't sound so loud, but maybe that's because they weren't so tall or so close.

He heard birds. A lot of birds. They were having a conversation and sounded upset. Maybe they didn't like people putting houses where they lived in their nests. There were other animals chattering too. Maybe squirrels. Maybe rabbits. Did rabbits chatter? He didn't know.

What he did know was that Frank and Cheryl were talking too much about hiking and camping. They were looking at each other's funny houses. And funny chairs. Cheryl's was just a seat. Frank's had a back. Tatum wondered if sitting in that one made it easier for Frank to cook. Because he really needed to get to cooking so Tatum could eat and go to bed.

"It's funny how I don't really think about food when I'm hiking," Frank said, which was not anything Tatum wanted to hear. "I'm too busy thinking about whatever brought me out here, that incredible journey thing, and the rest of my attention's on the trail."

"Tell me about it," Cheryl said, sitting on her chair without getting ready to eat. Tatum guessed he was just going to have to wait for breakfast. "Then suddenly I'll be thinking about sleep, and my stomach reminds me I've burned off all the calories I consumed during the day."

"I'll bet Tatum's ready for some food," Frank finally said, and Tatum sat up again, his ears perked, his tail sweeping the dead leaves and grass behind him. "I've got an emergency meal. One of the dehydrated ones that might work. Meat and some vegetables."

Tatum barked twice. He liked meat. He liked some vegetables. He liked Frank a lot.

"Okay, dude," Frank said. "Let me get some water boiling here, and I'll fix you right up."

That sounded like it was going to take way too long, but Tatum knew he didn't have much of a choice. He didn't know how to get home to his mum, or to cook his own food, but even if he did, she'd tell him he had to wait. Why did everything about eating mean waiting?

He didn't think Frank or Cheryl had a bag of kibble or a bowl to pour it in. He really did need to get home where everything he needed was. Like his bed and pillow and squishy toys.

Because now he was going to have to sleep another night without knowing his mum and dad were close, his dad snoring, sometimes his mum too.

She told Tatum he snored louder than everyone else in the house. If he knew how to stop, he would, but he liked sleeping and didn't want to stop and figure it out.

Jed had snored too. He wondered if Dr. Valerie snored. Or if the dog who had slept in the bed he used at Jed's house had snored. Did birds snore? Did birds even sleep? How did they not fall out of trees when their eyes were closed? He had a whole lot of questions, and he knew his dad would have all the answers when he finally made it back home to ask him.

Until then, he would just have to keep waiting. For everything.

"Wait a minute," Cheryl said teasingly, glancing across the fire toward Frank. He'd pulled his sleeping bag out in front of his tent to use as a pallet and was lying on his back, reading, with Tatum curled up at his feet fast asleep. "You read on an e-reader?"

"You betcha," he said with a grin. "I downloaded fifty books before heading out. The charge holds for days, and I've got a small cord and charger if the power runs out."

The moon above them was bright, the night clear, the stars twinkling and adding their own ambience. Cheryl was sitting cross-legged on the ground near the fire, using its light for reading. She had to admit to a bit of envy over Frank's digital backlight. And the cushion of his sleeping bag. She usually read in a similar position but hadn't wanted to abandon him.

The ground was hard, and the day's warmth gave way to a chill that was seeping into her bones. "I can't picture a bookstore owner not reading physical copies."

"This bookstore owner is a fast reader. Can you picture me lugging around fifty paperbacks? Even as thin as the one you're reading?"

"You read fifty books on a hike?" That sounded insane. She barely managed fifty books a year these days, sad to say.

"Like I said. Fast." He sat up and dimmed the device, giving her his attention. "But no. I don't read that many. I just like having options."

She closed her book around a flat leaf she'd found on the ground. It appeared to have outstretched arms. She'd thought it perfect for holding her place. "Fiction? Nonfiction?"

"Both. I like biographies more than anything. Those tend to be the size of doorstops." He smiled as if struck by a thought. "And I understand some people read them on vacation and then turn them into award-winning Broadway musicals."

Cheryl laughed. "Right? Oh, to be so talented."

"Hey, if we all wrote musicals, the world would be a very noisy place."

"Or, looking at the bright side, a very joyous one, all that singing and dancing."

"True. That was a good one though. I own the cast recording. And the mixtape."

"Do you bring earbuds and listen to music while you're out here?" she asked, tucking back her hair that had been caught on a sudden gusty breeze.

"I bring earbuds, but I listen to audiobooks. True crime mostly. You?"

"I have trouble focusing on audiobooks. Not sure why. My mind wanders to my to-do list's to-do list. But for me, reading's an escape. All genres. Science fiction, fantasy, romance, thrillers. I read too much serious stuff for school. My brain rebels if I don't feed it some fiction."

"School, huh? What are you studying?"

"I'm in my second year of grad school. Psychology."

"Nice."

"Except for all the work involved on top of my job that pays the bills. I work in marketing for a local hospital," she told him before he asked. "At least I can leave that at the office at the end of the day. I keep telling myself one more year. I can do anything for one more year."

"Four were enough for me."

"What was your major? Something bookish?"

"I wish, but no. I needed the business degree to make sure I knew what I was doing at the store," he said, leaning forward to rub his hand down Tatum's side. "I knew I'd be taking it over. I wanted to take it over, but that's because I loved reading. I didn't know squat about running it. My dad was the finance guy. My mother the artist. They made a good team."

She smiled, her heart full. It was so nice to hear the emotion in his voice, his love for his parents, his respect. "I have my dad to thank for my book habit. He got me hooked on Craig Johnson and C. J. Box. He loved Louis L'Amour, but I'm not a big fan of historical settings."

"And your mother?"

Cheryl suppressed the urge to roll her eyes. "The classics. I hated them. I love them now, but they were not what I wanted to be reading at twelve."

"*Robinson Crusoe*? *Treasure Island*?"

"More like *Little Women* and *Jane Eyre*. Too much Sturm und Drang for me."

Frank chuckled. "A place for everything and everything in its place. Or something like that."

"Sometimes I wonder if she was trying to counter my dad's influence."

"How so?"

"He said kids needed more fun in their lives. He grew up without a lot of that, so wanted to make sure I didn't lose out. He was my camping partner for years."

"Sounds like a great dad."

"I had a great childhood. They loved me a lot. They just didn't love each other so much."

"I'm sorry. That sucks."

Cheryl shrugged, and said, "It happens," just as Tatum let out a loud whuffing yip and started running in his sleep. "And here I thought he'd worn himself out."

"He's either ready to go again or racing to get home."

"My guess would be the latter. I hate him being out here with that injury. I hope the hike out isn't going to be too much for him."

"I can rig my pack to carry him on my chest. Use my tent as a sling. I've got plenty of rope. He doesn't look too heavy."

"Have you done that before?"

"No, but how hard can it be?"

"Too bad you can't ask YouTube," she said, and they both laughed.

Then they both groaned, missing the convenience of a world at their fingertips.

WEDNESDAY

CHAPTER 18

Dear vacation diary, I don't know who is writin' dis down,
but I hope you have a pen. I miss Mum and Dad. I am
havin' fun wif Cheryl and Fwank, but they isn't my best
fwends like Mum and Dad, also Dad didn't write nap all
day *on my list.*

"Anything new this morning? From any of the searchers up there?" Nicole had just gotten to school and was using the office's landline since cell service remained spotty. The school year was almost over, but she still had a class to teach until then.

"Nothing yet," Charles said, using the phone inside the farm supply store. He'd spent all of Tuesday searching for Tatum and had slept a second night in Dr. Hinton's RV.

Earlier that morning, Dr. Hinton had headed to the next stop on his route, and the store's owner had supplied Charles with coffee and the biggest cheese Danish he'd ever seen.

He'd taken it with him to share with Tatum on the trail, having gone out for a couple of hours, searching in case Tatum had turned around and come back.

He'd seen several campsites, but nothing that said one way or the other if the dog leavings he'd seen had belonged to Tatum. Even if he'd been there, with the camper, or after the camper, he wasn't there now. And Charles needed to head home.

The human-interest reporter was coming by that afternoon.

Nicole had set up the interview the previous night while he'd been out on the trail.

The fact that this was where Tatum had last been seen made it hard to leave.

"I'm sure he's close. I can feel it. I'll pack some things tonight and come back tomorrow. Dr. Hinton has my number, as does the store owner here. Someone will let us know if the kids find anything after school."

"Okay."

It was all she said and he felt her disappointment as keenly as his own. He stared out the store's front window, watching the shadows of the trees play across the parking lot. "We'll find him, Nicole. You have to believe that. I believe that. It may not be today, but we will."

"I believe in you," she said, which should've galvanized him but somehow left him doubting.

He wasn't sure he believed in himself, and that was hard to admit. So he shook off the feeling to ask, "Anything from the videos?"

"Not yet," she said, the sound of chatter in the background reaching his ears. "I'll check at lunch. I just hope they pay off. Or the interview does. It almost seems like a waste of time since he's so far away. Who knows if anyone up there will see the story."

He'd had the same thoughts, but Dr. Hinton had told him not to give up. "It's networking. Chris, Dr. Hinton, said a lot of lost animals are located this way. Someone up here could see the social media posts and get in touch. Don't give up. We can't give up."

"I know. And I'm not. I'm just . . . sad. Anyway, I've got to go. I love you. Call me later if you can get to a phone," she said, adding with a laugh, "I miss my cell."

"Will do. And I love you too." Charles took a deep breath, then hung up and turned to the store owner who'd just checked out a customer. "Thanks again. For the phone and the food."

The man's name was Earnest. He was older than Charles, closer to his father's age. His bowlegged gait had Charles thinking of a cowboy. Earnest reached beneath the counter for a brown paper bag. "Ruth, my wife, brought this over a bit ago. For you. For the road."

Earnest and Ruth lived behind the store in a farmhouse painted the same barn red. "Tell her thank you for me. I can't appreciate enough what your son and his friends are doing."

"Good bunch of boys," Earnest said, waving at two men who came in. "We'll all be keeping an eye out. Weather looks good from here on, and everyone knows to keep their eyes open."

Charles nodded, lifted the bag again with a departing "Thanks." It was all he could manage with so much emotion choking off his breath.

—————

Tatum slept so long and so hard he didn't even remember sleeping. He'd done it in Frank's tent, though he didn't remember going inside with Frank either. In the morning the blue walls looked like the sky. He sat up. He yawned. He shook his ears.

And he smelled food.

The door to the tent was closed. He pawed at it, then barked. A moment later, he saw a big shadow that might be a bear and growled low in his throat.

But it was Frank who unzipped the door. "Good morning, Tatum. Ready for some breakfast? Think you'll be able to walk today, or do you want me to carry you?"

Tatum cocked his head, his ears up, his tail slowing down and going still. He was ready for breakfast, but why would Frank carry him? Had he run too far in his sleep and hurt his leg more? He hoped not. He needed to be able to walk home today.

"C'mon, you. Time's a-wastin'."

He walked out of the blue tent and found Cheryl folding up

her yellow tent and packing it into a pouch like the one Tatum's treats came in.

He could really use a treat or ten right now.

"Good morning, Tatum. Did you get a good night's sleep? Are you ready for some breakfast before we head home?"

Home? Did she say home? And breakfast? At the same time? Now that was more like it.

He barked and ran to where she was cleaning up, but when he got there, all he found was more jerky and apples. He sat, then laid down with his nose against the pile she'd left for him on the T-shirt she'd worn the day before. At least the food wasn't in the dirt. Dirt tasted like dirt.

"What's wrong?" she asked, giving his head a scratch. "Is my shirt too smelly for you? I thought you liked the food better when it wasn't on the ground."

He did. And her shirt was fine. He just wanted more pot roast and carrots and gravy. Or more of the deliciousness Frank fed him the previous night.

"I think maybe he's ready to get back on his regular diet," Frank said, folding up his tent and putting it with his backpack.

Tatum wondered if Frank and Cheryl had other houses. Like with backyards and big comfy beds and couches with soft cushions. Or if they lived in the woods with the animals and the trees. If they ate jerky all the time and didn't have phones to call for pizza.

"I can't blame him. I've been thinking about pizza all morning."

Pizza? Had Cheryl said *pizza*? Because he had just been thinking the same thing.

Tatum sat up and yipped.

"You too, huh?" She laughed, stopping to rub his head again as she did more packing. "For now, we have to eat what we have, okay? The sooner we get going, the sooner we'll get somewhere and see if we can find your family."

Okay. He heard her say *get going* and say *family* and say *pizza*. He gobbled up the food because his stomach told him to.

"Good boy," Frank said. "And you look okay to walk. If you get tired later, I'll carry you. Ready to go?" Frank slipped his rope leash around his neck. He wasn't going to wander away. Never ever again. So he barked. Because he was ready to go home.

———•◦•———

Charles had wanted Nicole to do the TV piece with him but the timing turned out all wrong. He'd hoped, too, she'd be able to take a day off work and head with him back to Mayville that night.

But other teachers were out, and there was a shortage of substitutes in the district, and he was stuck. Nicole was so good on camera. And it wasn't like he didn't know his way around a video, what with all the posts he did for Tatum's social media accounts. But mostly he wasn't sure he could talk about what Tatum meant to them without his wife at his side.

Then again, if she was there, he'd probably break down. He really didn't want to break down. He'd been doing enough of that in the privacy of their home and in his truck during the drive.

"Is this spot okay?"

The program's host, Joshlynn Mays, was walking through the backyard with her cameraperson. She'd stopped near Tatum's doghouse, where his toys were scattered.

Charles wasn't sure if he should tell her Tatum rarely used it. Once in a while, when he napped outside, he'd lie half in and half out. Mostly, though, he curled up in his bed in the kitchen while Nicole cooked. Or his bed in the living room while she and Charles watched TV or read on their tablets or played games on their phones. Or in his bed in their room. He laughed to himself. Did all dogs have so many beds?

"Charles? Can you join us over here?"

Charles crossed the yard, his hands stuffed in his pockets. Nicole had chosen his shirt. She said it went with his coloring and was perfect for TV. He was more worried about the camera adding ten pounds. Or he would be, if that mattered at the moment.

He stood there while the video team wired him up. They would follow him and Joshlynn with a boom as they talked about Tatum.

"Ready?" she asked, and he nodded. "Smile, Charles. Don't be nervous. We're just two friends talking about Tatum, okay? I'll film the intro once we're done. I know that seems backward, but our interview will give me a feel for how best to open the piece."

He nodded again. That made sense. And then the cameras rolled. He fell into step beside Joshlynn as she walked from the doghouse toward the backyard's picnic table. "How long has Tatum lived with you and your wife?"

"He's been part of our family for a couple of years now."

"And you adopted him from a shelter?"

"Yes," Charles said, flexing his fingers around Tatum's tags in his pocket. They were a talisman now. A touchstone. "He was about seven months old, so pretty rambunctious once he got used to the place."

Joshlynn smiled, then sobered. "But he's not a fan of storms."

"He hates storms. The thunder when it cracks more than anything. I think a lot of dogs cower and hide from that noise."

"Other loud noises too. Fireworks. Motorcycles."

"Those don't seem to bother him as much. But the combination of the lightning, the thunder, the pounding rain, and the wind whipping and whistling is just too much for him."

Joshlynn nodded as if she completely understood. And maybe she did. He hadn't asked her if she had a dog.

"Do you think he was ever caught out in a storm as a puppy?"

"I really don't know. I just hate that he got caught out in Sunday night's storm."

"Monday's wasn't much better."

Charles really didn't like thinking about Tatum out for a second night. "No, but he was north of here by then, so he may have missed the worst of that one."

"That's right," Joshlynn said, and Charles couldn't tell if she was peeved that he'd let that bit slip. "You had a call about Tatum."

Nicole had explained the development to Joshlynn's team, wanting to be fully transparent. "Yes. A man who lives near Mayville had been here during the storm. Somehow Tatum mistook his truck for mine and made the long trip as a stowaway."

"But he ran off again," Joshlynn said, frowning. "Is that right?"

"Yes. The man who found him took him to a vet to check the Maine Pets registry. Something must've spooked him. No way to know if it was just unfamiliar surroundings or what. He does have a microchip, which any vet or shelter will be able to scan—"

Joshlynn held up a finger to interrupt. "Actually, we checked with a couple of places yesterday. Were you aware the storm has disrupted the registry's services? That they're currently offline waiting for their data to be restored?"

That would've caught Charles off guard had he not spoken about the registry with Chris Hinton. Even so, he didn't appreciate having the information sprung while he was on camera, though he supposed that was the twist Joshlynn had been waiting for.

He cleared his throat and wrapped his hand around Tatum's tags. "That doesn't surprise me. We still don't have reliable cell service. Hopefully we'll all be back online soon."

Joshlynn nodded in agreement. "Tell us a bit about Tatum's social media accounts. I understand he's got quite a TikTok following."

"TikTok. Instagram. YouTube. Just search *Tatum Talks* and you'll find him."

"And if you've seen him," Joshlynn interrupted to say into the camera, her plea imploring, her hands held tightly together in front of her, "please leave a comment on any of the posts. Charles will get the notification and be in touch as soon as technology allows."

"Absolutely."

Joshlynn asked him several more questions, and he stayed focused on Tatum, where he'd last been seen, what he liked to eat, how to get in touch. The rest of what she wanted to know seemed like filler. He didn't want to give her a chance to edit out what was important over what she decided was of more human interest, so he kept to his mental script.

Soon they were finished. Joshlynn walked back to the doghouse to film her intro while a member of the crew removed Charles's microphone. They chatted about dogs, and the man wished him good luck. All Charles could do was nod.

He'd held it together. He'd said what he'd needed to say. He hoped Nicole was proud of him. He hoped the segment helped bring Tatum home. More than anything, he wanted Tatum home.

And he'd do anything he had to to make that happen. Even if everyone watching could see the tears he tried so hard to keep from falling.

CHAPTER 19

HEY DIARY, CHERYL KNOWS WHAT PIZZAS IS AND I
DON'T REMEMBER ANYFING ELSE TO TELL YOU.

The farther Cheryl and Frank walked, the more storm damage they encountered. They were heading south, which is where Cheryl thought the worst of the wind and rain had occurred.

Branches littered the trail. Trunks of more than one tree showed the path the lightning had traveled to the ground. Pebbles and larger rocks had washed onto the trail, making for a more focused hike. Nothing she hadn't dealt with before. She just had to pay close attention.

And she wasn't able to lose herself in her thoughts as easily as she had the first day out. Then again, now she had a dog to look after. And a man for company. She'd have to get back to working through all she wanted to say to her mother once she was home.

"Wow," Frank said, bringing her head up. "I hadn't realized how bad those storms really were. Glad we're on the tail end, because this is a lot to navigate." He looked over to where Tatum walked a few feet away. "Tatum doing okay? You want me to take him for a while?"

Just then, Tatum lifted his nose as he caught a scent, but he didn't pull or bark or try to run. He just got back to walking as if he knew the end goal. "He seems fine, but I'm happy to hand him off. Stretch my arms a bit. He's good on the leash, but my shoulders are feeling it."

Frank came closer and took the rope, earning her thanks. "I've got a spare carabiner. I'll tie it to this end of the rope and hook him to my belt."

"Oh, that's a great idea. Wish I'd thought of it."

Frank reached into a pocket on his shorts. "I used to camp with our family dog. He was twice Tatum's size, a big goofy hound, so I've had that shoulder pain."

Cheryl held her arms out to the side, then lifted them overhead and stretched. "I don't have any trouble hiking or pitching my tent. Even hefting around a heavy pack. It's just the repetitive strain. Your way seems much more . . . ergonomic," she added with a laugh.

Frank grinned. "Yeah. Until he takes off and pulls my back out of whack."

Wincing, Cheryl reassured him. "I doubt we'll come up against anything to make him bolt."

"Unless his people showed up out of nowhere."

"That would be pretty amazing. And would help a whole lot. Especially if connectivity is still wonky. We might not be able to get him scanned until things are back to normal."

They kept on, covering another quarter mile, then a half, moving in and out of the trees, dodging more and more debris, which was seriously slowing down their progress.

The sun was warm and bright, and Cheryl adjusted her ball cap and sunglasses to better see. She reached for her water and sipped, really glad to have run across Frank. She'd have been out of water by now if he hadn't shown up to share his supplies with Tatum.

But it was going to take longer than she'd hoped to reach the trailhead at this rate. Which was going to delay her visit with her mother. And that was an explanation she'd rather avoid.

"Crazy, isn't it," Frank said into her musings, a welcome interruption if she were honest, "how fast we all became used to carrying around a computer? Like one day those who could afford it were plugging big corded phones into their cigarette lighters, and now five-year-olds are playing games on their parents' smartphones in restaurants." He shook his head, chuckling. "I always wonder what Ben Franklin would think. Or Thomas Edison. Galileo even."

"We do live in an amazing time. I can't even imagine what's going to come next." She thought about how often she worked from home, how she attended school lectures online, did her projects on her own time. "Do you think we'll become more and more hermitic? Everything delivered. Virtual meetings and doctor appointments. Those are the things I think about rather than flying cars. No face-to-face interactions. Online book and wine nights via Zoom."

"Hey," he said, his dark eyes twinkling. "Maybe I could host those from the store."

"Let me know the date and time. And the book. I'm totally there."

Frank let out a loud laugh that had Tatum jolting to a stop, looking back, and barking. Cheryl laughed too, completely captivated by both of her companions. She'd never met anyone like Frank before, focused on family, devoted to family, going out of his way to help a total stranger and a lost dog. Changing his own plans to do so. And their shared outlooks, their shared interests . . . Part of her didn't want the journey to come to an end. If anything, that was crazy.

Frank urged Tatum closer, saying, "I have friends from college I only talk to on Facebook. And we're like an hour apart. We could meet for a burger in the middle. It says a lot that we don't, if you think about it. It's like voluntary solitary confinement. Just with better amenities."

He had a point. And she had classmates whose focus was on the disruption of technology on society. "I get that, but between work and school, I honestly don't know what I'd do without all the gig drivers who bring me everything I need."

"You know, Tatum's family might've posted to social media and we'll find them that way. We can do a search once we're back in the land of networking."

Cheryl smiled. "I do love the instant gratification. I won't deny that. I'm a completely spoiled hermit."

"Aren't we all?"

———◦◦◦———

Tatum was starting to think the woods weren't as scary as he'd thought. Animals had crossed the trail, but they'd been there before he had and he didn't have to fight them off. Some were smelly enough he was pretty sure they'd be mean. But some smelled soft and furry. The kind of animals his mum loved to watch in videos like his because they made her laugh being silly. Squirrels and rabbits and possums.

He wasn't sure which smells belonged to which animals. Was there a smelling school for that? Like obedience school? Where a dog could learn which animals were the stinkiest? He was pretty sure that would be skunks. He knew about skunks from the dog park at home.

He'd played with a dog there who his mum told him later had found a skunk in his yard and scared it and it had sprayed him with its stink and that's why the dog didn't smell like himself. He'd had to have a lot of baths. A *lot* of baths. With all sorts of soaps and even tomato juice. Which was why Tatum knew he would run the other way if he ever saw a skunk.

Baths were right up there with vets in his book. Though he did wonder why anyone would take a bath in juice. He knew juice was for drinking, mostly at breakfast, but he'd never really been interested in trying it. He'd smelled it, and it smelled like fruit.

Like the apples Cheryl had fed him in the woods. He wondered how trees made juice out of the apples they grew. And how apples turned into snacks for the woods. He really was going to have to ask his dad so many questions when he got home.

And then he stopped suddenly, jerking the rope and making Frank and Cheryl stop too. He stopped because he not only smelled an animal, he saw an animal! It was sitting on top of a big boulder rock looking right at him like it was mad about him being in the woods.

"What's up, Tatum?" Frank asked, and Tatum took a step toward the boulder.

The animal started talking to him really fast and loud. So fast he couldn't understand what it was saying. He gave a loud bark. The animal stopped talking. Then ran toward a tree and jumped like it was flying, and scampering up so high Tatum couldn't see it.

Oh! It was a squirrel! He knew about squirrels from home, but this was a woods squirrel, and it was bigger and louder and a different color, so he hadn't recognized it until it had run and jumped. Squirrels were probably the best jumpers he'd ever seen.

"I think he saw a squirrel," Cheryl said, and Tatum barked.

The squirrel had stopped on a branch and was looking down at him and talking again, really loud and really fast. Frank and Cheryl were laughing and talking, but he couldn't really hear them because the squirrel was too loud. Tatum wondered if the storm had scared it. Or if its home had been blown out of a tree. He was glad it seemed okay.

He wondered if it was telling him about the storm and asking him if he was okay too. He barked once to tell it he was, except for the part where he'd run off and got lost, but was on his way home and missed his mum and dad a lot. But he didn't think the squirrel heard all of that because it ran off again when Tatum barked. Oh well. He'd have to make a new friend another time.

"C'mon, Tatum. Let's get going," Frank said, and Tatum thought that was a really good idea.

CHAPTER 20

Never mind, diary, Cheryl doesn't know I like pizza. Dad is no longer in charge of my list.

They walked in near silence for another hour as if both needed to let their conversation sink in. Frank held the straps of his pack, his expression strained. Cheryl wondered if he was lost in thought, or if he was in pain. If Tatum was hard on his back. Then again, he had talked about incredible journeys bringing them out here without cluing her in on his.

She should be using the time to focus on her own, but she was completely distracted by a dog and a man . . . And didn't that sound like a book title of its own?

She wasn't aware she'd laughed until Frank asked, "What's so funny?"

"Thinking about titles. Nothing really."

"I read the titles when I'm working the shelves. I kinda get lost actually. Hazard of the job."

"Not a bad one though," she said, and he agreed with a nod. "Every librarian I ever met had to run me out when it was time to close. I'd check out so many books my backpack would nearly break me by the time I got home."

"Sounds like you started your hiking training early," Frank said, tsking at Tatum to come back to the trail.

"Right? I walked everywhere," Cheryl said, smiling at Tatum's reluctance. A curious dog after her own heart. "I still do."

"Me too," Frank said. "Though I do own a truck. I need that for the boxes of books. And camping gear. I buy too much."

"Same here," she admitted ruefully, moving behind him to avoid a tangle of small limbs. "I hate being without something when I'm ready to go."

"I get that," Frank said, then asked, "You feel like stopping for a quick lunch?"

"I was just thinking Tatum could probably use a break."

"He'll never admit it." Frank pointed to a spot just off the trail with a row of small boulders perfect to sit on. There was just enough shade that they wouldn't bake while resting.

"I'm surprised you did," Cheryl said, following him and slipping free of her pack.

"What? I'm that transparent?" Frank laughed, shrugging off his own and swinging it to the ground. "I swear this thing gets heavier the closer I get to the end."

He was right about that. "It's a long walk. And as far as I know, you're human, not superhuman."

"And I was trying so hard to impress you," he said, fixing up Tatum's water. "Sorry, guy. This is it for now. We're in conservation mode. Even the puddles seem to be drying up."

Tatum stopped, jerking on the rope, looking from Frank to Cheryl, then down to the ground, where the remaining water reflected his gaze. He looked closer, as if expecting to find something in the puddle, but all he got for his efforts was a wet nose and a ripple of circles. He looked up again, and Frank laughed. "Nothing there, buddy. Just a bit of rainwater from the storm."

Tatum cocked his head as if confused, then shook his ears and sat, almost as if he'd given up on trying to figure out why anyone would want to walk through the woods.

"And why would you want to impress me?" Cheryl asked a

moment later, frowning as she looked at her own water supply. Things weren't yet dire, but they did need to pick up the pace.

"I was already hating the idea of our parting. It's such a sweet sorrow."

She laughed as she took a sip. "You have a phone, Shakespeare."

"Yes," he said, then drank. "But I don't have your number."

Funny man, but she had to admit a bit of a thrill at his admission. It was nice to know she wasn't the only one feeling the connection they'd made. She pulled her phone from her pocket. Even without a signal she could add him to her contacts. "What's your number?"

He rattled it off, and she typed out a text that would hopefully deliver once the phone picked up a signal: *Let's get this dog home.*

They got Tatum watered and ended up giving him a snack of dried apples, holding off on the sticky peanut butter and salty jerky that would mean needing more water. He gobbled them down, then emptied his bowl before stretching out at their feet. He was snoring almost immediately.

"What a life," Cheryl said, returning her bottle to her pack.

"What a dog," Frank added. "He needs to be the star of his own book series. Teach people about survival."

She watched Tatum's chest rise and fall as he breathed. Every once in a while, his ear twitched, then a paw. She wondered if he was dreaming or just draining his exhaustion. She wished she could grab a power nap. She might have if she'd been alone.

"Do you write?" she finally asked Frank.

He nodded. "Mostly for myself."

Oh, she was pretty sure there was more to this story. "Have you had anything published?"

He gave a careless shrug. "A couple of volumes of essays, one of short stories."

She closed her eyes and rolled her head side to side, the tightness in her muscles easing. "But you're working on the great American novel?"

"Not sure how great it will be, but yeah. The store can get really quiet at times, and I'm surrounded by all that inspiration." He shrugged again, drank again, then closed up his pack.

They spent a good twenty minutes talking about stories . . . movies, television, books, and funny vignettes from their childhoods. A lot of those about camping.

But just as many about dogs they'd owned and loved.

"I've thought a lot about adopting another dog," Cheryl said thoughtfully, looking down at Tatum. "I miss the companionship. I hadn't realized it until running across this guy."

Frank reached down and ran a hand the length of Tatum's body. He rolled to his back and offered his stomach, and Frank laughed and obliged. "How long's it been since you had one?"

"A while. When I left for college, my mother had a little mutt. Part poodle, part dachshund, part chihuahua. He looked more like a shih tzu than anything. His name was Jake."

"Bet he was cute."

Cheryl nodded. "He was my mother's best friend. And her sidekick when my dad moved out. When Jake died, I think she felt completely abandoned. It was not long after I left for college."

Cheryl listened to Tatum snoring, thinking back to how loud Jake had sounded when he'd been less than half Tatum's size. She and her mother had laughed about how such a small animal could make such big noises. "I hated that she was on her own. And that it was so hard for me to get back and visit. My schedule was crazy. And I was working part-time."

And that had been the beginning of their estrangement. Her mother already disapproved of her degree choice, and then that same choice kept her away.

Her mother hadn't gotten what she wanted out of life. Not from her husband. Not from her daughter. And Cheryl wasn't sure how to cross that great divide, even with Tatum helping.

"That had to be tough for her, but I'm sure she understood."

"Actually, she didn't. It was pretty much the beginning of the end of what our relationship had been. She said I was being selfish, leaving her alone after all she'd done for me."

Frank was silent, chewing a piece of apple she'd offered. It was a comfortable silence, a reflective silence. And so she said more. "I'm actually getting ready to go see her."

"Good for you."

She smiled to herself. "You make it sound so easy."

He huffed. "Parent and child relationships are complicated. I'm well aware how lucky I was. Not everyone has what I did."

She looked over just as he shook his head and dropped his gaze to the ground. Her heart ached, filling her chest with sorrow. "I'm sorry you lost them."

"Yeah," he said softly. "Me too."

Tatum stretched and sat up then, shaking off dead leaves and stirring up dirt and sticks. He sneezed, then stood, his tail wagging as he looked from Cheryl to Frank and back.

Cheryl smiled. She adored this dog. "I think he's trying to tell us something."

"Break time's over." Frank got to his feet and hefted up his pack. Then he clipped the rope to his belt and glanced at his watch. "Doesn't look like we'll reach the trailhead till this evening."

"We can pick up the pace if you want," she said. "I'm up for it, and Tatum seems fine."

The sooner she finished what she was now calling her incredible journey, the sooner she'd be free to visit her mother. In another year, she'd have her graduate degree. And she was looking at moving out of state. She had to make things right with her mother before she did.

It might be easier with Tatum along. Easier still with Frank along . . . a thought that came out of nowhere. She hardly knew him. But something told her he was one of the good ones.

"Let's do this," he said. "I've got places to go and people to see." Then he laughed and added, "Not really."

It was late afternoon when they reached the trailhead's parking lot. Six vehicles were there other than her own. Cheryl headed for her small SUV. Frank tossed his pack into the bed of a pickup, then caught up with her. "What are you going to do with Tatum tonight?"

She loaded her pack into the rear of her vehicle, then stopped. She hadn't really thought beyond this point. She should have. Her small apartment complex, they were all studios, really, didn't allow pets. She turned to Frank, then looked at Tatum, who was sitting between them, facing away as if taking in all the sights, sounds, and scents he could manage.

"I don't know." She added a laugh. "I'd made a mental list of what to do, calling shelters and vets, picking up dog food, stuff like that, but until this moment, I hadn't even remembered I can't keep a pet in my apartment. I mean, I suppose I could sneak him in for a night. Or I could if I didn't live next door to the world's nosiest neighbor."

"Why don't I take him home with me?"

She looked up at Frank's offer.

"I've got a house. I've got a fenced yard. We can touch base in the morning."

She glanced again at Tatum, who'd finally plopped to the ground on his belly. He looked as exhausted as she felt. It was a good exhaustion as always, but they both needed to sleep—

"I've got two guest rooms," Frank added before she came up with an answer. "You can stay too. It was my parents' house. It's way too big for one person. I don't use half of it."

She wasn't sure staying with someone she didn't really know was a good idea—

"Or if that makes you uncomfortable, which I totally get, I think the B and B at the edge of town allows pets. I'm happy to split the cost of a night's stay."

Who was this man, and why was he being so nice, so generous, offering perfect solutions? She sighed heavily and rubbed a hand over her forehead. "I don't know."

"Well, you have my number. Even if you can't reach me on it," he said with a laugh. "I'm going to pick up a pizza and head home. I'll give you my address if you want to come stay, but I'm pretty sure I'll be passing out as soon as I've stuffed my face—"

She let all of that settle, then asked, "What kind of pizza?"

⟶•⟵

Tatum really did like pizza. Or he was sure he would if anyone would let him have some.

He had come with Cheryl to Frank's house. They were sitting at Frank's kitchen table talking about calling people to find his family. And they were eating pizza. He was not eating pizza.

He had ridden to Frank's house in Frank's truck. Cheryl had to go to her house and get clothes, she told him. Then she had to stop and buy him some food. He really didn't know why she couldn't just buy more pizza. But he'd been really hungry, so he ate the kibble.

Frank had made him a bed in the kitchen out of sheets and blankets. Frank said he had a lot of extra ones he didn't use, and he probably was using too many but he wanted Tatum to be comfortable and to sleep well. Tatum was very comfortable. He was full of food and water, and he'd run around Frank's backyard. There had been so many new things to smell.

He thought he would just go to sleep and dream about his adventures. And then when he woke up tomorrow he'd ask for leftover pizza for breakfast. He would probably get kibble, but at least it would be a new day and maybe the day he got to go home to his mum and dad.

And to see Puddles. He hoped Puddles wasn't sad and missing him too much.

He woke up when Frank scooted back his chair and stood up to put the pizza box in the trash. It was all gone. Nobody ever saved him any pizza. Cheryl got up too.

"C'mon, Tatum. Let's go see where we're going to sleep."

Oh! He was going to sleep in a bed! Even better! He wouldn't be sleeping by himself in the kitchen, or outside in Frank's tent!

Frank was really nice to let him stay inside. He made Tatum think about his dad, and that made him sad and want to go home. But maybe he would get to see everyone the next day, after a good night's sleep. His mum always told him it was important to get a good night's sleep.

And at least they were out of the woods and he didn't have to keep watch to make sure Frank and Cheryl stayed safe. That had really been hard to do because he wasn't sure which of the smells were dangers and which were just smelly animals and stinky other people.

He jumped up onto the bed. It was a big one, and he moved over to the side by the wall. He knew Cheryl would need room to get in. He curled up and closed his eyes. He heard Cheryl moving around. The bed jiggled when she got in, then it was dark.

And he slept.

THURSDAY

Chapter 21

Dear diary, remind me to ask Dad what books is.
Remember how I said everyone on vacation has dogs, well
they never show them to anyone and talk about them like
they is on vacation. I don't know why all dogs is campin'
and I never did it before.

Tatum was ready to go. Cheryl was taking too much time. He'd ran around the backyard when he'd woken up and Frank had fed him while making his own breakfast.

But Cheryl was way too slow. Tatum must've run out all of his patience outside.

"She'll be out in a minute," Frank told him. He was standing at the sink, eating the same way Jed had done. "She had to call her mother, and sometimes those calls can take a while."

Tatum wasn't sure why but Frank was nice so he plopped down and wagged his tail. Frank had thrown a stick for him to fetch earlier. And ran with him back and forth across the yard.

It had been super fun. Frank had a really nice big yard. And Tatum never even thought anything bad about the stick. That had made him really happy. He had come to love playing with sticks and now wished he'd picked some up in the woods to save for later to make sure he had enough at home for his dad to throw.

Frank was a good thrower like his dad, though it wasn't the same as playing with his dad, but it had been fun and made him want a nap already. He guessed he was still tired from his hike.

He wondered if Frank wanted a nap too. He was drinking more coffee and looking at his phone. Tatum guessed that was just what people did. Coffee and phones. Coffee and phones.

Running and fetching and napping was a lot more fun.

People should pay more attention to dogs.

"Hey," Frank said then, and Tatum opened his eyes. "Everything okay?"

Tatum sat up. Cheryl nodded as she crossed to where he was sitting to rub his ears. She was really good at rubbing his ears.

"I told her I'd be there tomorrow. No going back now."

Huh. Were they going back somewhere? To the woods? Tatum really hoped not.

He'd decided he wasn't going to ask his mum to do more hiking.

It was too much work.

—————

"Tell me more about the book center. And about your store."

Before they'd reached the end of the trail, Frank had explained that he was scouting for a community reading location. Not a store, so much, he said, and not a library, though that was a closer description. But a place focused on every aspect of books.

Visitors could buy them if they chose to, some new, some used. Or they could sit and read as long as they wanted. They could bring friends and host discussions. They could bring their kids and let them curl up in blanket forts and fall into the pages of a fairy tale.

It had been a dream of his parents. And here he was fulfilling it for them.

"What do you want to know?" Frank asked, giving her a curious smile.

"Everything," she said, stopping short of throwing her arms out wide. She loved that she and Frank shared this interest, though *interest* wasn't the right word. Not for either of them.

Books were her passion, her best memories, her calm in every single storm. Even the one she'd gone through with Tatum, she mused. From where she sat in the passenger seat, she glanced into the back to see he'd settled in for the ride, his eyes closed as he drifted off.

She turned to the front again, catching Frank's eye, the butterflies in her stomach fluttering. "I've never met a book I didn't like . . . eventually. Maybe not love, but for sure like."

Frank chuckled. "I could probably fix that for you. I know some old tomes—"

"Which no doubt have some amazing insights and revelations." When he said nothing, just shook his head, she asked, "What's the name of your store?"

"Read Me," he said, smiling as he did.

Cute. "Has that always been its name? Or did you change it?"

"That's what it's always been. My dad thought Lewis Carroll was genius."

As, no doubt, did every *Alice's Adventures in Wonderland* fan. "Do you have a specialty? Do you sell everything?"

"We don't stock everything, but we can order anything. We stock the usual bestsellers. And we have a shelf for employee and customer recommendations. Fiction, any genre, nonfiction. All books deserve their due. And all readers deserve a choice."

She liked that motto. "All new books?"

"For the most part," he said, reaching up to adjust his visor. "I do have a section of collectible and out-of-print titles people look for a lot. Some Patricia Highsmith originals. Asimov. I have an entire shelf devoted to Winnie the Pooh."

"I love that," she said.

He surprised her at every turn. And almost always with something they had in common. It was pretty amazing to have run into a kindred spirit in the middle of the woods. "I had a plush Eeyore when I was little. Its tail unbuttoned. I lost it so many times my mother finally sewed it on. Which made it really hard for him to lose it."

"But it gave your mother one less thing to have to look for."

"True, though I really wished she'd attached it with a cord so I could still take it off."

She started to say that's what she would do for her son or daughter but thought talking about kids she might never have was too personal an admission to make to a man she'd just met. So she said, "Do they still make them like that? Or do you only stock books, not toys?"

"I have plush versions of all the characters, but they're not really for sale, since I have to have them cleaned once in a while. They gather a whole lot of dust."

"That didn't answer my question about the tail," she teasingly reminded him.

"Oh. Huh. I'm not sure I've ever noticed."

"Well, next time you're in that aisle, check. And let me know."

She looked at his profile as she said it and saw the corner of his mouth lift before he replied. "Or you can look when I show you around."

She felt giddy, like she was sixteen and looking forward to their first date. How silly was that? "As long as you show me your collectibles too."

"Absolutely," he said, checking his mirrors as he drove, then checking Tatum, before checking on her and getting back to driving. "Anything in particular you're looking for?"

She shook her head. "I just like old books. Ones that are real hard to find. Just promise you won't think poorly of me for my inability to read what I have before buying more."

"Where's the fun in that?"

"Oh, good. We're of like minds."

"I thought you might have figured that out by now," he said. "The hiking, the camping, the books, and getting this dog home."

All the things she'd been thinking. She liked that he was equally aware of everything they shared. "He'd make a good book-store dog."

At that, he gave a sharp huff. "As long as the bookstore had a backyard for him to play in. Otherwise, he'd gut Winnie."

"Ouch," Cheryl said, and looked back again. "Would you do that, Tatum?"

But he was passed out and didn't even lift his tail in answer.

"Did the dog you camped with hang out in the store?"

"He actually did. He was my dad's right-hand man. Dad had a rocking chair and a small table, round with an inlaid chessboard," he said, making a circular motion with one hand to explain, "and a small braided rug, and Walter took that over. It was near the checkout area, so everyone had to watch their step since he hung off both sides. Dad could sit and read or play chess with friends who stopped. Mom kept coffee and bar cookies in the small break room."

"And the dog's name was Walter," she said, and Frank laughed as he nodded. "Sounds like their home away from home. Sounds absolutely lovely. I'll bet you loved growing up there."

"It was. And I did," he said, a small break in his voice.

Cheryl didn't know whether to let it go but went ahead and said what she was feeling. "I can't imagine how hard it is to be without them."

He didn't respond right away, as if gathering his memories, sift-ing through them, holding close the ones that comforted him the most. "They epitomized the two halves of one whole dynamic. I mean, they had their differences, and their unique personalities, but they were so lucky to find each other. Their life together was amazing. They were so happy."

And her parents rarely had been when together. While apart . . . "I find relationships so interesting. Some couples with completely different interests are great together. Others, like my parents, couldn't stay connected. They grew further and further apart with time."

"That's tough."

"Sometimes I think both would've been better off with a more similarly minded partner. My dad was the impractical dreamer who would pick up and go camping on a whim. My mother was completely practical in every regard." She wished she'd been able to see that as a child. "It was like being raised on two planets by two different alien species."

"Pretty clear why you settled on psychology."

"It's been my own private therapy," she admitted, wondering how things between them had gotten so deep when the only reason they were here together was Tatum. "I understand them more clearly now. And I appreciate what each of them gave me."

"As it should be."

She shifted on her seat to better face him. "Did you get the best of both of yours?"

"I think I am them. Not reincarnated, but I see every bit of both of them in myself. Except for the part where my mother was female," he said, pausing to chuckle. "They were similar in so many ways, different in just as many others. And none of us could get enough of dogs."

"Dog people are my favorite people."

"Absolutely. I mean, I have good friends who are not, but there's just a common ground it's impossible to share with them. I love them, just not sure they would've gone out of their way to rescue an injured dog lost in the woods."

CHAPTER 22

Dear diary, remind me to tell Dad about my list and how he didn't write it good. Cheryl talks all day long about vets, shelters, and whatever books is. Vets is fine, but I like other fings too. My family don't talk about shelters 'cept when Dad talks to people when they write about me or to tell them where I used to live.

"Those storms could not have had worse timing," Cheryl said as she opened the back door of Frank's truck for Tatum to jump in. She climbed into the front and fastened her seat belt. "Then again, without the storms, Tatum would probably still be home and we wouldn't need to get his chip scanned."

"But without the storms, we wouldn't have met," Frank said as he climbed behind the wheel. He looked over and smiled. "The bright side, remember?"

They'd stopped at the only vet in Mayville, who hadn't been seeing patients at all. They were cleaning up after an extended power outage had ruined their refrigerated supplies. Frank's house, luckily, had not suffered. Neither had Cheryl's apartment. At least as far as losing electricity.

The cell towers, on the other hand . . . "I hate putting you out."

"You're not putting me out," Frank said. "My manager is running things this week. And it's Thursday. The store is closed on Thursdays."

Cheryl looked over, amused. "Is that a thing? Like hair salons closing on Mondays?"

He laughed. "I don't know. My parents just never opened on Thursday since Friday and Saturday were the busiest days of the week and they said they needed to be ready."

She loved hearing him talk about his parents. "You must miss them terribly."

He nodded. "They were the best people I've ever known."

"Did you ever wish you had siblings?"

"Not even once. It was like living with my two best friends. And we always had dogs. They were young at heart, but I swear the dogs kept them even younger."

"It's hard to say no when they want to play. And it's impossible to say no when they need to go out."

"Which almost always results in play."

"Except in the dead of winter."

"I don't know," he said, signaling to turn. They were on their way to a nearby shelter they'd been told might have a list of dogs reported missing during the storm. "I had a couple who would've romped through the snow all day long. I was the one who was ready to get warm and dry. They thought the snow had fallen just for them."

Cheryl glanced back at Tatum, who was staring out the back window, his nose up, sniffing through the crack Frank had left him. "What about you, Tatum? Do you love the cold and the snow?"

He wagged his tail on the seat but didn't look toward her.

"I'll take that as a yes."

"He's so good-natured," Frank said. "Lots of lost dogs would be timid and scared. Or aggressive."

"I'll bet he's got a great family. I hope the shelter can help."

"They know we're on our way, so fingers crossed."

Every single one of them, Cheryl mused silently. Dogs often adapted easily to change, but she knew Tatum had to be longing for home.

What a journey he'd stumbled on. Since his remaining tag only had his name, no address or phone number, she had no idea where he'd come from, how far he'd traveled.

He'd obviously been under a veterinarian's care, and she was happy to know his leg was healing well. But had he been injured before becoming lost? Or had a kind soul seen his wound and taken him in?

"That was a heavy sigh."

She glanced over at Frank. He hadn't shaved, and his face sported a dark stubble to match his black hair. There were a few strands of silver, but she knew he wasn't but a few years older than her. He was also incredibly observant, a trait she put in the good column, amused at herself for keeping track.

She wondered if he was keeping track of hers. "Did I sigh?"

"Pretty loudly, as a matter of fact," he said, his grin all too knowing.

She felt seen, exposed, but in a good way, a sharing way. "Thinking about dogs and families and strangers who care for the lost ones."

"It's quite a calling. I've had friends who spent all their free hours working with rescue groups. It was as if they had two full-time jobs. But they hated the idea of an animal in need of food or medical care. And yet that's the circle of life."

"I guess it's different when it's a domesticated animal. Especially a pet. I don't suppose they lose their survival instincts. They just get used to couches."

Frank laughed so loudly at that he snorted. "I think I've seen that meme. But it's true. I mean, look at this one back here. He's about to fall asleep but can't quit sniffing the air."

"I loved dog books when I was a kid. Jack London's. Lassie. I knew to avoid the tearjerkers, though we did read *Old Yeller* one year in school. Pretty sure that teacher never assigned that one again."

"I can imagine. I knew what was going to happen and read it anyway and don't think I slept for a week after I finished it."

"Imagine a class of twenty sleepless grade schoolers and their sleepless parents descending on your classroom."

"They really worm their way into our hearts, don't they? Whether they're real or not."

Which was why Cheryl had everything crossed in hopes that Tatum was on the shelter's list.

"Whoa," Frank said, drawing her attention back to the road ahead. He slowed, then braked to a stop. "What have we here?"

It was a horse. And it had gotten tangled up in a downed tree's branches near the fence at the edge of the road. The tree, in fact, was the only thing keeping the animal from wandering off.

Tatum's nose was going a mile a minute. A low growl rumbled in his throat.

"It's okay, buddy," Frank said. "It's just a horse. And I think she may be lost like you."

———⊷◦⊶———

Tatum had never heard of a lost horse. He thought other dogs might get lost from their mum and dad sometimes. And he supposed cats did too, even though he saw them wandering around like they knew exactly where they were and nobody could tell them otherwise. He'd chased some out of his yard. He wasn't sure about fish like Puddles.

But he didn't know how a horse would get lost from a barn. Horses were pretty big. Anyone could see them anywhere. And big animals didn't live in houses with their families anyway.

Did horses have families? Did the big animals in the woods have families? Did they live on their own with nobody?

Until he'd found Cheryl, he thought he'd have to be a woods dog forever. And even with all that walking, he'd never found any food that was good, or water that wasn't full of dirt from the ground.

He wouldn't have made a very good woods dog. Especially since he'd have to sleep on the ground. He wouldn't have his own funny little house. If he did, though, his would be green.

He would have to ask his dad about these things once he got home. Maybe the horse had been scared by the storm too. He thought probably so since it had run into a tree.

He waited in the truck with Cheryl. She had given Frank the rope Tatum had walked on. He wondered if the horse could smell him. Maybe it would make him feel better to know another animal had been taken care of by Frank with that rope.

The horse was gray like the stormy sky with some splotches that were dark and some that were light. Its tail was really long and swishy like a brush or a broom. Tatum wondered if he could wag it very well when it was probably heavy because that was the point of a tail.

Frank was talking to the horse. Tatum couldn't hear what he was saying, but his voice was very soft and low. Tatum sniffed the air. He thought the horse was scared.

He wanted to go out and tell it everything would be okay because Frank was a nice man like his dad. And Cheryl was a nice lady like his mum. And together they were extra nice.

Even if they talked too much.

"It's okay, Tatum," Cheryl said, reaching back and patting him. "Frank's going to take care of the horse. Then we'll have to get her home too. Just like you."

⟶⊷◆⊶⟵

"She got caught in the tree's branches," Frank said, gesturing toward the mess left by the storm. "It hit the fence and left her an out. Looks like a grass-is-always-greener situation. She made her way out here and decided a snack was in order."

Cheryl had joined Frank at the rear of his truck, leaving Tatum to sniff the air through the cracked windows. The horse was gorgeous. Like Tatum, well cared for and no doubt missed.

"Now what?" she asked. She knew nothing about horses.

Frank nodded, pointing beyond the truck. "Looks like a farm road up ahead. If you want to drive on, I'll follow with her. Maybe you can find out if she belongs there. Or if they know where she needs to go. Because if she decides she wants to head in the other direction, I'm not sure me and this rope are enough to stop her."

"I can do that," she said, turning to look in the direction he'd indicated. There was a big mailbox at the turnoff. It wasn't far. "You want me to wait at the entrance? Or drive on in?"

"Go on in. Find out if they're missing this girl. If not and they know where she belongs, maybe they can make a call. I'm assuming they have a landline out here. Have the owner come after her."

"As long as you trust me with your truck," she said as he led the horse to the edge of the road and waited for her to climb behind the wheel.

Tatum leaned his head over the front seat to check out the change in the routine, and Frank laughed.

"I'm pretty sure, Cheryl Stratton, I'd trust you with my life."

———⟫•⟪———

Cheryl wasn't sure how to react to what Frank had said, but it was all she could think about as she drove. No one else was on the road, so she crept along to keep Frank in sight. Should the horse bolt, she wanted to be able to get back to him and help.

His admission had come out of nowhere, and her heart had yet to quit pounding. She'd never reacted so strongly to someone she hardly knew. She wasn't sure she'd reacted so strongly to anyone she did. And that made what she was feeling hard to reconcile.

Right now, she didn't have time. Tatum sat in the seat behind her, looking out the back window as she drove. "What do you think, Tatum? Is Frank a nice guy?"

Tatum wagged his tail on the seat, then put his front paws on the seat back and stood for a minute, pressing his nose to the back glass and whining.

Cheryl smiled. "Aww, don't worry. We're not leaving him be-hind. We're just going up here to see if we can find who owns the horse. Frank will catch up in a minute."

Tatum wagged his tail again, then sat down as Cheryl slowed to turn into the farm. She rumbled over a cattle guard, reading the name MILLER in big blocky letters on the mailbox.

It occurred to her then that she needed to call her mother again. Cheryl had made arrangements to visit this afternoon, but this detour might just turn into a full-blown delay. She was begin-ning to doubt they'd make it to the shelter before they closed today.

"Life just has a way of throwing the unexpected into our paths, huh, Tatum? You found me in the woods. I found Frank in the woods. Frank found a horse in a tree." She laughed as she braked to a stop in front of the big white farmhouse at the end of the road. "Who knows what's going to happen to any of us next?"

———✦———

Tatum didn't know what Cheryl was talking about, but he sure hoped Frank and the horse would be okay out there all by them-selves. He could see them in the distance. They were walking down the road toward the truck and the house where Cheryl waited.

It was a really big house. And there was a really big barn. That was probably the barn where the horse lived. Tatum imagined it would be pretty loud during a storm attack.

He thought he saw some goats, and he knew he smelled chick-ens. They were kind of stinky. Then he saw the best thing in the entire world next to seeing his mum and dad.

He saw dogs.

CHAPTER 23

Dear diary. We found a horse cuz her fence is not like my fence at home. I haven't seen my mum or dad or Puddles or my bed or nuggets in forty-three years. Also I found some dogs, so they is not all on vacation.

Abby Miller saw movement outside the living room's front window where she sat on the cushioned seat reading Diana Peterfreund's latest book. This was her favorite spot to sit and read. No one ever used the living room during the day. Her parents would come in later to watch TV and the evening news, though sometimes they ended up reading and watching online.

Her mom had a tablet set up in the kitchen so she could listen while she cooked. Abby and her brother and sister cleaned up after dinner, and a lot of times her dad stayed at the table with his laptop. He had a lot of work to do with spreadsheets and reports and emails related to the farm. That night it had been Sarah's turn to set the table while Abby finished her homework and Doug did chores in the barn.

The window seat was filled with red, yellow, and orange pillows in all sorts of patterns and shapes. Abby always felt as if she were sitting in a flower bed. And the light was perfect all day long. She pushed aside the lacy curtain to look out and saw a man walking up the farm's road. A big black truck was in front of him. A woman was driving, and a dog was in the front seat with its head out the passenger-side window, sniffing the air as if he'd never been on a farm before.

The strangest part was that the man was leading her family's horse. Shaking her head, Abby smoothed out the ribbon she used to mark her place in the book and closed it. Silly horse.

"Dad! Lucy got out again!"

In the kitchen, chair legs scraped the floor. Her father had been talking to her mother and finishing up the table since Sarah had gone upstairs to work on a paper due the next day. Or that's what she'd said. But when Abby called, her dad came running. He leaned over her to look out. He smelled like feed and diesel fuel and garlic bread. He'd been snitching slices again.

"What in the world? I swear I'm going to fire that kid. Can't fix a fence to save his life."

Abby rolled her eyes even though he didn't see. "You can't fire him. He's your son."

"True," he said with a laugh, ruffling the hair on the top of her head. By last count, he'd fired Doug ten times already this week. "Feel like going out and bringing Lucy to the barn? I'll be right behind."

"Sure," she said, reaching for her boots and shoving her feet inside. She left her book on the seat. It was due back to the library the following day, and she'd really wanted to finish it that night. She'd have to sneak it under her covers and read by the light of her phone.

It would've been easier to read it *on* her phone, she thought, pulling open the front door and heading across the porch. But it was from the school library. The county library's waiting list had been crazy long. Like so long she'd have been eighteen and ready to graduate by the time her turn came around. She'd been lucky to get her hands on it at all. She'd decided that was because she was thirteen. So far it had been the luckiest year she could re-member.

She raised a hand and waved at the man, who waved in return. "Thanks for bringing Lucy home. We hadn't even realized she was gone."

"Oh, good," he said, smiling. His hair was dark and kinda messy. He had glasses with black frames and his smile was friendly and seriously cute. "I was hoping she lived here. Or at least that you'd know where she belonged."

"She's ours," Abby said, nodding.

He was really tall. Even taller than her dad and Doug. Tall like a basketball player.

"My brother did a crappy job fixing the fence."

"Lucy's a great name for a horse. I'm Frank, by the way," he said, and pointed toward the truck. "That's my friend Cheryl driving. And I think this was the storm's fault more than your brother's. You've got a tree down across the fence, and Lucy took advantage."

"Oh. Okay. Well, I'm Abby. My dad's on his way," she said, having heard the echo of the front door closing and his boots pounding the porch. "You can tell him where it is. Is that your dog?"

"Actually, no," he said. "Cheryl found him in the woods when she was hiking. We're taking him to the shelter in Floyd to see if he's on their list of dogs reported missing since the storms blew through. Hopefully we can find out where he belongs. Guess the storm sent a lot of animals running."

Abby heard her dad coming up behind her at the same time the woman—Cheryl—got out of the truck with the dog. "Does he have a name? The dog?"

"Tatum," Frank told her. "He still had his collar and his name tag but not any others."

"Can I pet him?"

"Sure." It was Cheryl who said it.

She was pretty young, Abby thought, because she reminded her of Sarah. She wore a pair of hiking shorts with athletic shoes. Her T-shirt had a picture of a mountain, maybe one she'd hiked or something. Her hair was pulled back in a ponytail. It was brown like Sarah's too. "C'mon, Tatum. Say hello to . . ."

"Abby Miller."

"Hi, Abby. I'm Cheryl. You already met Frank. And this is Tatum."

"Hi, Tatum," Abby said, kneeling on the road's hard dirt track. She scratched his head and let him sniff her. He was really cute with bright yellow-brown eyes. His coat was reddish brown. He had good teeth and a fun smile.

"I'll bet you'd love to meet Rufus and Skipper. They're our dogs, and they're supposed to keep an eye on things around here. I guess they didn't notice Lucy had gone missing."

"Hello, folks." Abby's father came up behind her, his long evening shadow reaching all the way to Cheryl's truck. He was wearing a ball cap, and the brim looked like a wing on the side of his head, and the tops of his boots made it look like he was wearing buckets on his feet. Abby laughed at that. "Randall Miller. Thanks for getting our Lucy home."

"Not a problem," Frank said, holding out his hand. "Frank Ouelette."

"Cheryl Stratton," Cheryl said, shaking too. "Glad we found her before she got hit, or hurt."

"We really appreciate it. She's our only horse, and I'd hate to have lost her." He rubbed a hand down Lucy's long face. "Lucky us you came across her."

"We were on our way to Floyd with this one here," Frank said, nodding toward Tatum. "We couldn't reach the shelter there on the phone so decided to make the drive. They've got a list of dogs reported as missing. And you've got a tree down on your fence. Lucy got tangled up in the tree limbs but she seems okay."

"Abby'll take her to the barn, and I'll head down in a minute to check her out. Why don't you two come on up to the house?" her dad said, turning that direction. "How about some supper? We have plenty. Garlic bread and spaghetti. Helen makes the sauce from her garden's vegetables. Tomatoes, onions, green peppers. It's something to behold."

Abby took her dad's hand when he stopped and offered it, getting up with a last pat to Tatum's head. She took the rope from Frank. "I'll bring back your rope in a minute."

"Thanks, Abby," Frank said, rubbing Lucy's neck. "Be good, Lucy."

"If Doug's still in the barn, have him take the ATV out and look at the fence real quick."

Abby nodded, "Okay. C'mon, Lucy," she said, leading her away while her dad kept talking to Cheryl and Frank. "Let's get you brushed down and fed. Bet you're hungry. That green grass tastes just the same no matter where you eat it, you know. Or if you didn't before, I suppose you do now. But it's still never going to be as good as spaghetti."

<hr />

With Frank and Cheryl doing so much talking to the farm people, Tatum turned his attention to the girl Abby as she walked to the barn with the horse, Lucy. He watched the other dogs running after them. Curious, he moved farther away from Frank so he could see more of what was behind the house. Farms had a lot of buildings. And a lot of fences. And a lot of room to run. And a lot of animals. And—

Wait! Were those . . . goats?

He walked away from Frank and Cheryl and the man they were talking to. The girl had gone to the barn with the horse. The other dogs had followed her. He hoped they'd come back to play. It had been forever since he'd played with anyone.

He was an expert at playing. And he knew for sure that's what the baby goats were doing. They were having more fun than he knew goats could have. There were two little ones who made funny noises like they couldn't talk very well yet. And their legs were pretty wobbly.

His mum would for sure laugh at that.

One was smaller than the other, and he kept running and jumping on the bigger one's back and then ran off when it fell over like it wasn't his fault at all. Tatum cocked his head and frowned. But the big one didn't seem to care. He jumped up and ran at the little one and butted it with his head. Then they both fell over and Tatum laughed inside his head.

Beside him, the girl Abby laughed out loud. He didn't know she'd come from the barn. "They're pretty silly, aren't they? That little one is Levi. The other one is Wyatt. Maybe later you can have a drink of the milk we get from the mama goats."

Milk? From goats? Not from a refrigerator? He had never heard of such a thing.

"My mom makes cheese from the milk. It's really good. Especially on pizza."

Now that was just getting crazy. She'd said *cheese* and *pizza* both. He didn't know farms were better than grocery stores, like the one where Jed had bought bacon. Or the one where his mum bought his food and his treats and things for his dad that his dad shared.

"Mom's making spaghetti for dinner, and she puts the cheese in the sauce. I don't think my brother knows that. He loves her spaghetti, but he swears goat cheese is gross."

The little Levi goat started running again, going in circles round and round the bigger Wyatt goat. Tatum almost got dizzy watching, and then Levi jumped and stood on Wyatt's back, and then they both fell over. He wondered if the goats liked to play with dogs. Then he wondered if he could find a bigger dog at the park to jump on top of—

"Abs! Bring Tatum back over here, will ya?"

"Yes, sir!" Abby waved at her dad, then looked down at Tatum. "C'mon. I guess we're done watching the fun. But I'll do my best to get you some cheese or milk."

Tatum decided then and there he was sticking close to the girl Abby's side.

CHAPTER 24

Diary, Rufus and Skipper is dogs too, and I am tired fwum runnin around.

While Frank walked with Randall toward the house, Cheryl excused herself to try to call her mother, and was surprised to find she had a signal, though weak. She moved several yards away from the truck, watching Tatum romp in the yard with the two dogs who belonged on the farm, Skipper and Rufus. They were gorgeous.

He was having so much fun she found herself laughing, and her mother picked up the phone to hear her, asking, "What's so funny?"

"Mom, hi. Sorry," Cheryl said, closing her eyes for a moment to refocus.

"You sound breathless."

"A bit, I suppose." *Because I have bad news and don't want to tell you.*

She hated so much disappointing her mother. They had to fix this rift. They had both crushed too many eggshells already. She was her mother's daughter, but she wasn't a little girl. She needed her mother to accept her choices. But she also had to be certain her mother understood that she respected her viewpoint, even as she went her own way.

She glanced again at Tatum. He and the Millers' dogs were running full tilt between the truck and the house and back, as if they had endless energy and never ran out of breath. Which she supposed was part of being a dog. "I've been delayed by a lost dog and a found horse."

And a really nice man named Frank who trusts me with his life. Or at least with his truck, she mused privately, glancing toward the house where he stood talking with Randall and his wife.

"You'll have to tell me the whole story when you get here."

Cheryl leaned against the truck, rubbing the stress from her forehead. Her mother sounded anxious, or maybe even insistent. Cheryl feared she'd gone to trouble preparing dinner when she'd told her not to. Her plans were so up in the air. She took a deep breath and plunged in.

"It may be tomorrow before I make it. Part of the story with the dog I told you about earlier. The registry who has his microchip data is offline so we're headed to a nearby shelter who has a list of dogs reported lost in the storm. I actually just got the first cell signal I've had in a couple of days. Anyway . . ."

After an uncomfortable silence, her mother responded. "I see. The dog comes first."

Enough, Cheryl mused, standing straight and shaking off her anxiety. It was ridiculous and wasn't doing anyone any good. "Actually, the horse came first, but we got her home—"

"We?"

"The friend who's helping me with the dog. His name is Frank." Cheryl took another deep breath. "I think you'd really like him. He owns a bookstore. Like a store with shelves that hold actual books. He even has a collection of plush Winnie the Pooh characters."

Her mother said nothing for a long moment. Cheryl knew she was rambling. She also knew her mother was disappointed, but that wasn't new. Still, she hated how awkward it made the few conversations they did have. She really wanted to mend this downed fence and was employing all the tools she had. If only her mother could—

"You're welcome to bring him along. If you still plan on coming."

"Of course I plan on coming," Cheryl said, caught completely off guard by her mother's invitation. "And thank you. This is just a delay."

"One I'm sure you believe couldn't be avoided."

"I suppose it could've been," she said truthfully. "I didn't have to make this choice. But all I could think about was that horrible trip when we thought we lost Bear. I was hoping to get Tatum home and keep his owners from feeling any of that. Or more of that than they already have. Because I know they're missing him. He's part of someone's family."

For a moment Cheryl feared the connection had dropped, but then her mother came back, saying, "I'll see you tomorrow, then. With Frank and with Tatum."

Then she hung up, leaving Cheryl hugging her phone to her chest, her heart filled with an incredibly unexpected joy.

⊸•⊷

"Sounds like the storm blew down that old maple near the fence section we just repaired," Randall Miller said, gesturing toward a pasture in the distance. "I'll make sure it gets patched up tonight, though Doug and I'll have to deal with the tree tomorrow when he gets home from school." He glanced at Abby, who'd rejoined them and handed Frank the rope. "Lucy likes to wander. Abby says she's free-range, like the chickens."

The girl blushed, and Cheryl smiled at her as Frank said, "Thanks," and tossed the rope into the truck. "I'll bet you two have some great rides."

Abby nodded. Her hair was a deep auburn, the same color as

the smattering of freckles on her nose, and she wore it in a beautiful French braid. She was almost Cheryl's height. A lovely young woman.

"I've been riding her for years. She's the sweetest horse I've ever known."

"I used to read all the horse books when I was younger," Cheryl told her. "All the dog books too. Okay. Any book with an animal," she said with a laugh. "But I dreamed of living surrounded by my own herd. Sadly, I only had a small backyard and room for a dog."

"Like the Chincoteague ponies," Abby said. "I loved reading about them. But Lucy's enough work. I would hate to have to take care of that many." She looked off toward the dogs. "Dogs are so much easier, though brushing out all the snarls and burrs takes a while."

"I'll bet," Cheryl said, following the direction of the girl's gaze.

Tatum was running like the wind, racing with the family's two dogs toward the barn. "I wish we knew more about him than his name. We don't even know what happened to his leg. The vet we saw took a look and said the wound was healing well. So there's that, at least."

"He seems like a smart one," Randall said, watching the trio wrestle and romp. "In good shape too. Doesn't look like a stray."

"If he's not on the shelter's list of lost dogs, I guess for now he can stay with me," Frank said, glancing at Cheryl. "I've got a big yard, so he can stay there. Cheryl's apartment doesn't allow pets."

"And here I thought you two were a couple." It was Randall's wife Helen who spoke, having joined them earlier. Smiling, she moved her gaze between them. She wore an apron over her jeans and yellow plaid blouse. Her boots matched Abby's, and she was half a head taller.

"We actually just met while hiking," Cheryl said lightly, looking over at Frank, who wore the most beatific smile. "And even if we make it to Floyd today, and Tatum is on the list, I have no idea where his family is. We might not be able to get him home tonight anyway."

"I'd say that's a fair worry," Randall said, adjusting his cap after scratching the back of his head. "I'm pretty sure the shelter in Floyd closes around five."

"Would've been nice if someone had told us that," Frank said, giving Cheryl a grim look.

She nodded. "I guess we should've thought to ask."

"Yeah," he said. "It's been a crazy few days. Being unable to get in touch with anyone other than in person has made this quest a bit of a challenge."

"And if you two have been hiking, you're probably pretty worn out," Helen said, lifting a hand to shade her eyes and looking off across the big yard. "Tatum's fine with Rufus and Skipper. Come on in and I'll set two more places at the table. We've got more than plenty food and room."

Cheryl looked at Frank, who shrugged. "We don't want to put you out."

"You won't be," she said, turning to Abby. "Tell your sister to come downstairs. Grab the extra chairs from the dining room and put out two more place settings."

"Yes, ma'am," Abby said, heading for the house.

"Thank you for the invitation. I'm on board if Frank is."

"Everything's ready. Just waiting for some hungry customers." She looked at her husband as she said it, and Cheryl smiled. It was obvious the two had a great relationship. Farming was a hard life, one where the work had to be shared by the entire family.

That was what she wanted in her life. What she'd thought as a child her parents had but hadn't. What it seemed Frank's parents had enjoyed for decades.

She wasn't even sure why her thoughts had drifted to the future. Her current life was a bit of a mess. But she supposed love could show up out of nowhere . . . and why in the world was she thinking about love?

She smiled as she looked at Frank. They were in this together now. "You think Tatum will wander? Should we secure him outside?"

But before he could respond, Helen said, "Skipper and Rufus always spend the supper hour on the back porch waiting for their turn. I'm sure he'll join them."

Randall agreed, nodding heartily and saying, "He'll be fine, but Abby can keep an eye out while she eats. Okay, Abs?"

The young teen had paused at the front door. "Of course. Would it be okay if I took videos of him and posted them to Tik-Tok? I have a few followers there, and some on Instagram, where I post photos. People enjoy seeing what it's like to live on a farm. Maybe someone who knows him will see them. Then it won't matter if the shelter is closed."

"Thank you, Abby," Cheryl said as she walked beside Helen up the stairs. Frank and Randall followed, their voices low and unintelligible as they talked. "That would be great. And I'll cross my fingers you get a gazillion hits and we can get him home."

Chapter 25

Diary, I am still tired, and the new people on vacation does not have pizza either. Rufus and Skipper doesn't eat nuggets cuz whatever a farm dog is. Abby is Dad's fwend I fink, cuz she has TikTok. I wonder why him is not here too.

Tatum sat on the porch between Skipper and Rufus. He was out of breath and had drank a bunch of water with them. They had a giant metal tub, and the water was really cold and delicious. Their dad had turned on a faucet outside and filled it up.

Now they were all waiting for supper while Cheryl and Frank ate inside with the farm family. Tatum liked them, the dad and the mum and the girl Abby. There was another girl and a boy, but he didn't remember their names yet because he hadn't seen them until they came to eat. He was pretty sure they were having spaghetti. It made him hungry and think of pizza.

Tatum thought Rufus was a dog called a border collie. He was black and white and furry and about Tatum's size. And he never stopped running. He was always busy going here and there. So Tatum had to follow, of course. He needed to find out everything he could about the farm so he could tell his mum and dad and Puddles what he'd learned when he got home.

Skipper was a bunch of colors. Mostly white but he had a lot of brown and some spots that almost looked blue. Tatum didn't think blue was a dog color, but he didn't know about farm dogs.

Skipper did a lot of pointing at things. He would stop and his tail would go up and he'd raise one paw. Tatum never could see what he was pointing at. Maybe his eyes were better.

They were both probably a lot of help on the farm.

He thought he could be a lot of help too. He would just need someone to teach him what to do. But he might not be on the farm that long. And if he went home the next day, he wouldn't need to know. But he would have a lot of fun learning while he was there.

He was pretty sure farms were a whole lot of work. There were so many animals to keep track of, and he thought Skipper and Rufus might not take as many naps as he did.

He plopped to the porch to wait for his food. He closed his eyes. He missed home, but he did like making new friends and having so many adventures. He couldn't wait to get home and tell his family everything he'd seen and smelled since he'd escaped the storm.

He really hoped his dad was okay. That he'd fought back when the storm attacked.

And that he'd won.

———⊷◦⊶———

Tatum had been sitting on the porch with Rufus and Skipper, watching the girls Sarah and Abby help their mum and Cheryl get supper ready for everyone to eat.

Everyone, he was beginning to think, but him. His new friends had already given up and run off to the barn, where Frank was with the boy Doug and his dad.

He didn't know if they'd given up too, or if something was happening down there and that was what Skipper and Rufus had gone to check out. He'd find out later, though he did cock his head as he wondered if they were getting food down there and he was missing out. Maybe he should go to the barn and check it out for himself, but it was hard to move when all he could smell was meatballs that smelled almost like they were made of pizza.

As he watched, Abby's mum put them into a great big bowl on the table. The bowl was pretty close to the edge, and the table wasn't all that tall.

He considered those things for several more seconds, and then he looked at the chair. Just the one chair. The one the girl Abby pulled away to make room for another.

She'd never pushed it back in.

He crept closer to the screen door. He'd already figured out he could open it with his paw. It didn't shut all the way, and his paw fit in the space like someone had left it there just for him.

He slipped his paw in enough to make room for his nose, then the rest of his face, then his whole head. It squeaked a little bit, but everyone in the kitchen was busy with the food and doing a whole lot of talking. He could get in and out and no one would ever even see him.

If he wasn't about to starve to death, he would've had patience. Like his dad was always telling him to have. But he'd been eating woods food, then kibble with no pizza or gravy.

Sometimes a dog had to take matters into his own paws.

His shoulder was through the door now, then both front legs, and the rest of him was pretty skinny, so he ran, he jumped, his nails skidded on the chair, and his butt fell off the other side.

He caught his balance and turned, just as Cheryl yelled, "Tatum! No! Get down!"

Then Abby's mum yelled, "Bad dog!" and that really hurt his feelings.

But he was a dog on a mission, and his mouth was ready. He sunk his teeth into the meatball on the top, scooped it into his mouth, and ran, skittering across the floor with the girls Abby and Sarah running after him. He bounced against the screen door and leaped off the porch.

And when he was safely beneath Frank's truck in the front of the house, he swallowed.

It was the best meatball he'd ever eaten in his life.

———◦———

"What did Tatum eat while you were hiking? I mean, you obviously didn't pack for a dog."

It was the Millers' son, Doug, who asked. He was closer to his oldest sister Sarah's age than to Abby's, and was his high school's star baseball player. He was tall like his dad, and lanky, his hair more brown than Abby's red, but he had the shoulders and arms of a ballplayer. A lot of that, Cheryl was certain, came from working the farm.

She stabbed a fresh cherry tomato with her fork. She'd seen the family's vegetable garden through the back door when calling Tatum onto the porch, and wondered if they sold the excess through a co-op, or at a farmers' market. Or if they canned and froze what they grew. There was a giant freezer in the mudroom along with empty produce crates.

She could eat like this every day. "Jerky, peanut butter, and dried fruit. Apples mostly. Frank had some vegetable soup, but you're right about not packing for a dog. Neither one of us. If not for the rain, we might've run out of water for him."

"I'd be stealing the first meatball I came across if that's all I'd had to eat too," Doug said, earning a sharp "Douglas!" from his mother, and Cheryl tried not to laugh.

"Gotta say I'm sorry I missed that," Frank said. "He's been so well behaved, I guess we can forgive him this once."

"And now I'll be getting on fixing that door," Randall said, as Helen nodded and added, "You got that right."

"His wound didn't get infected in the woods?" Abby asked, twirling her fork through her pasta as if she hadn't paid any attention to the previous exchange.

"No," Cheryl said, loving the girl's concern. "The vet thought whoever stitched him up gave him a long-acting antibiotic. Maybe even pain medication. Injections."

"That's good," Abby said, reaching for her water glass. "It's easier that way than to try to get pills down them on a schedule. I've had to do that with Skipper, and he ends up spitting them out or throwing them up every time."

"Abs here has her heart set on veterinary school," Randall said, pride thick in his voice.

"But when we're at the supper table with guests, she doesn't have to talk about dogs throwing up," Helen said, giving Abby a cocked brow. "Not everyone is used to farm talk with their spaghetti, you know."

"It's okay," Frank said, cutting into a meatball with his fork, his gaze focused on his plate. "We're all animal lovers here. I could tell tales about the wolfhound I had as a kid . . . but I won't," he added, winking flirtatiously at Abby, who dropped her gaze.

Cheryl wanted to kick Frank under the table—that was not how to set the girl at ease—but was afraid she'd miss and hit someone else. The table was large and round. There was plenty of seating room for seven, and plenty for the family-style platters of food in the center.

She knew he would never purposefully embarrass Abby. Men could be so clueless, and girls her age so easily ruffled. But she changed the subject anyway. "What schools are you considering?"

Abby shrugged as she got back to eating. "I might not be able to go. It costs a lot, and I don't have the money, though I'll start saving when I get a job. I know there are grants, but I doubt I can get a scholarship. My grades aren't as good as Sarah's. And I don't play sports like Doug."

Cheryl felt a hitch in her chest. The girl, the young woman, was so poised and smart and self-aware. "I guess after-school jobs are hard to come by out here even when you are old enough."

"Sarah does tutoring after school, and Doug works weekends at the pharmacy in Shireton," Helen said, handing Frank the serving bowl of salad. "Abby is just finishing up junior high, so I'm sure more opportunities will come her way next year."

"Plus she's doing her TikTok thing."

The comment came from Doug, whose focus was on his plate piled with more meatballs than noodles, and Frank asked, "What TikTok thing?"

"She set up an account last year, I guess. She posts videos from around the farm." He dug into his food. "People who don't know how hard farming is love it. Like it's entertainment."

"Oh, right." Frank looked at Abby again. "That's where you wanted to post about Tatum."

Abby nodded. "I'll take some videos after supper. And it's not really that popular, but most of my followers are animal lovers, so maybe they can help network Tatum."

"Can you monetize that?" Cheryl asked. "I know you can make money on YouTube, but I don't know much about doing it on TikTok."

"I only have TikTok and Instagram right now, but I'm going to spend the summer setting up a YouTube channel. I've got a lot of longer videos I can upload there. But I want to have more of a plan when I go into it. A platform, I guess. I want to get it right. Focus it toward animal husbandry and not just silly goats, though people do love them. Maybe use it somehow when I do apply to college."

"That's very smart," Frank said. "You could become a farm influencer."

Randall laughed. "I don't even know what that is, and I'm afraid to ask."

"Google can explain it a lot better than I can," Frank said. "But I know there's money to be made through social media."

"Even for teenagers?" Randall asked, glancing at Abby, who was frowning as if working through her idea.

"Absolutely," Frank said. He reached for his water glass and drained it. "I was just reading a book about it. I'll find you the title when I get home. Or just give me your address and I'll send you a copy."

"Frank owns a bookstore just east of Mayville," Cheryl said.

She'd only lived there a year herself, and being caught up in work and school, she hadn't gotten out to explore as much as she would've liked to by now. Kinda wild to think she'd met Frank on the trail instead of surrounded by Winnie the Pooh titles.

"For real?" Sarah asked. She'd been quiet through the meal, observant. This was the first time she'd spoken. "With everything being digital, do you have a hard time staying open?"

"I would, but I inherited the store from my folks when they passed. So it was already well established. And it's a bit of a hobby as much as it is a job."

"That is awesome," Sarah said, toying with her salad. "I'm not sure who reads more, me or Abby, but we're never without a book."

"If you lived close, you could probably hire Sarah on the spot to work for you," Helen said. "Randall and I have always been readers, and the kids inherited those genes."

"Interesting you should say that," Frank said. "My parents loved this area. One of their dreams was to open a sort of community reading center up here. Kind of a cross between a library and a bookstore. They knew folks living in more rural areas, the ones who don't read digitally, have a harder time borrowing some titles."

"Are you going to do that?" Abby asked.

"I'm planning to look around, revisit a lot of the spots that were important to them. It's kinda my summer project."

"Who's working at your store while you're not there?" Sarah asked.

"I have a manager, but my next-door neighbors are a retired couple. Both are lifelong bibliophiles. They knew my parents, and they love to hang out in the store."

"Like volunteers?"

"Exactly."

"More bread, Frank? Cheryl?" Helen asked, offering the basket of toasted slices.

"I'm fine," Cheryl said, wonderfully full. "I haven't eaten this much or this well in ages. Thank you again for having us."

"It's the least we could do after you brought Lucy home," Randall said, pushing back his plate and finishing off his water. "Now. Unless you have somewhere you need to be, why don't you two stay the night? You can get back on the road in the morning. I mean, I doubt you'll make any progress finding Tatum's family until then. And he's having a great time with the others. We've definitely got enough room."

"We wouldn't want to put you out," Frank said, and Cheryl quickly added, "I'm sure we can find a place to stay near Floyd."

"Maybe, but not sure you'll find any place that's pet friendly," Randall said, scooting his chair away from the table and gathering up his dishes to carry to the sink. He scraped his scraps into a pile that included tomato cores and discarded lettuce leaves.

Cheryl figured it was for the dogs. Tatum was going to eat well that evening.

"We have two extra bedrooms. It's not a problem."

"If Cheryl's up for it, I'm game," Frank said, wiping his napkin over his mouth. "We didn't really have plans except to get to the shelter and head home. Well, Cheryl was going to see her mother but . . . Here we are."

"I called her earlier to explain the delay," Cheryl said. "I'd love to stay, thanks. It'll definitely be easier in the morning to start from here."

"What are you going to do with Tatum if he's not on the lost dogs list?" Sarah asked.

Before Cheryl could respond, Helen said, "That's a bridge they'll cross when they come to it. In the meantime, Tatum's safe and cared for. That's all that matters."

CHAPTER 26

Diary guy, farms is busy. Everyone is lookin' for my family, but I didn't see where I dropped it, also I don't know what families is. Abby has a mum and a dad, but they go on vacation together, but they call it farm . . . I don't know if it not the same as campin'.

"What *are* you going to do with Tatum if you can't find his family?"

Helen asked the question of Cheryl as they walked toward the vegetable garden. It sat behind the house, to the left, while the barn was off to the right, away from Lucy and the goats. The chickens were closer. They had a pen, but it was almost like a small pasture. Cheryl watched them pecking at the ground for bugs and imagined their eggs were amazing.

"We actually haven't talked about it beyond him staying with Frank for now," Cheryl said. "This whole adventure has been so strange. Meeting Tatum, meeting Frank, running across Lucy, and now spending time with all of you. I'd been camping to clear my head, and things just got crazy."

Helen paused for a moment, lifting a vine to check a not-quite-ripe tomato. She looked at the leaves, turning them over, then moved on. "You said you were supposed to see your mother. It's none of my business, but I hope the delay hasn't caused problems for you."

Cheryl took a deep breath. Gardens smelled like nothing else, the earth and the greenery and the ripening vegetables. She wasn't the least bit hungry but swore her mouth was watering. She wanted to bite into a pepper and taste the tang, into a tomato and feel the burst of juices. "Not at all. Please don't worry. My problems started a long time ago. I'm hoping to finally get things worked out. It's a long story, but family troubles usually are."

Helen nodded knowingly. "This garden is where I clear my head. I love walking through here and checking to see what I can harvest. I do it every evening. The kids are busy with homework, and Randall's finishing up chores or reading the news, and it's so quiet and peaceful out here. And the vegetables smell so good," she added with a laugh. "I think that's my favorite part. The way they smell. I love the peppers most of all."

That had Cheryl smiling. Must be a universal thing. "Frank and I ate pizza last night, but the two days before, I ate mostly freeze-dried camp food. Things that are easy to carry and easy to prepare. I love being in the woods but wish I could haul fresh food with me. It's just impossible when hiking. I have to keep my pack light. It's different when setting up a site to stay."

"Do you camp on your own?" Helen asked, leaning down to move aside a squash leaf.

Cheryl nodded as Helen stood and looked over, showing off a zucchini. "My father would take me out when I was young. We'd hike for a couple of days and camp overnight. I've loved it ever since. I don't do long treks. Most of the time, I only have the weekend free. Luckily I had this week off. It's just good to get away. Breathing the fresh air. You must love living up here."

"I do. But that doesn't mean I wouldn't like more conveniences. Like overnight delivery."

Cheryl thought back to her conversation with Frank and how fortunate she was. "I'm completely spoiled to instant gratification. I admit it."

Helen chuckled. "It can make life easier in a lot of ways."

"Sure, but your kids have skills I doubt I do."

"I guess the secret is balance." Helen moved farther into the rows of staked vines, bringing a handful of string beans to her nose and inhaling. "Sarah's just biding her time until she graduates and can get out of here. She's smart, savvy. She'll be fine. Doug too. He designed and built my greenhouse last year. He's a quiet thinker. It makes him seem absent-minded at times. I'm not sure what either of them will end up doing."

"Farming doesn't interest him?"

"Not like it does his father, but I won't be surprised if it's what he finds himself doing in a few years." She stared into the distance for a moment, smiling softly. "I worry the most about Abby."

"Why's that?"

Helen shook her head, shrugging off her thoughts. "*Worry* isn't the right word. She'll be fine too. She's still young, so she has time to come into her own. But she really does love the animals and wants to go to veterinary school. I'm just not sure that's an option."

"I'll bet there are grants, like she said. Maybe even small scholarships. Lots of related industries offer them. And it's never too early to start researching those. See what the qualifications are. But I doubt I'm telling you anything you don't already know."

Helen smiled. "I do, but thank you for the push. I keep thinking there's no rush, but one day I'll turn around and she'll be eighteen and then it will be too late."

"I don't know," Cheryl said. "Sometimes we have to put off what we want to do until all the pieces are in place. Sometimes we don't even know what we want to do so . . ." She shrugged, thinking of her life, the lives of friends, thinking of Frank. What had his plans been? "Then sometimes life takes a sharp left turn and plans go flying out the open window on the right."

"That's very poetic."

"It's what happens in the woods," she said with a light laugh. "I'd been walking and thinking of how best to deal with my mother's disappointment over my career choice. I'm a grown woman. And she's still waiting for me to change my mind and do what she wants."

When Helen raised a questioning brow, Cheryl went on. "She's a bookkeeper. She thought I'd follow in her footsteps, but I'm getting my master's in psychology. Family therapy."

"I imagine that keeps you busy."

"Most of my classwork is online. And my job is set up where I can do a lot of work from home. Pretty sure I'd make a perfect hermit."

"It's a good time to be one," Helen said with a huff. "Then again, I guess I've always been one. We work dawn to dusk, and now that the kids get themselves to school, I don't go to town very often. If we run out of milk, Doug can grab it on his way home. I can whatever produce we don't eat, or make sauces and soups to freeze. I guess it's good I have the dogs for company."

"Do you bake your own bread?"

Helen grinned, the smile lines at her temples adding to the sparkle in her light green eyes. "Does a bread machine count?"

"Absolutely," Cheryl said. She really liked this woman. "It's fresh. You chose the ingredients. You're just saved the manual labor."

"I actually like that part. Kneading, pounding out my frustrations," Helen said, reaching for a cantaloupe. She offered it to Cheryl. "Smell this."

Cheryl took it and brought it to her nose. "Mmm. It's like dessert."

"Let me find another one and we'll go cut them up. I just need enough to share with the dogs. They think it's the best treat in the world."

"I'll bet they love all the produce. The things they can have anyway."

"They do. And there are only a few things off-limits. Onions for one."

Cheryl glanced back toward the house. Skipper was stretched

out panting while Tatum and Rufus tumbled across the yard. As she watched, they got up and Tatum scampered away, looking back to see if Rufus was chasing him. Which after a stop at the watering hole, he did.

"Those three are having a good time. I'm glad your two accepted Tatum."

"They don't get a lot of company. And Tatum's a great dog. They're good judges of canine character."

"He really is. I was thinking of taking him to see my mother, but with all he's gone through, it might be best if he waits with Frank." It had been a while since her mother had owned a dog. Her house was no longer set up to minimize exuberant canine breakage. He'd need to stay in the yard, and there was the issue of watching him to clean up any mess he might make. Then again, she had included him in the invitation. "We didn't plan to be away this long. It was supposed to be a quick day trip then back home."

"You know, Tatum could stay here. After you get back from Floyd. We've got the room. He's comfortable. It wouldn't be any trouble."

Funny how her first reaction was to say no. To want to keep Tatum with her when he wasn't even her dog. She couldn't have him with her at home anyway. And even though Frank had room, he had the bookstore and now the reading center to focus on. As much as he loved dogs, he wasn't in a position to take on one with Tatum's exercise needs.

Cheryl had to do what was best for Tatum. She adored him, she loved his company, but he wasn't her dog. She had to remind herself of that. Again. "Thank you. I'll think about it."

"Do. Because it could solve a lot of your problems," Helen said, handing her another cantaloupe. "Let's go have some fruit with our ice cream. It's homemade."

CHAPTER 27

Diary, dis vacation is wicked long, but the food fing is fine cuz it so diffwent. Dad put take pictures of Tatum on my list, which I like cuz it just like home times. Rufus and Skipper is always runnin', always, and don't stop for rides in the car or the nuggets place.

Nicole sat sideways on one end of the sofa with her iPad, scrolling through the comments on Tatum's news story on the station's website. The internet was back, at least for now, and Charles was using the Wi-Fi to check notifications coming through from TikTok and Instagram.

There were hundreds of them, hugs and hearts and crossed fingers and stories of families being reunited with lost pets after months, years even. The outpouring of support choked him up. Tatum had touched the lives of so many strangers. To this day, the love for Tatum amazed him and Nicole both, when all they'd wanted to do was share their good fortune at finding him and giving him a forever home in their hearts.

Charles didn't want to wait months or years to get their dog back. He didn't want to wait a week, or even another day. He wanted Tatum home now. He tossed his phone to the side.

It hit Nicole in the shin. "Ouch?" she said, the question in her voice deserving an answer.

"I hate this. Every bit of it. I want him home." Charles reached for his phone, softly rubbing her leg in apology. "I don't want to keep worrying. I don't want to keep trying to come up with new things to try. I mean, we know where he is. Or where he was last seen anyway. I hate that work picked up and I have to wait to head back up that way. I just want life to go back to normal. Now."

"You sound just like Tatum," she said, and Charles looked over to see her face lit with a soft smile. "Always impatient. Always wanting what he wants now."

Charles knew exactly how Tatum sounded. He was Tatum's online voice after all.

"Look at these comments. The love, the concern. How can that not bolster your resolve?"

He didn't respond, just shook his head, so Nicole started reading them aloud.

"Here. Listen. 'I'm making a donation to my local shelter in Tatum's name. Best of wishes.' How sweet is that? And here's another. 'Same goes for me. I can't imagine how many amazing dogs like Tatum are waiting to be loved forever.' You did this, Charles. Tatum did this," she said, her voice breaking. "I know you miss him. I know you're hurting. But doesn't this reach, the impact you've made, inspire you to keep going?"

"It does, and I will," he said, which was the absolute truth. He added more honesty. "But they don't really help with the fear. That's the worst part. I'm afraid things aren't going to go our way. And that's why I'm so impatient."

She was silent for a moment as if letting that settle. Then she asked, her voice soft but insistent, "What would he say to you right now if he was here? What do you tell him all the time?"

She was right, but he wasn't sure he could shake off this funk. It went bone-deep because that's where his love for Tatum lived. "If he was here, I wouldn't be impatient."

"Charles . . ."

He sighed and leaned back, dropping his head against the cushion. He tried to think like Tatum, to find Tatum's voice. "I can't. Not right now."

Nicole set aside her iPad and sat straight, rubbing a hand up and down his arm. He'd put a frozen casserole in the oven earlier while she changed into a T-shirt and shorts after work. They were just waiting to eat. "Okay, then. As you. What do you need to tell yourself?"

He pulled in a deep breath. He knew what she wanted to hear. It was one of his favorite pieces of advice, one he'd actually seen on a meme, and he paraphrased. "Worrying doesn't change anything. It doesn't make things get solved more quickly. It doesn't make the outcome any worse. Worrying is a useless emotion. A waste of energy."

"But you can't stop."

He shook his head. "Can you?"

"Of course not. But I don't want you to worry that I blame you either. I never would. I never could. Look what happened with Mr. Allen. He had Tatum for less than twenty-four hours, and the silly little goof jumped and ran just like he did with you."

"He didn't know Tatum. I do. I am never going to get over this, Nicole."

"Yes you will. And when he's home, we're both going to be even more diligent than before."

That was an understatement, he mused, then sat forward, his heart jolting, and reached for the remote, caught by his image on the TV. "Look! They're running the story again."

He hated seeing himself on-screen, hated hearing himself talk. He supposed a lot of people did. But mostly he hated seeing the backyard so empty. Tatum's toys didn't even look the same. They looked like they'd been discarded, that they were litter, when they were loved by a dog who wasn't there to remind them how very much.

"I miss that dog," Nicole said, her voice barely a whisper. She leaned into Charles and he wrapped his arm around her shoulder, hugging her close.

"Me too," he said softly. "Me too."

"You sure you're okay spending the night?" Frank asked as he and Cheryl walked along the fence near the road. The Millers all had evening chores to take care of, along with school- and house-work to finish, and Cheryl had needed to walk off the pasta.

She'd sleep good that night, and the food had been amazing; she wasn't sure she'd ever eaten as good in a restaurant. But she'd feel like a lump the next day if she didn't burn off a few calories before going to bed. Especially the ice cream's.

Tatum ran in front of them, sniffing the fence posts and the grass growing just on the other side.

Always greener, Cheryl mused. She had to admit to being nervous. He wasn't on a leash. Hopefully, he'd want to stay with her and Frank, and the Millers' dogs, and not go walkabout.

"If you're sure. But if you need to get back to your scouting quest, I can figure out getting Tatum to the shelter," she said with a shrug. Transportation was the biggest issue with extending this trip to two days. "I might be able to borrow Helen's car. Or have her drive me to Floyd and rent one there or something."

For whatever reason, Tatum had come into the woods and found her. She'd kept him close, accepting the responsibility that came with his trust. She didn't want Frank to feel obligated. He was the one with plans. All she had to do was go see her mother . . .

"I thought we were in this Tatum thing together," Frank said, his hands stuffed deep in his pockets. "The three hiking muske-teers and all that."

He made her think of a dejected little kid. Had she hurt his feelings? "We are. I'm so appreciative. But I know this wasn't how you'd planned to spend your time up here."

"My time is my time. I can spend it working or on Tatum or with you."

She let that settle, the way he separated her from Tatum. It made it hard to focus, hard to think. It made her stomach flutter, and she sighed. "Helen said we could leave him here if the shelter doesn't tell us anything."

"Huh. Really." He followed Tatum's antics as he chased grasshoppers and moths, creating havoc in the insect world as he played. "I'm sure he'd love it."

"That wouldn't mean we'd have to stop looking for his family." If he could spare the time, she wanted him included. This quest wouldn't be the same alone. He'd been along almost since the beginning. "But he'd be well cared for while we did."

Frank grinned, and gave an *Aw shucks*–sounding huff. "I like the way you say *we*."

That made her smile. "Well, I figured when you attached yourself to us in the woods we were in this together till the end."

"Attached. Is that what I did?"

The question hung unanswered as she looked ahead to where Tatum was rolling around and scratching his back. Rufus came running toward him, and Tatum hopped up as if his legs were made of springs.

"He fits in so well here. I just know I'm going to miss him whether he's here or with his family. I wish my living situation allowed for a dog. I really miss having one."

"You could always keep one at my place. If you don't want to move. I've got plenty of room, and we don't live that far apart." He stopped walking and looked over at her, all tall shadow. "I can't believe how close we actually do live. And have never run into each other. Like in the grocery store. Or the sporting goods store. Or, you know, the bookstore."

"I hate to admit how little of Mayville I've seen since I moved there," she said, lifting her gaze and searching out his. "And I don't need to adopt a dog for us to spend time together, you know."

"I do know. Just wanted to make sure we were on the same page there."

She hooked her arm through his as they walked, her shoulder bumping him, her strides so much shorter than his. "So first thing in the morning, we take Tatum to the shelter in Floyd."

"Right. If he's on their list, or if the registry's back online, we call his family and I guess make arrangements to meet them."

She nodded. "But I still need to go see my mother, which is now putting you out."

"No, it's not," he said. "My time is your time. And tomorrow evening, whichever way things go with Tatum, we take Helen up on the offer. He stays here, and we go home. Once they're located, the family comes here to get him. You and I get on with our lives."

"Why does that seem so easy?"

"Why does it have to be hard?"

She looked at Tatum, who seemed to have no problem keeping things simple. She needed to adopt his attitude. "I guess I've kinda gotten used to things being difficult. It's been that way a few years now, so I keep waiting for the other shoe to drop."

"That's tough. I'm sorry."

"I could write a paper," she said, and laughed. "I keep thinking about how many lives Tatum has touched in the last two days."

"Says a lot about his family."

"I really do want to meet them."

"Well, let's get tonight behind us and see what tomorrow brings," Frank said before he whistled for Tatum. "C'mon, boy. Let's see where you're going to be bunking tonight."

"I've got a feeling Abby's going to plead to have him sleep with her," Cheryl said, remembering how much she loved having a dog at the end of her bed, warming her feet, keeping her company. It had been someone to talk to, to read to, to cuddle with.

"Which I'm sure he'll love to do."

———✦———

Tatum came running toward Frank and Cheryl. Skipper followed him, but Tatum was faster. He would win all the races they had. But he wouldn't win against Rufus, and that was okay. He was just glad they both liked to run. It was fun to run with friends.

He wondered if Frank would run with him back to the house but thought probably not because he looked like he was too busy talking to Cheryl. That was okay too. They always had a lot to talk about. And he'd rather they did it when he was playing and he didn't have to hear them.

The sun was going down, and Tatum was getting pretty tired after all the running and playing he'd done that day, and riding in Frank's truck forever, and finding a horse. He'd never found a horse before. Or eaten cantaloupe before. He'd heard Cheryl tell Frank it grew in a greenhouse, but Tatum hadn't seen a greenhouse anywhere.

Cantaloupe was almost as good as a Puppuccino. He had eaten a lot of good food here on the farm. And drank milk from goats with Skipper and Rufus. It had been warm and not as sweet as a Puppuccino, but it was really good. He could still smell it on his nose.

Even with so much fun and food he still wanted to go home. Maybe the next day he'd finally get there. And the farm day would be like a vacation he could dream about. A farm was a better vacation than the woods. It wasn't scary at all, and he didn't have to stay on a rope.

But next time he took a vacation, he wanted his mum and dad to come along with him. That would be the most perfect vacation in the world. With pot roast and gravy and cantaloupe.

CHAPTER 28

Diary, please remember to ask Mum if she has any cans of lope—it tasty. Also horses isn't dogs either, Lucy is a horse like Tatum is a dog. It weird.

"He's a pretty cool dog," Doug said, sitting next to Tatum on the top step below the back porch. Abby sat on Tatum's other side. Tatum had stayed out with Abby so she could take some pictures while her mom had showed Frank and Cheryl the extra bedrooms upstairs. Doug had just finished his chores, and he smelled like he'd been rolling around with the goats. It was pretty gross. "I'll bet he'd be good with the goats with some training."

And then he'd smell as bad as you do, she thought, smiling to herself. "Probably, but I don't know if Dad will let us keep him if we can't find his family."

She knew Tatum was going to stay if Frank and Cheryl didn't get what they needed at the shelter. But she didn't know how long, or if they'd have to give him up. She hoped not.

"Did you make a video?"

She nodded, her phone in her hand. "I posted a short one, though I probably didn't add enough hashtags. I'll look through the rest after I do the dishes."

"Hey, I'll trade you. I'll do the dishes. You fix the fence."

"I'd do it right the first time so there wouldn't be a need to fix it again."

"Ha. Funny. Dad checked it the first time. So you can blame

him for Lucy getting out, though it was probably just the storm and that tree being really old."

"I think Dad's just tired. He and Mom work too much." And they worried about having three kids to put through college. Abby had serious stress about that.

After a long quiet moment, Doug leaned back on his elbows and stretched out his legs. "It's almost summer. We'll be done with school in a couple weeks and be able to do more. Though I really wish summer meant sleeping in. I would love to sleep in."

"You get to sleep in on Saturday. Like most people who work."

"I'm sixteen. I'm supposed to be sleeping in all summer," he said, and Tatum gave a little yip.

Abby laughed. "I think he likes sleeping too."

"Name me a dog who doesn't. Animals have the right idea. Eat and sleep. That's their life."

"Is that really all you want to do?" She knew it wasn't. She was just having a lot of anxiety about the future. She had it all the time, but talking about school at dinner made it worse.

"Well, no. Though sometimes it sounds really good. And animals don't know any better."

There were times Abby actually felt sorry for Doug. Not many, but she knew he worked just as hard as their dad. And he had school, which meant homework. Then there was sports. He played baseball and hockey both. That meant practice almost every day.

She'd heard their parents talking about his shot at a full scholarship. They lived in such a remote spot, the fact that he'd been noticed was pretty amazing. Her chances at college were pretty slim. Unless she could make some money and save it up. She was a good student, but that wasn't enough. What she needed was a way to get involved in volunteer work, or community service. And she wasn't sure how to do that living way out here.

"The vids you uploaded. Did anyone comment about Tatum?"

She shrugged. "A couple of people. Just to say how cute he is. And wish him luck getting back to his family."

"Yeah, check your hashtags. I swear some posts I see are almost all hashtags."

"I added some, but I'll add more next time," she said. "I was probably in too much of a hurry. I'll take more time tonight."

Doug wrapped an arm around Tatum's neck and pulled him closer. "How about that, Tatum? We may be able to get you home after all."

"I think I'll miss him. And I know that's silly."

"Nah. Dogs make it easy to like them."

"I guess so."

"You want me to help you make a video?"

"Do you want to?"

"Sure. Or, you know, I wouldn't have asked."

Tatum sat on the porch between the boy and the girl. Abby and Doug were their names. He had met so many people since he got lost from his dad's truck during the storm. He didn't like thinking about the storm, so he thought about the people. He liked all of their names.

Jed and Dr. Valerie. Cheryl and Frank. Now Doug and Abby, and there were more people here. Sarah and their mum and dad, who he only knew were Mom and Dad. Also there were so many animals he could hardly keep his tail still from excitement.

There was his new friend Lucy, who he had found when she had gotten lost. And there was a goat name Levi who kept jumping on top of the other goats. Especially on top of the goat named Wyatt. They were both pretty little. Like babies. And fell over a lot. Like babies.

He'd seen a cat in the barn, Abby's dad had called her Charlie. She was big and orange, and Abby said she was fierce. She wasn't like the cats who came into his backyard. He was kinda afraid of her. She hissed at him when he came close. So he didn't. He let her have the barn all to herself. She didn't hiss at Skipper or Rufus. But they didn't go very close either.

He liked making new friends, people friends *and* dog friends and horse friends. He smelled chickens and knew there were eggs in their pen, but Abby said he couldn't play with them, so he guessed he wasn't going to get to be friends with them. That was okay. He wasn't sure he could keep up with more than he already had. And he had to leave room for Puddles.

When he ran away in the storm, he never knew he'd make so many new friends.

It was pretty awesome.

———

Abby laughed at Doug and Tatum rolling around on the grass. Doug was laughing too, and Tatum would yip at him when Doug didn't get up fast enough. They ran in circles, Tatum chasing Doug, then Doug would throw a stick almost halfway to the barn and they'd both take off. Her brother had as much energy as the dog. Tatum always won but Doug was pretty fast.

That's one of the reasons he was so great at sports. And all that exercise would help Tatum sleep all night. She'd watched him sleeping in the yard. He could be pretty wiggly.

"What's going on?"

Abby kept her focus on the camera as she answered her sister. She was really surprised Sarah had come outside. Or cared enough to ask. She stayed wrapped up in her own world most of the time. She had one year of school to go and was making all sorts of plans.

To be honest, Abby was kinda jealous. Things for Sarah always seemed so easy. "Doug's helping me make a video of Tatum for TikTok."

"Did you post any others yet?" Sarah asked, sitting where Doug had been.

"A couple. I got a few comments on the first, but not from any-one who knew him," she said, as Doug came running full blast to-ward the house, Tatum smiling as Rufus ran on the other side.

"Have you thought about calling Dr. Lindsey?" Sarah raised a hand to shade her eyes. Abby shook her head. It wasn't even that bright. "Sometimes owners report lost animals to their vets. And then the vets share the information."

"I will tomorrow. Dad suggested the same thing, but it was too late tonight."

"I can help. If you want."

Wow. Now Abby was really impressed. Maybe it just took a fun-loving dog to get Sarah out of her room. Rufus and Skipper were fun too, but they didn't play as much. They'd been part of the family forever. Plus, they were older. Tatum seemed pretty young. He had a lot more energy.

"Thanks," Abby finally said, standing up and walking away from the house to get a better angle. The barn was in the back-ground, the setting sun lighting it to look like a painting.

Sarah came up beside her, lifting her hair and wrapping a band around it. Her ponytail swayed, the shadow looking like Lucy's tail. "Do we need to check on his leg or anything?"

"I heard Dad tell Cheryl we could take him to see Dr. Lindsey in a couple of days. Since he's lost, he thought he'd take a look at the stitches for free."

"Yeah, he's pretty nice like that. Or even one of his techs or in-terns could check."

That's right. Sarah was friends with Kate, Dr. Lindsey's daugh-ter. "Is Kate still going to be a vet too?"

Sarah shrugged. "I don't know. She's thinking now about being a psychiatrist."

"For animals?"

"No, but I've heard that's a thing."

"Animals are easy to understand."

"You really do need to go to vet school, Abs. You're better with animals than anyone I've ever known. Better than me for sure. And really better than Doug."

Out of nowhere, Abby's eyes filled with tears. She didn't think Sarah had ever said anything so nice or so supportive about her love of animals. Abby had always thought Sarah considered her a silly dreamer, that she needed to be more practical. But since she'd never said anything, maybe Abby had it all wrong. Maybe Sarah was in her corner after all.

She blinked and rubbed at her eyes. She was going to have to edit the video. She hadn't been paying enough attention and had captured her whole conversation with Sarah.

Good grief. She stopped recording and yelled, "I'm done!"

"Okay!" Doug yelled back.

"He seems good with Tatum," Sarah said.

"Well, yeah. Tatum is fun, not work."

They stood side by side as Doug collapsed onto his back, and could hear his labored breathing from here. Tatum sat beside him as if he was ready to keep going. Doug reached over and patted him, then didn't move again. Abby figured he'd fallen asleep. He could do it anywhere, and he did. Then their dad would do something like tie his shoelaces together before heading to the barn and calling him. She thought he would've learned to check by now, but he never did.

After a minute, Tatum wandered over to the paddock her dad had repaired earlier. He sat there and watched Lucy walk around, her tail twitching.

He cocked his head to one side, his ears perked up as if he wasn't sure what to think of her. But he didn't move, even when she started toward him.

"You need to film this," Sarah whispered, nudging her.

Abby raised her phone and focused in on the two animals. The summer breeze ruffled Lucy's mane, the strands of grayish white blowing and making Abby think of books she'd read as a kid. *Misty of Chincoteague, Black Beauty*, and others.

She'd loved reading about horses because she knew how they smelled, how they sounded, how funny they could be, how sweet and soft. She wondered what Tatum was thinking. He didn't seem alarmed, just curious.

Lucy came closer, whuffing. Tatum stood up then, but he didn't move. It was like he wanted to be ready to if something happened. Then Lucy stuck her nose through the slats in the fence and even looking at her camera's screen, Abby could see her nostrils flaring.

Tatum stepped closer and lifted his snout.

"Are you getting this?" Sarah asked.

Abby shushed her and watched as the two animals came within inches of each other as if saying hello, getting to know each other, becoming friends. It was the sweetest thing she'd ever seen and it made Abby cry for real, and she swore she heard Sarah sniff back tears of her own.

CHAPTER 29

Hi, diary. Tatum is not farm dog; running is fun sometimes, but Tatum is nap dog. Sleep is now my favwit cuz I still like food but I get more food than sleep.

After talking to Sarah and Doug, Abby went upstairs. She lay across her bed with Tatum beside her while she finished her homework. She'd heard her mother and Cheryl in Sarah's room, looking for something for Cheryl to sleep in, and a change of clothes for the next day since she and Frank hadn't packed for a night away. Abby's mom had told Cheryl she could wash their things, but Cheryl said tomorrow would be fine. It was late. Abby didn't know what Frank was going to do. He was too tall to borrow from Doug or her dad. Or maybe that didn't matter with guys' clothes.

Her mother had argued against Tatum sleeping inside, even though that's what he was used to. They knew nothing about him, where he'd come from, stuff like that, she'd said, but her dad had said it would be fine. He'd been to a vet. He was obviously in good health. Abby figured her mother was more worried about his shedding and one more thing to have to clean.

He was already snoring, soft whuffing sounds that made Abby smile. With the day he'd had, she didn't blame him. Between school and homework, the excitement over Frank and Cheryl finding Lucy, then chores and the photos and videos she'd taken, she was ready for bed.

She might have to wait till the morning to post Doug's video, since she needed to edit the sound. It had been pretty exciting watching all the comments come in on her earlier photos. No one had recognized Tatum yet. Hopefully soon.

She reached over to plug in her phone, and just as she did, a notification buzzed. Her heart blipped, and she checked the comment. She was still getting a lot of them, more and more now that she'd posted a short vid of Tatum romping with Skipper and Rufus. That one hadn't needed editing. It was just a lot of dog noises, Rufus barking mostly.

She was going to have to turn off notifications when she uploaded the video of Doug. She already had too many followers who liked looking at him on the farm. Most of them seemed to be girls. Not really surprising. His phone never stopped buzzing with texts. It had gotten so bad their dad made him leave it in his room during supper.

At least he turned off the sounds and only allowed vibration when they were all upstairs doing homework or getting ready for bed. Their rooms were next to each other, and it was bad enough that she had to listen to him laughing. He sounded like some comic book villain, like he was plotting and planning evil deeds. Sarah's room was on the other side of hers. She was quiet almost all the time. She also wore headphones almost all the time.

Not all of Abby's friends had phones, so she didn't have as many people to text with. She was lucky she had a phone, but living away from town, it helped a lot when her mom was going to be late picking her up. That was usually on the days she had to stay after school for tutoring.

She really hoped this would be the last year she needed the help. Honestly, she didn't know why she had to study math anyway. She knew how to measure things, how to weigh things. Why did she need algebra? Why did she need geometry?

Then again, maybe she'd need more math than she thought if she did make it to veterinary school. She hadn't researched the required courses. Maybe she should. Her mom told her it was important for college. Sarah and Doug said the same. They were both just better at math.

It was just going to cost a whole lot of money to go to college that long.

She'd have to set up her YouTube channel as soon as school was out. If she started getting subscribers now, by the time she used it as part of her school applications, she might have hundreds of thousands. She was dreaming big, but why not?

And she could probably make more money there than at a minimum-wage job. She couldn't work at any of the restaurants because she'd need a car to get to Floyd or to Shireton, and she didn't want to waste money buying one. She had to save every penny.

Her phone buzzed again. She reached over and after checking the newest comments, she silenced it for the night. Sarah's room was quiet now. She figured Cheryl had gone to hers. Abby changed her clothes, then decided she'd better set her alarm earlier than usual.

She wanted to get to the shower before anyone else made it downstairs. With this many people, there would never be enough hot water if she didn't.

FRIDAY

CHAPTER 30

Diary, it's okay that I get really busy and don't always remember to tell you what to remember to tell Dad and Mum, right? I miss dem but they is havin' fun on vacation, and I'm busy. They didn't tell anyone where they went cuz everybuddy is lookin' for them. Dad didn't put on my list that they will be back; Mum tells me every day they will always come back.

Tatum had never walked to a bus stop before. He'd seen buses stop on the corner by his house. He had to bark at them sometimes to remind them they didn't need to be so loud. They had bright blinking lights, and he'd seen kids get out of them when he'd been behind in his dad's truck. His dad told him they had to stop so the kids could safely cross the street. His dad had also told him he didn't need to bark. He did need to, but he stopped when his dad asked.

Walking with Abby down the road from the farmhouse to the fence and gate at the end was a new adventure. Skipper and Rufus were used to it. They came along, but they ran off chasing things in the tall grass. They didn't stay with Abby.

He stayed with Abby. He wanted to be up close and see what happened when the bus stopped. But mostly he stayed with her because she was talking to him like she'd done the night before when she'd let him sleep in her bed. And he was a really good listener.

"I'm sorry no one has found your family yet. Lots of people are trying. I'm sure with so many people involved you'll be home very soon. Would you like that?"

He barked because he thought she wanted him to say something. But then he smelled something new in the grass and took a few steps away.

Abby smiled at him. "It's okay. You can go play with Skipper and Rufus. The bus will be here in a minute, and then you can all run back to the house. Have you ever gone to school? You're very well behaved, so it makes me wonder if you had lessons. Or if maybe your family was just really good at training you."

Tatum hadn't gone far and had still been listening to Abby talk. Now he came back because he was pretty sure she'd said he was a good boy. Usually his dad gave him a snack when he said that. But Abby just kept walking without looking for anything in her pocket.

"Oh, there's the bus," she said, pointing down the road. "We're right on time. I have to go through the gate, and you have to stay inside, okay? Then go find Skipper and Rufus and just do what they do. Then I'll see you this afternoon when I get home. And maybe someone will see your pictures and videos and post a comment. Wouldn't that be amazing?"

Tatum didn't know what *post a comment* meant, but Abby was excited so he was excited too, and he barked. She laughed and leaned down to scratch his ears.

"Be good. Don't cause Mom any trouble because she's got enough to do already. Dad too. They work really hard, and you're really lucky they invited you to stay. That means they think you're a good dog too."

He barked again, then ran away down the road because the bus was stopping with almost as much noise as the attack storm. It squeaked super loud and wheezed like it couldn't breathe and creaked and groaned like it was really old.

Abby waved back at him as she climbed up the steps. Then the door closed, and the bus swallowed her. He hoped she was safe in there. But she'd said she'd see him when she got home, so he ran off to play with Skipper and Rufus and be a really good, good boy.

⟶•◦•⟵

Abby checked her phone on the ride to town. She was the first person on the bus in the morning and the last one off in the afternoon. She had time to look at her notifications before her friends got on closer to town. The sun was up, and the air was crisp. The tops of the grass stalks looked almost yellow. She hated having to get up so early, but the quiet time was nice.

And the view really was pretty. She was really lucky to live on a farm. She thought she might like to be a large-animal vet, taking care of horses and cows and goats and the like. She'd see dogs and cats too, of course, but she'd get to travel to farms. Maybe she could work for the wildlife service and deal with wild animals, tagging bears and deer.

She really was going to have to do some research. And get her YouTube channel going.

She read through the comments that had come in since she'd checked when she'd gotten back to her room after her very warm shower. Nothing much really. Just comments wishing Tatum good luck. She thought he'd had some of the best luck a dog ever could.

He could've gotten lost in the woods but had run across Cheryl, then they'd run across Frank before they'd found Lucy. And now he was living on a farm. Even if it was temporary.

Tatum had a whole lot going for him. And as she put her phone away, she hoped things kept going his way. As much as she'd miss him, she knew his family missed him more.

Falling in love with the animals she treated when she was a vet was something she'd have to be careful about. She thought it probably happened, maybe when treating one that was really sick. Maybe she'd talk to Dr. Lindsey about that. Or do some research on that too.

She dug out her phone again and launched her note app and began making a list of all the things she needed to research. Things she would never have thought of if Lucy hadn't escaped and Tatum brought her back.

———◆———

"Now all I want to do is crawl back in bed and sleep for the rest of the day," Frank said, patting his stomach.

Randall laughed. Helen laughed. Cheryl shook her head and grinned.

After the Millers' kids left for school, Randall had returned from the barn for breakfast. Helen had served the four of them thick buttered slices of toasted homemade bread, crisp bacon, and eggs that had come straight from the yard to the frying pan. There had also been fresh blueberry jam. Cheryl was feeling Frank's pain . . . but loving it.

Frank went on. "How do you eat like this every morning and get any work done?"

Randall chuckled, sopping up the last of his egg yolk with his toast then finishing off his coffee. "It's eating like this that makes it happen. Spend a day with me and you'll see."

"For another breakfast like this, I might just take you up on it. Especially since I'll probably find myself over this way more often in the coming weeks."

"You're welcome any time," Helen said, cradling her coffee mug, her elbows on the table. Her loving gaze followed her husband as Randall got up and cleared the dirty dishes, scraping scraps into a big bowl Cheryl knew would be mixed with the dogs' breakfast kibble.

Nothing was wasted in this house. She got to her feet. "Let me help you get the kitchen cleaned up before we leave."

But Helen waved her off. "No need. You have a big day ahead of you."

They did, but Cheryl couldn't walk out without doing something. Not after the helping hands the entire Miller family had extended. "Then at least let me feed the dogs."

"You can do that, sure. Kibble's in a bucket in the mudroom. Bowls are on top," Randall said, handing her the scraps and giving a nod toward the back door. "Mix it up in here. One scoop of kibble for each."

Frank finished off his coffee, then carried his cup to the sink. With the back door open, Cheryl could hear as he spoke to the Millers. "You've been so generous. I'd love to repay you somehow."

"Get books into the hands of everyone up this way who wants them," Helen told him. "I know it'll be appreciated. That's all you need to do."

"That's the goal," Frank said, moving to the back door as Cheryl set the bowls on the porch. The canine trio who'd been so patiently waiting attacked, scattering kibble as they wolfed down the food, then carefully licking up every piece they could find.

Grinning, Cheryl looked up at Frank. "I guess we won't have to wait for him to finish eating."

"Fingers crossed you find out where he belongs," Randall said, washing his hands at the sink. "But bring him back by if not. And the two of you are always welcome."

The way he said it made it sound as if Cheryl, Frank, and Tatum were a family. And strangely, the idea of them being one left Cheryl elated. Oh, she was in trouble here, she mused, returning the bowl to the sink and washing up.

"Thank you again, for everything," she said, as Helen gave her a hearty hug.

Lifting one hand in farewell, Frank placed his other on the small of her back and guided her across the porch. He grabbed Tatum's leash from a hook there, then whistled.

Tatum came running, Skipper and Rufus on his heels, and Frank shook his head. "I'm not sure I've ever seen such a happy dog."

"Could be he's happy because he knows he's about to go home."

"Do you think dogs are able to work out things like that?" he asked as they walked around the house and toward the truck, Tatum's nose to the ground as if he might've missed something.

"They've got great intuition, so who knows? I like to think so. It makes me happy."

"I was wondering about that spark in your eyes."

She kept quiet and let him think her happiness was for Tatum. She was happy for Tatum, sure. But mostly she was happy for all the things Frank made her feel.

What an unexpected gift Tatum had brought into her life. She had so much to thank him for.

CHAPTER 31

Hi, diary guy. Back in the car wif Fwank and Cheryl. No buddy tells me when we leavin' for more vacation, I fink it's a surpwise pawty vacation.

The drive to the shelter in Floyd didn't take long. Unfortunately, when they got there, they found it closed. A sign on the door said they'd return next week but were dealing with the fallout from the storm. Some of the animals remained, but they had relocated most to area kennels.

"Well, that sucks," Cheryl said, at a loss as to where to go next. "I suppose there's a vet in town, but if things were that bad over here, who knows if they're even open. Or have a copy of the lost dogs list."

They were parked in front of the building. It had a brick facade and a chain-link fence that extended several feet on either side. The fence continued down the length of the building and beyond where, from the parking lot, Cheryl could see a number of kennels. Empty kennels.

"There's something smaller written on the sign," Frank said, opening his door and walking to the shelter's entrance. In the distance, Cheryl heard a barking cacophony. And in the back seat, Tatum was whimpering, then growling, then whimpering again, his head out the window.

"It's okay. Just a lot of dogs wondering when they're going to get to go home," she told him, shifting in her seat to reach over and pat his back.

He wagged his tail, then gave a single bark. She couldn't imagine what was going through his mind.

Frank was back in moments and rubbed Tatum's head before climbing behind the wheel. "It says they've made arrangements with the shelter in Chester for intakes. Not sure where exactly that is from here, but Google will get me there. If I can connect."

Cheryl huffed. "I know exactly where that is from here. My mother lives in Chester. I grew up in Chester. I don't remember a shelter there, but I haven't lived there, or visited, in years."

"Sounds like serendipity to me," Frank said, grinning at her as he started the truck and put it in reverse. "Point the way and we'll kill these two birds with one stone, uh, so to speak."

The drive from Floyd to Chester took an hour. Thankfully, they'd started out early enough that they arrived before the noon closing time. Temporary hours, a sign posted at the entrance had said, to accommodate the unexpected influx of displaced animals.

The place was a madhouse, the parking lot nearly unnavigable. Frank found a spot off to the side in an empty lot and waited with Tatum while Cheryl checked in.

Now it was a matter of waiting their turn.

"I'm not sure I've ever seen a storm cause this much damage and havoc in my entire life," Cheryl said, rejoining Frank and Tatum. "I mean, it's nothing major anywhere. Just a lot of inconveniences all over."

"I guess running across Lucy was a blessing in disguise. We found a place for Tatum to stay and didn't waste a trip coming this way last night," Frank said. He turned to Tatum, who came up to sniff his ear, his wagging tail slapping Cheryl on the back. "Fate works in mysterious ways."

They were sitting on his truck's open tailgate waiting for their number to be called. She figured with this crowd, they were going to be there a while. Frank held Tatum's leash as he stood in the bed, taking in all the activity. "How far from here does your mother live?"

"Not far. A mile or two."

"Do you want to take the truck and go see her while I wait with Tatum? You can give me the address and we'll walk over when we're done here."

She started to say no. The word popped onto her tongue. But Frank's suggestion made a lot of sense. "Are you sure?"

"About you driving my truck?"

She rolled her eyes. "No. About me leaving you here. But yes. That too."

He hopped off the tailgate and dug into his pocket for the keys. "Go. Text me the address. And I guess her number in case I need to find a landline again."

Cheryl slid from the tailgate and pulled her phone from her pocket. "I might be a while."

"Then I'll come get the truck and take Tatum to a park," he said as his phone buzzed with her text. "We'll be fine. We'll wait."

She took the keys from his hand. How in the world had she ever lucked into meeting such a nice man? "It's a corner lot. A white cottage with dark green shutters. And this time of year a gorgeous flower bed in front."

"What type of flowers?"

"Anything she can get to grow. Gardening has always been her favorite hobby," she said, thinking of Helen Miller's vegetables, wondering if her mother used her flowers similarly, and wondering, too, why it had taken her so long to figure that out. "Probably a bit of therapy too."

"It's all about being outside. Same thing with hiking."

"Yeah," she said with a smile she felt to her bones. "I know that very well."

⟞━◆━⟝

After Cheryl drove away in Frank's truck, Tatum and Frank walked around. Frank looked at his phone. Tatum listened to all the dogs barking and sniffed so many places they'd been.

He thought they were sad. Or mad. Or some of both. Like they were missing their families and wanted to go home and didn't know how to get there. He wanted to tell them all to be patient, that maybe Frank could help them after he got Tatum back to his mum and dad.

But being patient was hard. He wasn't very good at it. So he didn't say anything to them.

He wasn't sure where Cheryl had gone, but he thought he'd heard her say something about her mum. He would go see his mum too, if he could, but right now he was waiting for something with Frank. He thought they were going to go into the building. It had a lot of animal pictures on the walls like Dr. Valerie's. Even if this place was a vet too, that was okay.

His nose was getting so tired, and his ears were starting to hurt. There were too many dogs here. It made him want to hide.

"It'll be our turn soon, Tatum. The storm was really bad, and other dogs got lost too. The people who work here are trying to get them all home."

Tatum wagged his tail.

He knew Frank and Cheryl were trying. He knew Abby was trying too. And Doug and Sarah. But mostly Abby. He liked her even if she took a lot of pictures like his dad.

"Number forty-two!"

"Hey! That's us," Frank said, turning toward the building. "Let's go see if the good people working here can tell us where to find your family."

Tatum yipped and pulled Frank forward. Frank laughed. He sounded as happy as Tatum felt, like all the Puppuccino cream in the world was tickling his nose.

CHAPTER 32

DIARY, it not surpwise pawty vacation, Fwank bringed me to the shelter. I don't fink Fwank even has my list at all. Is it home time yet, I'm MISRABOW.

Cheryl slowed for the turn into her mother's driveway, realizing how strange it felt to think of the house as her mother's when she'd grown up there, when her father had lived there. When, good or bad, they'd been a family here for eighteen years. And then they hadn't.

She'd fallen in love with hiking and camping during her years in this house. Reading had become an essential part of her life thanks to her parents' influence. She'd become a dog person thanks to them too. But no. This was not where she belonged.

She'd been a daydreamer from the very beginning. It was why she was so suited to hiking, thinking while alone on the trail, while alone at her campsite, working out her problems to the music of the wind in the trees, the smells of fresh growth and decay, to the feel of crisp dew on her skin, the sight of stars twinkling above the canopy of trees.

Her father had shared all of those loves, but she was pretty sure she would've found her center in the same way on her own. And she'd wonder forever what it would've been like for her mother to join them, for the camping trips to have been the three of them toasting marshmallows for s'mores, playing card games, spending time in their own minds, connecting.

Her mother was standing on the front porch, a cup of what Cheryl knew was tea in one hand. The other was wrapped around the porch railing as if she needed the support.

Cheryl parked, took a deep breath, and shut off the truck. She stuffed her phone and the keys in the pocket of the shorts she'd borrowed from Sarah, leaving her backpack on the floor.

"Nice truck," her mother said, breaking the ice of Cheryl's approach. "I assume it's Frank's?"

"Hi, Mom," Cheryl said, putting off her mother's question. "You look great."

It had been far too long since Cheryl had seen Betsy Stratton, and she appeared as perfectly put together as the last time, and the time before, and most of Cheryl's life.

She was five foot six and thin. She made sure of that. Made sure, too, to wear clothes to show off her shape. Most were designer label, at least the ones she wore to leave the house, or to invite company in. Cheryl wondered when she'd become company instead of family.

"And, yes. It's Frank's. We used it to drive Tatum to the shelter since it has more room."

"Is he leaving Tatum there?"

"No. Like I told you, we're hoping they can tell us how to contact his family and get him home."

"And if you don't find them? Are you going to keep him?"

She shook her head, accepting that truth. "I can't have him at my apartment. Frank has a big yard, but he's got commitments that keep him away. The family who owns the horse we found said he could stay on their farm. Hopefully he won't have to be there long."

"Well, let's go inside. I've made some crab salad for lunch. You can tell me more about this reading center of his. I wasn't quite sure what you were describing when you called."

Cheryl grabbed the door before it closed on her and went inside. As always, her mother's house—and there she went again—

was spotless. She kept two windows partially open to get a cross breeze through the living room, and another in the kitchen and the back of the house. The whole place smelled clean and fresh and made Cheryl strangely homesick.

It was so much the smell of her childhood. Rather than bacon or canned air freshener or cigarette smoke, all of which made her think of her father, the scent she remembered was the wide outdoors. She wondered if it had been her mother's way of reminding her father of what he loved. Or if she had loved it as much, just in her own way, one that came with flowers.

"Read any good books lately?" her mother asked, settling the bowl of chilled seafood on the table along with bakery-fresh sandwich rolls, plates and cutlery, a bowl of green salad, a cruet of dressing, and a dish of mayonnaise because she knew Cheryl liked extra.

Cheryl had never understood why they couldn't pour salad dressing from the bottle, or scoop mayo out of the jar, but this was who her mother was. Who she'd always been.

And part of the reason her father was no longer there.

Her mother rarely left home. She had a dedicated office where she did bookkeeping for a number of clients. It provided her a more than decent living, but it also kept her working very long and isolated hours. More hours than she'd put in if she were working for a firm. And, Cheryl knew, that was the root of their estrangement. Those hours and her wish for Cheryl to join her, to share the workload and the income, to eventually take over when she retired.

She'd assumed for years Cheryl would major in accounting, or business, and get her CPA license, one thing her mother never had done. But Cheryl had no interest in debits and credits, in bank balances, and definitely not in taxes. Her father had known that and had broadened her horizons, another reason her mother had resented her relationship with him.

As she had mentioned to Frank, it didn't take a rocket scientist to figure out why she'd chosen to major in psychology. What drove human beings fascinated her.

She reached for a sandwich roll and the serving dish of mayonnaise. "I took an old Ian Fleming and Barbara Cartland when I went hiking but didn't have much time to read."

"That's a strange combination," her mother said, fanning out her napkin in her lap.

Cheryl shrugged as she spooned up the mayo. "Every book deserves a read, and those were in easy reach. I'm halfway through a great tech sci-fi title in hardcover, but it's about eight hundred pages, so I had to leave that one at home. What about you?"

"A lot of domestic thrillers, though I think I'm ready for a change. They're getting too hard to buy into. Honestly. The coincidences and supposed red herrings are like red flashing lights."

Yeah, Cheryl had read a few of those. "Are you still taking summer vacations with Wendy and Maya? I know summer is usually an easier time to get away."

"Usually, yes, but I've taken on a number of new clients since we last spoke. Whenever that was." She gave a dismissive wave. "Wendy canceled anyway. She fell in love or something."

"I'm sorry. About the plans."

Her mother made a poofing noise as she dished up a saucer of salad. "I'm used to people putting themselves first, no matter the arrangements others have made."

Bristling, Cheryl finished spreading more mayonnaise than she needed before she spoke. "We're all guilty of some of that. Looking out for one's self is human nature. Survival."

"Of course you would defend her."

"I'm not defending her. I'm offering an explanation for her choice, one with more layers than simple selfishness. Not knowing her, I can't speak to her motives," she said, pulling the dish of crab salad closer. She'd known everything her mother said was going to be barbed, but she couldn't believe how calm she felt after days of crazy anxiety.

Even if she did sound like a counselor more than a daughter. "Finding a new love can consume one's thoughts. Whether that new love is a person, or a new career, or a lost dog."

Her mother drizzled a teaspoon of dressing onto her salad. "I suppose I won't see you again for a while, then, since you've added Frank and Tatum to your schedule."

A grin tugged at Cheryl's mouth. Baby steps. "Mayville's not that far away, Mom. But I guess with all these new clients, you'll be too busy to meet halfway."

Her mother forked up a small bite of salad and chewed, then ate another before dabbing her cloth napkin to her lips. "Does Frank live in Mayville?"

"He does. His bookstore's in the township to the east."

"I'm surprised he can make a living with a bookstore these days."

"His parents left him set," Cheryl said with a shrug. "The store is more a hobby. And a homage. Like the reading center. It was something his parents had wanted to do for ages."

"Interesting. Sounds like you've met your perfect match."

Cheryl laughed. "I've only known him a couple of days, so I wouldn't go that far. But he's a very kind man. He hikes. He loves books. He adores dogs. I'm sure I'll discover some trait that will annoy me. I'm sure I've got plenty he won't like. But it's nice to have a friend. Which is why you should still go on that vacation."

Her mother frowned as if Cheryl had lost her mind. "Alone?"

"Why not? It's not like you can't afford it. Or aren't capable of traveling alone. You may meet someone amazing."

"I'm not looking to meet someone, amazing or not."

"A friend, Mom. Someone to text with in the middle of the night when you're struck with an idea, or when you can't remember the lead actor in a movie."

"There's IMDb for that."

"But a friend is much more interactive," Cheryl said, biting into her sandwich.

"You know there are enough calories there to last you all day."

"I've been hiking and eating dried fruit and peanut butter." She left out the part about Helen Miller's spaghetti and fried eggs. "I needed your crab salad. It's the best comfort food ever."

"It was my mother's recipe," her mother said as she added a helping to her salad. "I'll write it down for you if you like."

"You could email it to me. So I don't lose it."

"I suppose I could."

"But it still won't be as good as yours."

"It's a recipe, Cheryl. Anyone can get the same result."

"Not when yours is made with so much love."

CHAPTER 33

Diary, day 903, still nobuddy has any pizzas.

Tatum walked with Frank to the door of the loud animal building. The one where he knew there was going to be a vet. If he had to see a vet he would rather see Dr. Valerie.

He'd changed his mind about a vet being okay.

But Frank didn't know Dr. Valerie, or Dr. Albert, who Tatum went to for his regular checkups. Frank didn't even know Jed. Frank only knew Cheryl and Abby's family. Tatum hoped Cheryl came back soon. Before he had to see the vet.

That would be really great actually.

Frank talked to the girl inside the door. Tatum couldn't see her because there was part of a wall between her and Frank. He could hear her, but it was hard to listen because of all the dogs barking.

Frank leaned down. "It's okay, buddy. I'm not leaving you here. If I could, I'd take all the dogs with us and help find their homes. A lot of them got loose in the storm like you did."

That made Tatum feel a little bit better. He liked being inside his house, and inside Frank's house, and inside the house at the farm with Abby. He liked Jed's house and Jed's pot roast. And Dr. Valerie's office was okay because no dogs were barking and he'd made friends with the fish. He hoped Puddles was doing okay without him.

Frank squatted down beside him. Then the girl he'd been talking to came around the wall. "This is Ginger. She's a good friend. She's going to put her tool on your neck, okay? It won't hurt at all. You won't even feel it. But since hers is working now, it might tell us where to find your family."

A tool could do that? Tatum thought that must be the best tool in the world! He wondered if his dad had a tool like that in the garage. Maybe he could bring it to the shelter and help Ginger find the families for all the dogs who wanted to go home.

"Hi, Tatum," Ginger said, handing him a cookie. It smelled really good, but he waited until Frank said it was okay to eat. His mum had always told him he was a good dog when he was patient and waited for permission. Sometimes it was pretty hard, he had to say.

While he chomped on the cookie, Ginger used her tool to find his mum and dad. The cookie was loud, and the barking was loud, and he wasn't sure what Ginger and Frank were talking about, but Frank used his phone to take a picture of something Ginger showed him on an iPad like his mum had.

Then she sat down on the floor.

"I'm going to take a look at your leg now, Tatum. Frank said he doesn't know what happened, and I just want to make sure whatever the bandage is covering is in good shape, okay?" She handed him another cookie and he took it while she lifted his leg into her lap.

She unwrapped the bandage the vet he'd seen after getting out of the woods had put on, and she and Frank looked at his stitches.

"Ouch," the Ginger girl said. "Whatever you did, that had to hurt. It looks good though. No swelling or signs of infection." She wrapped his leg back up with bright orange tape. "Sorry, Tatum. We're all out of blue."

Then she got up and walked with them to the door. "You're

good to go. With the towers back online, you should be able to reach his people. Good luck to both of you. And thank you for getting him home. Too many people wouldn't bother."

"A lot of them probably aren't dog people."

"True, but it still takes someone special to spend their time and money on an animal who's not their own."

Tatum wasn't sure what they were talking about, but they'd said *family* enough times that he figured he was probably going to go home now to his.

"Let's go find Cheryl and get my truck," Frank said as they started walking. He decided that Frank really liked to walk. First in the woods, then to take Lucy home, then around the farm, and now to find Cheryl. But that was okay.

Because at the end of the walking, Tatum would be home.

⟫•◦•⟪

"Abs! Hey, Abs!"

Standing in line to catch the bus home, Abby turned to see her two best friends hurrying toward her. The high school was next door, and the busses drove up in front of the gym. That meant they were close to the fields where the high school athletes practiced after school.

"Hi, guys!"

Jill reached her first, squinting as she looked at the baseball diamond. "I guess Doug's staying late again for practice?"

Abby shook her head. A lot of mornings she rode to school with Sarah and Doug, but her classes were over earlier than theirs. And a lot of time they had to stay for extracurricular activities.

"Doug has tutoring, and Sarah's doing tutoring."

Stephanie laughed, her silvery-blond hair swinging around her chin. "Do you ever wonder if athletes don't have room for regular studies because their heads are full of playbooks?"

"Probably," Jill said. She was shorter than both Steph and Abby and had more hair than both of them. It was a big poofy cloud of brown curls. She was pretty adorable.

Though her friends rode home on the same bus, they both lived closer to town. Once they got off, Abby had the rest of the long ride alone. Sometimes she wished she didn't live on a farm, though that was because she missed out on things she needed a car to get to, but most of the time she knew it was the perfect life for her.

"So what's the deal with your new dog?" Jill asked, as the bus rolled to a stop to load up. "I saw your TikTok."

"He's just staying with us until we can find his family. That's what the videos are for."

"You think anyone who knows him will see them?" Steph asked.

"I don't know," Abby said, hitching her backpack higher on her shoulder as the line began to move. "I hope so. Lots of dog lovers follow my account."

"You're TikTok famous!" Jill said, laughing. "You probably have more followers than the school has students."

"We live in the middle of nowhere, silly," Steph reminded Jill as she stepped up into the bus.

"Ugh, I know. I can't wait to get out of here."

"I'm hardly famous. I only started my account a few months ago. I didn't think I was ever going to get a phone." And she hadn't until she'd turned thirteen, just before school had started. Even then it had only been because of coordinating rides with Doug and Sarah.

Abby followed her friends down the aisle. They always sat right in the middle of the bus, each in their own seat. There weren't that many riders, and it was the easiest way to sit and talk.

"I like living here. Most of the time." Though sometimes she wished she could be lazy during the summer when school was out. Go to the coast. Go swimming. Read for hours and hours.

Sleep for the rest. Wasn't that the life Doug had described? A dog's life? The sleeping part anyway.

Sometimes she'd sleep over with Jill at Steph's house. They'd watch movies and eat junk food all night, then sleep till lunchtime the next day.

That never happened at home. "I mean, you know. We get to ride horses—"

"And get up at the crack of dawn to milk goats and fetch eggs."

Abby shrugged. "It's just part of the job. And the cheese is really, really good."

"For stinky goat cheese," Steph said, her and Jill cackling.

Abby rolled her eyes. It was fine. Her mom had told her more than once that not everyone was cut out for their life. Even Sarah, who'd grown up on the farm, wanted a different career.

Abby did too, but hers was still related to farming. Or animal husbandry really.

"Hey, Abs. You know we're kidding, right?" Jill asked.

Stephanie nodded. "Yeah, it's not like we live a life of luxury. We just have different chores."

"But we don't have to do them at the crack of dawn," Jill said, laughing again.

"And at least you're famous." Steph thought for a minute, her head cocked to the side. "I could probably get up at the crack of dawn to be famous."

Abby tried not to laugh. Her friends were so silly, she mused, grabbing her seat as the bus swung wide for a turn. "Anyway, I'm not that famous. That's all I was trying to say. People just like animals. There are tons of TikToks with gazillions of followers."

Jill grabbed her backpack before it hit the floor. "What if you don't find Tatum's home? Are you going to get to keep him?"

Abby shrugged. "I guess, maybe, if he can be trained to work. Like Skipper and Rufus."

"What if he can't?" Jill asked. "Will you have to give him up? Like to a shelter?"

"I don't know." She doubted it. Frank would probably come get him if that happened.

"Maybe my mom would let me have him," Steph said. "Our yard is huge. And Mikey would have so much fun playing with him."

Steph's little brother was in third grade. Abby thought he was kind of annoying, but she supposed she'd been annoying too, when she'd been that age.

The bus jolted over a pothole, then the brakes screeched as it pulled up to the next corner to stop. Fumes that smelled like diesel and something burning came in through the open windows. Abby waved her hand in front of her nose.

Jill and Steph both got off here. They gathered up their stuff to go.

"See ya Monday," Steph said.

"Text ya later," Jill said. "And I really hope you find Tatum's family."

"Then you'll be even more famous, and I'll need to get your autograph," Steph said, laughing as she and Jill ran to the door.

"No running!" their driver yelled. "Jill! Stephanie! You two know better!"

That made Abby laugh. Their driver was like a hundred years old. He was Tod James's grandfather or something like that. He always made Abby think about one of those tall advertising things with arms that waved around when they bent in the wind.

Or maybe Ichabod Crane.

He closed the door and took off again. Abby thought about what her friends had said about her being famous.

At lunch, she'd posted the video of Lucy and Tatum. And she'd posted the one of Doug. She'd just cut it off before she and Sarah had started talking. She'd kept it all, of course. She'd actually listened to it twice last night before going to bed. She'd probably save it forever.

Even if she could make money somehow on TikTok or You-Tube, it was always stuff she thought was surprising that got the most views. Stuff that Jill and Steph thought was too weird for words.

That was funny too, because she couldn't imagine buying eggs in a store. She supposed that was why she had the followers she did. Her life was so different from theirs.

Soon she was the last student on the bus. She sat back for the ride to the farm and pulled out her phone. She silenced it during the school day, so when she saw the number of notifications, she about lost it. A lot of them were on the video of Doug playing with Tatum. Those she ignored because they were girls asking about him, not the dog.

But the video she'd posted of Tatum and Lucy touching noses... Her heart felt like it was going to explode. There were dozens of comments!

> *Good luck finding his home!*
> *My furbabies have all their paws crossed!!*
> *PeePie says he'll be keeping his eyes and ears open!*

Abby knew from comments in the past that PeePie was a tiny rat terrier who looked like he'd caught his tail in an electrical outlet. That one made her laugh.

But it was the next one that made her suck in a sharp breath.

> *I think I've seen this dog before. Let me see if I can find where it was. #lostdogs*

Oh! Oh! The comment wasn't from anyone she knew, but the hashtag gave her a clue as to how the girl posting had found her video. Maybe her social media would pay off!

She read the comment again and again then returned her

phone to her backpack. Then she held her backpack in her lap and hugged it tight to her chest, holding on because she didn't know what else to do.

Tatum might be going home really soon. She was so happy for him. But all of a sudden she wanted to cry. How could she be so sad and miss him so much when he hadn't even left? And he wasn't her dog? She wasn't ready for him to leave. And yet she knew he had to.

That he missed his family. That his family missed him.

If they came to pick him up at the farm, she'd make a video of the reunion. All the commenters would love watching that. They would probably cry too.

CHAPTER 34

*Sowwy, diary, I almost overreacted a little bit. Fwank had to
ask the shelter what Dad's phone number was. Mum calls
him all the time, he could just ask me, his number is face time.*

Having read Frank's text, Cheryl tucked her phone away in her
pocket, smiling. With all the ups and downs, the disappointment
and frustration, the anxiety she'd been carrying around for far too
long, today was going to end up being a great day.

"Good news?" her mother asked, lifting her cup to her mouth.

They were sitting outside on the top step of the front porch,
drinking tea. Hot tea because it was her mother's favorite thing to
drink year-round. She'd made a pot of Earl Grey, which was
Cheryl's favorite flavor. She'd taken that as a good sign.

Cheryl had already told her some of Tatum's story, but filled her
in on the rest of what she knew while they'd waited for the water
to boil. About the farm, and the wonderful Miller family. About
Helen's vegetable garden, Abby's love of animals, her social media
effort to reunite Tatum and his family. About the way Randall
doted on his wife and kids. It might be hard for her mother to
hear, what with their family history, but it was a lovely, lovely truth.

Most of all, she told her about Frank and how generous he
was. How kind and caring.

"The registry is back online. Frank has the contact info for Tatum's
family." She was absolutely giddy. She wanted to laugh. And she
wanted to cry. She wanted to do cartwheels across the yard.

"How wonderful!" her mother exclaimed before sipping more of her tea. "Has he called them yet? Are they close?"

Cheryl shook her head, having memorized Frank's text. She didn't think she'd ever forget it. "He wanted me to do it since I'm the one who found him. And they live in Bangor."

Her mother gasped. "Bangor! How in the world did he make his way up here?"

"We may never know. Or maybe there's a piece to the puzzle we're missing and we'll find it when he goes home."

Her mother nodded. "Do you need to go pick them up? Frank and Tatum?"

"Actually, they're on their way over. It's not a long walk."

"It's a couple of miles at least."

"Yes, but Frank's a hiker too, remember?"

"Hiker, dog lover, bookstore owner. I remember," she said, looking down into her tea. "If he's setting up his reading center in the area, and focusing his attention there, that might be a reason to move back. If you won't do it for your mother, maybe you can do it for a man."

Cheryl breathed in. This was her life. She wasn't living it for Frank any more than she was living it for her mother. "I have to be in Mayville for work and lectures I need to attend in person. Frank doesn't change that. He and I can stay in touch. You and I can stay in touch. I don't have to be here in person to love you."

"Or him?"

"We're friends," she reminded her mother. "If we grow closer, things might change. But I'll always be here for you. Anytime you need me."

"We have different ideas of what *need* means, Cheryl," her mother said, pouring another cup of tea for them both from the pot on the tray at her side.

"I'm so grateful we live in the here and now. It's different from when you left home for college. You and I can video chat. We don't have to rely on landlines or the Pony Express. We can text anytime. I know it's not the same as sitting here drinking tea, but we can drink tea at the same time on video chat. And I'll get back here as often as I can. I've told you that. You know it's true."

"I suppose," her mother said after a long moment of silence.

It was the first time she'd budged, softening her stance, and it gave Cheryl hope.

"Is that them?" her mother asked, and Cheryl looked in the direction she'd indicated. "He's quite tall, isn't he?"

They hadn't walked; they'd jogged, a slow jog, but Tatum's tongue was still dragging. Frank's too, Cheryl thought with a laugh.

"I'd better go get a bowl of water for Tatum."

"And I'd say a glass for Frank," her mother added. "I'll never understand why people love to run so much. Maybe because I grew up walking everywhere I never found it necessary to add the extra exercise."

"You don't remember how many miles we biked when I was in grade school?"

"Hmm. I hadn't thought about that in a while. Now, biking I could get behind."

"We need to do that, then. I'll have to check the garage and see what shape the bikes out there are in."

"Pretty terrible, I imagine. They haven't been used in ages. It would probably be less expensive to buy new ones."

"Next weekend, then. We'll go shopping, okay?"

"Okay," her mother said, standing to smooth down her blouse and slacks. "You'd best get that water. I think your Tatum may collapse any moment now."

"Your mother's great," Frank said once they'd pulled out of her driveway. Tatum was stretched nearly the full length of the back seat, snoring. Poor guy, being dragged all over creation. He was going to sleep for ages when he finally got home.

Cheryl was pretty exhausted herself, all her pent-up anxiety having drained away to puddle at her feet. The last couple of days had been a whirlwind. And that on top of hiking.

"She thinks the same about you."

"Nice," Frank said, grinning broadly as he checked traffic at the corner stop sign. "A mutual admiration society—I can get behind that."

He maneuvered through the neighborhood, making his way toward a park he'd told her he'd seen. She knew the one. "We're going bike shopping next weekend. We used to ride when I was younger. Seems a good way to keep making progress with her."

"I'm happy to come along," he said, then frowned and added, "I mean, if I won't be butting in. We can take my truck. Load them up in the back."

"Thanks," she said. He was so cute when doubting himself. "And, no. You won't be butting in. I'll do some shopping online this week, then check with Mom and let you know."

"Maybe you could vid chat and shop together."

"That's a great idea." Her mother was as tech savvy as she was so the only problem would be finding a good time. "It'll get us in the habit. Which we should've been in all along."

A smile pulled at the corner of his mouth. "You're on the right track. That's what matters. "Now. Let's call this pup's people and give them the good news."

They'd reached the park, and he turned into the parking area, choosing a spot at the far end, away from the playground. "I thought it would be great for them to see him happy and having a good time rather than just calling them from the road."

"You're just full of all sorts of fun ideas, aren't you?"

"That's because I'm a fun guy."

Cheryl shook her head at his fungi joke. "How in the world did Tatum end up here if he lives in Bangor?"

"My guess is he hitchhiked. Like he was hiding from the storm, somehow got into an open delivery van or whatever. Then jumped out and ran when he saw you."

"That is so random," she said. "I'd just crossed the two-lane between Mayville and Shireton when I heard him. All the times I've walked that trail, I've never seen a car on that road."

"I know the spot," Frank said, shutting off the truck. "The mobile vet was parked at the farm supply store not far from there. I'll bet that's where he was when he saw you."

"I guess it doesn't matter now, though I'll always be curious."

Frank opened his door, the noise waking Tatum. He stretched and sat up, his tail wagging as he looked around. "There's a free table over there."

Cheryl followed the direction of his gaze. "You sure you want me to make the call?"

"Absolutely," he said, holding her gaze, his filled with an infectious happiness. "You found him. You do the honors."

Tatum may have found her, but she still felt as if Frank had done just as much to care for him, feed him, transport him, then get him scanned. She took a deep breath and exited the truck, pulling her phone from her pocket. "Why am I so nervous?"

"It's excitement," he said, grabbing Tatum's leash as he hopped down from the back seat. "You're the psychology major. You should know that."

"Ha ha," she said as she walked to the picnic table. She climbed up to sit, placing her feet on the bench, watching Frank walk Tatum from tree to tree. Then he sat on the ground, his long legs stretched out in front of him, and played tug-o-war with a stick.

Tatum's tail was wagging like mad. She wished his family could see him running free as he'd done on the Millers' farm, but it was safer this way. She certainly didn't want to risk him dashing off at this point in his journey. She tapped out the number and held up the phone.

"Cross your fingers," Frank called to her, but since she'd already done that, Cheryl held her breath instead.

CHAPTER 35

Diary, Fwank could just ask Cheryl how to call Dad, but he doesn't pick up. They forgot Dad is on vacation. It fine, sometimes Dad forgets to feed me three times a day even though him and Mum agweed on two times a day.

Tatum couldn't believe he was going to get more play time with Skipper and Rufus!

He really wasn't sure what was going on with Frank and Cheryl. They'd been really quiet since leaving the park after leaving the other lady's house with flowers after leaving the vet and the Ginger girl and her cookies. He was happy to be going back to the farm.

Just not as happy as he would be to be going home, but maybe his mum and dad would come for him soon. And the farm was a lot more fun than the park he'd gone to with Frank and Cheryl. He hadn't even been able to run because of his leash. It wasn't like the park at home where he could play with other dogs. It made him think of the woods. He was not a woods dog, but he was pretty sure he could be a farm dog. Like Skipper and Rufus.

Now that the storms had stopped attacking, he was having a great time on his adventure. It would be okay for another little while, but he was getting pretty homesick. And he knew his mum and dad and even Puddles were missing him and were worried.

He was worried about them too. And he hadn't known how bad missing could feel. He'd always missed his dad when he was at work until he got home. His mum too. Puddles never went any-where, so he had him for company, but it wasn't the same. Pud-dles didn't talk to him or play. He just made bubbles and swam around and stared at him with his big eyes.

He missed Jed and Dr. Valerie, but that wasn't the same either. When he went home, he would miss Frank and Cheryl too. He thought he'd miss Skipper and Rufus most of all, but he had other dogs to play with, and he could tell them about the farm. But he had to say, he was pretty sure he'd miss the girl Abby most of all.

He liked sleeping on her bed. And he liked the way she talked to him, like he was part of her family and not just a visitor. She was a great dog person. Skipper and Rufus were lucky to live with her and her mum and dad and the other girl Sarah and the boy Doug.

Frank turned his truck onto the road, and Tatum's tail went all crazy with excitement. He couldn't even imagine what would happen when he saw his family again.

It would probably fly right off his butt.

———≫•≪———

"I guess this is why it's good to keep a landline," Randall said after Frank explained that they couldn't get through to the num-ber on Tatum's chip. Randall had met them at the truck when they'd parked. "At least for folks living up here. I suppose in the city it's easier to rely on a wireless connection, cable and all. Any idea when you'll be able to get through?"

Cheryl shook her head, defeated. She couldn't believe they were running into connectivity issues again. "What we heard is that some of the initial repairs require upgraded parts. Like the lines and towers had been due for maintenance already, so they're going back in to take care of it. Everything should be up and run-ning tomorrow, but could be later today. We tried again when we got here, but nothing yet. Just dead air."

It was early afternoon. Cheryl and Frank had arrived back at the Millers' farm not long after Abby had gotten home from school. Tatum had seen her with Skipper and Rufus near the barn and taken off. Cheryl was glad he was so comfortable here, that he felt at home. That he belonged. It would ease the sting of leaving him. Because it wasn't going to be easy.

"Well, I know Abby's glad to have Tatum here for however long it takes to reach them. Skipper and Rufus too," Randall said. "You two going to stay another night?"

Frank looked at Cheryl. "We could, but I have a couple of appointments I need to keep tomorrow. I'm looking at two properties, and I don't want to miss out if either of them suits."

"Well, since he's going to be here, we can keep trying to reach his people too. We'll let you know if we do."

"Thanks," Frank said. "We'll do the same."

A mix of emotions swirled through Cheryl's chest. She and Frank had already talked about what was in Tatum's best interest. Yet here she was, second-guessing that decision because the idea of leaving him was tearing her apart. "I know Tatum will love being here, and I know we're not abandoning him, even though part of me feels that guilt."

"You're not," Randall said, shaking his head. "We are opening our home to him."

Cheryl nodded, her throat tight. "There's also a part of me that feels I'm leaving him because it's easier for me. But I can't keep him in my apartment, and he needs room to run."

"Then that's a yes?" Frank asked. "You're okay with him staying? And we can go?"

She nodded. "Yes. And thank you again," she said to Randall. "He's going to be so happy."

"You have our numbers," Frank said. "We'll all keep in touch." He turned his gaze on Cheryl, his eyes filled with compassion. "I have a feeling we're about to get him home."

⇒►◆◄

Tatum sat with Skipper and Rufus next to the barn and watched Frank and Cheryl drive away in Frank's truck. He hoped when they came back they brought his mum and dad. He was going to miss them. He'd had so much fun with them. Even if he'd had to be in the woods for some of it. And go to so many vets. Even more vets than when he'd been with Jed.

"You're going to have a good time with us, Tatum." It was the girl Abby. She'd come out of the barn. She sat down beside him. She wrapped an arm around him. She rubbed her head against his. "I don't think you'll be here long. I'm really going to miss you when you go home."

He didn't like it that Abby sounded sad, but he did like hearing the word *home*. It made his tail start swishing through the grass, and he really wanted to bark, and if she hadn't been holding him, he would've chased the bugs that jumped away from his excitement.

He liked Abby a lot. He liked sleeping in her bed. He wondered, now that Frank and Cheryl were gone, if he'd have to sleep with Skipper and Rufus. He supposed that would be okay. He knew they were happy living with their mum and dad and their very own kids.

Plus they had goats and chickens and a horse. And a cat he didn't want to think about. He only had Puddles. He didn't think a horse would fit in his backyard. And the goats didn't smell so good, and his mum wouldn't like that. She'd like the eggs from the chickens though.

Mum loved eating eggs. Dad too. And Tatum too most of all, though he wondered if they wouldn't taste even better with gravy. Maybe when he got home he could find out.

———⸎———

"He'll be fine," Frank said once Cheryl could no longer see the Millers' farm in the truck's passenger-side mirror. "But if you don't want to leave him—"

"No. It's fine." She pushed loose strands of hair from her face and sighed. "I'm just . . . tired."

"Emotional overload."

"Yes, Dr. Ouelette. I know." She sighed again. "Sorry. That sounded crabby."

"You did a good deed, Cheryl. A great deed, getting him out of the woods and to a safe place. Imagine if he was still there foraging on his own."

"I'd rather not imagine that," she said, shifting in her seat. The rural landscape zoomed by. She wished she was in a better frame of mind to enjoy it. "He's a bit of a goof. He'd probably try to make friends with the first animal he got close to. And I really don't want to think about that."

Frank laughed. "He may not have been raised on a farm, or even used to living on one, but he'll adjust in no time. Next time we see him, he'll be herding goats."

Would they see him again? Together? Because she couldn't ignore Frank's use of the word *we*. She leaned her head against the seat and closed her eyes. "The Millers are super people."

"Like with superpowers?"

That had her smiling. "Hey, they've got three teenagers who do chores and homework and engage in conversation at supper. I'd say that's some pretty powerful parenting."

Helen and Randall were lovely people, a lovely couple. Their three kids were so fortunate. In the same way Frank had been fortunate. Even Tatum was fortunate, she mused, feeling less unbalanced about her own situation.

Things with her mother would take time . . . and a few bike rides.

"I'm glad you had a good visit with your mother," Frank said, as if reading her mind.

"She's been through some rough years, but yes. We'll be fine," she said, breathing in and imagining the aroma of Earl Grey tea. "And she's pretty super herself."

"Did she say she might like to have another dog?"

"We never got around to talking about that."

"Well, now you have a reason to drop by."

"One does not drop by on my mother," Cheryl said with a laugh as memories of friends showing up unannounced rushed back. The house had not been in order. Her mother had not been in order. And yet only her mother had cared. "She does not like surprises."

"And you?"

She thought about the surprise of Tatum, the surprise of Frank, the twist her plans had taken over the past few days. "They used to stress me out. I'm sure that was a takeaway from witnessing her reactions. But I'm better about them now. I kinda like them in fact. The way they come out of nowhere and turn the everydayness upside down."

"The bad ones do that too, you know."

She knew he was thinking of losing his parents. She reached over and took his free hand in hers, squeezing then letting him go. "So what are you going to call your community center?"

"I'm not sure. I've got a lot of ideas tumbling around."

"You can tumble them by me if you want."

"I probably will," he said, and this time he reached for her hand, and she let him hold it.

"Are you going to move? Or commute?"

"Long term, I'll hire a manager. Or I'll turn over the bookstore to my manager there and move up here. Things are still up in the air. I'll figure it out once I have my location."

"I was curious because I'll bet my mother would love helping out."

"You think?"

Cheryl nodded, suddenly loving the idea. "She's a bibliophile of the highest order. And she needs something more in her life than work. Something to get her out and involved. She needs to meet people."

"What about you?"

She glanced over, surprised. "Would I want to work for you?"

"Not for me. With me."

He knew of her plans, of the pursuit of her graduate degree. She knew he wasn't asking her to give up her dream. But what he was asking . . . It unarmed her, left her breathless.

Had her entire future been changed by finding a lost dog in the woods?

She took a leap of faith and laced their fingers together. "Yes. I would."

CHAPTER 36

Hi, diary. I don't live at Abby's house, but I haven't left yet. Remember me to tell Dad vacations is too long and I am ready to go home and I don't like camping. Fwank looks at Cheryl like Jed looks at Val like Dad looks at Mum, so I fink them is going to get a dog.

"My name is Abby Miller. Most of you already know that since you follow me. But some of you might be new because of the vids about the dog whose family I'm trying to find. He found his way to our farm while trying to find his way home. I hope some of you might be looking for him and can help reach out to his family. More in the comments."

Abby posted the video she'd taken of Tatum this afternoon. He'd been romping in the yard with Skipper and Rufus. He really liked to play.

She knew she didn't need to make the plea. Her dad had the number for Tatum's family in Bangor. But it felt like something to do while she waited for Tatum to go home.

Her followers were animal lovers or enjoyed learning about life on a farm. She didn't know why. It was a lot of work, though she supposed it was fun in a way. Animals were always fun. Plus there was so much room. So much privacy. She never felt crowded, or in anybody's way, except in the mornings when she needed a shower and Sarah wouldn't get out.

She would hate having neighbors who could see everything she was doing.

The winters weren't as much fun because that was when the work was the hardest. For one thing, they had to make sure the animals had water. She had to break the ice on Lucy's trough every morning before going to school. Sometimes again when she got home.

Same with the goats. Some of those videos got the most likes and comments. People were amazed at how hard it was to care for the goats year-round.

She put her phone on the charger and her backpack into the closet. She'd look at her homework tomorrow, though she thought it should be against the law to have homework over the weekend. Then she went downstairs. Tatum followed her, and she let him out through the back door. He caught sight of Skipper and Rufus and took off. They would make sure he didn't get in trouble, running too far or chasing the chickens or the goats.

He wasn't a farm dog, that was for sure. Skipper and Rufus knew to leave the animals alone unless they were herding the goats. They played with them sometimes. Especially the babies. But they never chased them to be mean. Abby thought the baby goats were the best part of the farm. She didn't think she'd ever in her life seen anything cuter.

"C'mon, Abs. This table isn't going to set itself."

"Coming, Mom." She looked out to where Tatum had stopped to say hi to Lucy. "See ya later, Tatum. Have to go earn my keep."

"I heard that," her mother said, but her voice was full of laughter.

Abby laughed too. She didn't mind helping in the house. Her mom did the work of ten moms really. Sarah was up in her room doing homework, but she had a lot more than Abby did. And Doug was outside doing chores with their dad. He didn't have practice on Fridays.

One thing Abby did wish they had was a dishwasher. Every

time she said that, her mother reminded her that they did, and her name was Abigail Grace. That always made Abby roll her eyes and Doug and Sarah laugh. But their dad was good to take up for her and tell them their hands could use some practice. Abby loved her dad so much. He was the best.

She was setting the forks next to the plates, her mother at the stove frying chicken, when she heard Sarah stomping from her room to the top of the stairs. Then she yelled down.

"Abby! Get up here! Your phone is going off like it's the end of the world or something!"

———※◆※———

Tatum was lying in the grass between the back porch and the fence that kept Lucy in her big pen. He had smelled the food in the kitchen and had come to wait with all his patience for his supper, but nobody was bringing out the bowls. He would probably have to wait forever.

Skipper was chasing bugs that came up from the ground when he ran through. Some were moths, Tatum knew. He almost got up to run after them too, but he was pretty tired since he hadn't had his supper yet. His leg felt okay. The Ginger girl with the cookies at the place he'd gone with Frank had looked at it and said it was perfect.

He rolled to his side and stretched out. The ground was cool. The grass tickled his nose and smelled like all the things that lived outside. Different things than he smelled when he was home.

His ears perked up at the sound of Lucy making snorting noises. Maybe she'd got a moth in her nose. He liked Lucy. He knew the big-attack storm had scared her too. And she'd run away to escape from it like he had. And Frank and Cheryl had found her and brought her home.

Maybe Frank and Cheryl would come back the next day and bring his mum and dad. Or maybe Jed and Dr. Valerie would drive to the farm and take him back to his house in Jed's truck.

Maybe if he lay in the grass for a very long time, his mum and dad would look for him on the farm and find him.

Maybe they were still looking for him by the store and the bushes where he'd tried to hide. It would probably just take them more time to get here. But he could wait.

Waiting to come home would be his job now. He'd be good at it. They'd see.

⟶·❖·⟵

"Great. Okay. Thank you. I look forward to hearing from you."

Abby's father hung up from his call and looked at her, then at Doug, Sarah, and their mom.

"Okay. All done," he said.

"Sweet!" Doug said.

"Awesome!" Sarah said.

"This is great news!" That was from their mom.

Abby didn't say anything. She didn't know what to say.

After Sarah had yelled about her phone, Abby had rushed upstairs to find like a gazillion new notifications. But one commenter had left a note about the news story. And the best part was they'd included all the specifics.

She'd nearly fallen down the stairs hurrying back to the kitchen. When she got there, her dad was sitting at the table with his laptop. Her mother was telling him to hurry up so Abby could finish setting the table. They'd both looked at her and asked what was wrong.

It had taken forever for her to tell them. She was laughing and crying, and then Doug and Sarah were there, and it had been like Christmas morning with all the craziness.

They'd all watched the story together on her dad's laptop. Then they'd backed it up and watched it again. Then they'd moved to the living room to sit while her dad had called the station, hoping they could get through to the Fraziers. He'd had no luck with the cell number he'd gotten from Frank, and he'd been unable to find a landline listing for them.

He didn't sit. He paced back and forth.

Abby was shaking so hard. She couldn't believe everything had finally worked out.

She wanted to call Cheryl and Frank and tell them, but asked, "What now?"

"They'll get in touch with Tatum's family, and I imagine we'll hear from them soon."

"You think they'll come pick him up right away?" Doug asked. He was sitting on the floor in front of Abby and smelled like he'd been rolling around with the chickens *and* the goats.

"Would you pick up Skipper or Rufus right away?" Sarah asked. She waved a hand in front of her face. "And you really stink. Could you maybe go do something about that?"

"How long will it take them to get here?" Abby asked. "From Bangor?"

"Not that long," Doug said. "Especially as fast as they'll probably drive."

"So tonight?" she asked, her voice shaky like she was about to cry.

Her dad walked over and sat beside her on the window seat. He wrapped an arm around her and kissed her forehead. "You've done a great thing here, Abs. You are the one who made this happen. I'm so proud of you. Be proud of yourself."

"I am, it's just . . . I really like him."

"He's a great dog," her mother said from where she stood in the doorway. "But he's not our dog."

"I know," she said, leaning her head against her dad's chest. It was dumb to be so sad. She should be happy, and excited. And she was. For Tatum.

"Is there a reward?" Doug asked.

"Douglas." It was all their mom said, but Doug shut up.

"If there is," her dad said, "it goes into Abby's college fund. She did the work, so it's only fair."

"I starred in one of the videos," Doug reminded them.

"Tatum was the star. You were an extra."

Sarah snorted at that. "You get to be the baseball star. Not the star of Abby's animal antics."

"You know," her mom said in that voice she used when she'd come to a smart conclusion, "that would be a really good name for a YouTube channel. School's almost out. Summer is the best time for videos. There's so much going on and lots of hours of sunlight."

"Your mom's right. You might make enough money to help with school in a few years."

"This is what I was talking about. The extracurricular activity you need," Sarah said. "It's educational. Schools will love that. And if you start now, think how many episodes and subscribers you'd have to list on your applications."

Abby felt like she was riding a Tilt-A-Whirl. She was dizzy and out of breath and hardly able to hold back the excitement. And all of that on top of being sad and happy about Tatum.

She had so much to do. "I need to start an episode calendar. I'm not sure I've got the right equipment for editing though. I can do some, but I'm not very professional."

"Maybe if there's a reward that's what you could use it for," Doug said as he got to his feet. "A MacBook."

"I doubt a reward would be that much, but sure," her dad said. "It would still be an investment in your education. If you're set on being a vet."

She nodded, her head bouncing, all of her bouncing.

And she would have Tatum to thank for every bit of it.

"I need to finish up supper," her mother said, turning for the kitchen. "Doug, you've got time to shower—"

The ring of her dad's phone cut through the room. Everyone

went still and quiet, the only noise that of Tatum, Rufus, and Skipper barking outside as they played.

Her dad put the phone on speaker and answered. "Hello?"

"Mr. Miller?"

"Speaking."

"My name is Charles Frazier. I think you found my dog. His name is Tatum."

Her dad grinned, looking from their mom to Doug, to Sarah, and finally to Abby. His grin took over his whole face. He looked ten years younger than he was. "Yes, Charles. He's here with us, safe and sound and waiting to get back home."

The sound of a woman crying came over the phone. And when Charles spoke again, his voice cracked. "Can we come get him tonight? How long is the drive, do you know? I'm sorry. I could look that up—"

"It's okay," Abby's dad told him. "Depending on how fast you drive—"

"As fast as I can get away with," he said with a laugh.

"Then I'd say four hours. That's about how much daylight you've got left."

"We'll be there."

"We'll leave a light on. Even if you don't need it."

Chapter 37

Okay, diary, please dial face time for my dad cuz I am ready to go home. Mum doesn't like to sleep wifout me in the bed and Dad says I always am standing right where he needs to go so nobuddy is standing for Dad. Vacation too long. Fank you.

It took forever to drive from Bangor to the Miller farm near Mayville and Shireton. The longer Charles and Nicole drove in silence, the harder and harder it became to believe Tatum had made this trip in the open bed of a pickup during a raging storm.

There was still evidence of the storm's strength along the highway. The more densely populated areas had cleaned up all but some of the larger trees, but the parts left to the local counties to clear away would take a bit longer.

What would've happened to Tatum if he'd jumped from the back of Jed Allen's truck in the middle of nowhere? If the rain had lightened up and Jed had slowed down or stopped for gas and Tatum had felt safe enough to try to find his way home?

"You okay?" Nicole's concerned tone mirrored that of Charles's thoughts.

He wasn't even aware he'd shuddered until he felt her hand on his arm. "Just thinking about all the ways this could've gone wrong."

"That's not a very productive use of your time, you know." She reached up to rub his neck. "We're almost there, and we'll have him back, and we won't ever let him out of our sight again."

"You got that right." Charles was still having a lot of trouble forgiving himself, but he knew that wasn't productive either. They were almost at the end of this nightmare. He needed to let the worry go. Tatum was safe. He was being taken care of. Nothing had happened to him.

That didn't mean Charles wasn't dying to know everything Tatum had been through.

Hopefully the Miller family could fill in him and Nicole on how Tatum had gotten from the farm supply store all the way to their farm. How had he gotten out of the woods? Had he done so on his own? Had he had help? What had he eaten while out there—

"This looks like the place," Nicole said, pointing toward a big red barn.

Charles slowed for the turn ahead. His hands were shaking. His heart was pounding. There was a big silver mailbox near the entrance. On the side in blocky black letters was printed the name: MILLER.

"I can't believe how nervous I am," Nicole said, sitting straighter to look around. "My stomach just did a gold-medal flip."

Charles didn't say anything as he made the turn, gravel crunching under the car's tires. He didn't say anything because he couldn't. His fingers felt as if they'd melted to the wheel, his grip was so tight. His throat was tighter. His chest the tightest of all.

Slowly, he drove the long driveway toward the house. It was a storybook-style two-story, white with black shutters and a covered wraparound porch. A swing hung to the left of the front door. Off behind the house was a fenced paddock with a beautiful gray horse. To the side of that was a pasture with what he thought were goats.

"Are those goats?" Nicole asked.

"Think so," he said. "And that looks like a pen of chickens."

"I'll bet Tatum's been having a ball."

Charles nodded, wondering where everyone was. He parked and shut off the engine. He got out and rounded the car. Nicole did the same, and they both stood in silence, taking in their surroundings. The sun was nearly out of sight, the sky a darkening indigo, cloudless.

Then movement in the distance caught his eye. A big dog speeding toward them, and two others right on its heels. One was black and white. And one was . . .

"Tatum!" Charles took off, running full blast toward the three dogs.

Tatum was barking now, running faster, passing the other two dogs as if they didn't exist. As if nothing in the world was as fast as he was. As if there was no possible way anything was going to keep him from his dad.

"Tatum!" Charles yelled again, waving.

Behind him, Nicole called out too.

In moments, he was there and Tatum leaped into the air, his legs still running as he landed on Charles's chest and took him to the ground.

Nicole skidded on her knees, stopping beside them, wrapping her arms around Tatum's neck while he bathed her face in slobber. She laughed. Charles laughed.

And then he heard other laughter and the pounding of running steps. He sat up, not quite ready to stand and let Tatum out of his lap.

He was never going to let him out of his sight again.

"I'd ask if you're Charles and Nicole, but Tatum pretty much answered that for me."

It was the man Charles had spoken to on the phone, Randall Miller. Charles lifted his hand and offered it to the other man. "Yes. Charles Frazier. This is Nicole. And I'm not sure I have breath for more at the moment."

"That's okay," Randall said, laughing as Charles collapsed onto his back, the grass soft beneath him, Tatum's weight such a welcome feeling. He was never going to complain about him eating too much again.

"These are our dogs, Skipper and Rufus. They've been showing Tatum the ropes and keeping him out of trouble. And by out of trouble I mean away from the chickens."

Nicole stood, dusting off her jeans. "There's no way we can ever thank you enough for taking him in."

"Other than the stitches in his leg there, he's in good shape. You can thank Cheryl Stratton for getting him out of the woods in one piece. Frank Ouelette too. Not sure how he got this far from Bangor."

"I can't wait to meet everyone involved in this reunion. I don't even know who Cheryl and Frank are. I have so many questions. We want to know everything."

"Well, let me introduce you to Abigail, our daughter," Randall said as a young teen walked up to his side. "Abby's social media accounts helped with all of this."

"Only a little bit," she said. "We saw the news story and found you that way."

"Thank you, Abby," Charles said, his arms still around Tatum, whose tongue was hanging nearly to his chest as he panted. "After we talked to your dad, we looked up your TikTok and IG and saw your photos. Well, Nicole looked while I was driving."

"It takes a village," said the woman who'd walked up on the other side of Abby. "I'm Helen Miller. And if Tatum will let you up, I've got a late supper waiting. And don't even try to object. I have to cook for this bunch anyway so just whipped up a little bit more."

"Thank you, Helen," Nicole said. "Honestly, neither one of us has eaten much of anything all week."

"Well, Tatum hasn't missed a meal. And now he's a big fan of cantaloupe and zucchini. You may need to add those to your shopping list."

"Anything he wants," Charles said, nuzzling his face to Tatum's. He didn't even bother to wipe the tears from his eyes. He just let them fall. "Anything he wants."

THREE MONTHS LATER . . .

CHAPTER 38

Abby wasn't sure there'd ever been a day in her life when she'd been as happy and excited. Maybe when she was little and had been waiting for Christmas morning. Or maybe the day her dad had brought Lucy home for the first time and she finally had a horse.

Every year, the last day of school was pretty fun, but that didn't last long. She still had to get up early, though not quite so, and she still had reading to do over summer break. She didn't mind that because she loved to read. But she did wonder what it would be like to have a vacation. A real vacation. The entire family. To go somewhere they'd never been.

Hawaii. Or the Grand Canyon. Or Yellowstone. Those all sounded like fun. They did spend a couple of days each summer at the coast, but they couldn't be gone long because her mom had the cheese and the vegetables to look after, and her dad had everything else. Even with friends stopping in to feed the animals, the rest of the work couldn't be put on hold for long.

But that day had been the best Labor Day ever. It had been amazing in so many ways. It still was. She never wanted it to end. Everyone who'd been involved in getting Tatum back to his family had come to the farm for a cookout. She couldn't remember ever having so many people on the farm at once. At least people who weren't family, or hadn't come to work.

Jed and Dr. Warren had brought Jed's new dog, Guy. He was a rescue dog that someone had found and left with Warren Veterinary. Jed said Tatum had made him realize how much he missed having a dog, so he'd adopted him. Abby had never met Jed, but that made her want to cry and hug him. And then he'd told her how much he appreciated her getting Tatum home, and he'd cried a bit because he'd been the one to lose him after taking him away.

They'd ended up hugging and crying, and Abby didn't feel bad about it at all. It was like hugging Santa Claus. Jed was big and round and Abby thought a jolly good fellow. She was so happy that Tatum had changed his life. That thought had her eyes filling with tears again, and she looked up from the picnic table where she sat to where Tatum lay at Charles's feet.

Or he laid there until Rufus and Guy ran past him at like a hundred miles an hour. He took off after them but lagged behind the whole way to the barn. Abby wasn't sure she'd ever seen a dog run as fast as Rufus, but Guy was crazy fast. She supposed that's what happened when two border collies raced. Skipper had stopped trying to keep up and had fallen asleep under the table after sniffing out all the scraps that had fallen.

Dr. Warren had answered all of Abby's questions about being a veterinarian, and had asked Abby quite a few of her own, things Abby hadn't known enough to consider. But now she did, and she had almost as many notes on her phone as she did pictures. Thanks to Tatum. He might not have wanted to be away from home, but he'd met Dr. Warren and brought her into Abby's life. She was so happy to have her as a resource.

Frank and Cheryl had brought Cheryl's mother, Betsy. She reminded Abby of an English teacher she'd once had, very proper, very smart, and always challenging Abby, Sarah, and Doug with questions about what she thought they should know. There had been so much talk of books while everyone had eaten. Abby had loved that. Frank too.

She didn't think she'd ever met anyone who loved books more than she did. And knew so much about them. About the authors too. Frank would've made a great teacher, she thought. She wondered if he'd ever wanted to be one. She had his number and knew where to find him on social media. Maybe she'd leave him a comment on one of his book posts and ask.

Charles and Nicole, of course, had brought Tatum. They were going to spend the night since they had the longest drive home. Her mom was showing the garden to Valerie, Nicole, and Betsy. Cheryl had seen it before but she had gone with them, her arm hooked through her mother's. Abby didn't know what had gone on with them, but they seemed great now.

Her dad had taken Charles, Jed, and Frank to the barn. Abby had no idea what they were doing—maybe watching Doug do chores. School started in another week, and her brother already had preseason practice, but he was off that day because of the holiday. Sarah too. Sarah had spent most of the summer tutoring incoming students, but she had helped Abby and their mom get things ready for their guests. Abby thought her sister had been as excited as she was.

Abby's siblings had a lot going for them with their extracurricular activities. It would all look good on their college applications. Just like the pictures and videos she'd taken of the day would look good on hers. Or her social media outreach would, as soon as she got it off the ground.

She'd done a lot over the summer but had been limited by her equipment. She'd upgrade everything as soon as she could. Her parents had promised her they'd cut all possible corners to make it happen. She felt guilty about that. The family's corners were already pretty round.

It might take longer to reach her goal than she'd hoped. She could get in most of her basic classes at community college, and that would add another couple of years to her online footprint.

It would work out. She was absolutely sure of it.

Dr. Abigail Miller would not be stopped!

———❖———

u still @ the table
ya why
stay there coming down

Abby couldn't imagine where her sister thought she might have gone, or what Sarah might want, but she knew she was going to need to help clean up the leftovers and get them inside pretty soon. Maybe that was it. Sarah making sure she wouldn't have to do it all herself.

Doug and her dad had moved the family's two tables together and used plywood and sawhorses to set up a third for the food. It had still been pretty crowded, so Doug and Frank had grabbed chairs off the back porch and sat in those. It worked out since they were the two who kept getting up to refill their plates like they hadn't eaten a meal in days.

Everything had been covered up to make sure it stayed clean, but people kept stopping by to snitch bites of things. She guessed that was the way of cookouts. And why at the end of the day everyone complained about being miserably full.

Abby had been too excited to eat much but had been grabbing cucumber slices while sitting there, looking through the day's photos and vids, deciding which ones to post later that night. She wanted to do a special holiday and Tatum reunion series. She had thousands of new followers on TikTok and Instagram and knew they'd love to share Tatum's day.

Sarah didn't say anything when she got there a few minutes later but moved aside several dishes to clear a space in front of Abby. "What are you doing?"

"Just cleaning up a bit."

"Like without being asked to? That's a miracle."

Sarah shrugged, and Doug came up a few seconds later. He reached for a clean paper plate and dished up a helping of baked beans, then sat beside Abby to eat, moving more of the dishes to the side before shoveling the beans into his mouth.

"Remind me to stay downwind," Sarah said, and Abby snorted a laugh.

A moment later, Tatum ran by, followed by the other three dogs. Those four were seriously going to sleep good, Abby thought, as a shadow fell over her from behind. Charles walked around the table to sit across from her. He had a big box in his hands and set it between them. Something in Abby's stomach started tumbling around.

Whatever was going on, Sarah knew. Doug knew. And now Nicole was standing at Charles's side, Jed and Dr. Warren had come up too, as had Betsy and Cheryl and Frank. Abby felt her father's hand come down on her shoulder, and suddenly felt surrounded. But not in a bad way. Just a very nervous way. And she was pretty sure whatever was coming was all about Tatum.

Charles cleared his throat. "Abby, Nicole and I owe you more than we can ever repay. You gave us back the missing piece of our family—"

"I really didn't do anything. Jed and Cheryl did more than I did," Abby said, and Jed gave a loud guffaw.

"All I did was lose the little fella after taking him hundreds of miles from home." He shook his head as if he couldn't believe his part in Tatum's adventure.

"You took great care of him," Nicole was quick to say to Jed. "And you kept him safe. You didn't take him away on purpose. We don't blame you for anything."

"We don't," Charles assured him, echoing Nicole's words. "We never will. I started it all by leaving my door open—"

"Okay, you two," Dr. Warren said, laughing. "We're not here

to play the blame game. Tatum's back where he belongs. That's all that matters."

"And he wouldn't be if Cheryl and Frank hadn't gotten him out of the woods," Abby said. She was just the final helping hand on Tatum's journey. "All I did was post to social media."

"And that's how the connection was made. The networking, your networking got Tatum home, especially since Cheryl wasn't able to reach us," Charles said, his expression grateful and serious in a way that made her uncomfortable.

Her stomach was really going nuts now, like a thousand butterflies and grasshoppers were fluttering around. She hated being the center of attention. At least in person. Probably why she'd taken to social media so quickly and completely. She was able to stay behind the scenes.

Charles laid both hands on the box between them. "Your parents told us about your dream to be a veterinarian, and how you plan to use your social media channels to finance as much of your education as you can."

Abby nodded. "It's probably going to take a while. I was just thinking earlier I might take some of my basic required courses at community college while I continue to save."

Her dad squeezed her shoulder. "That's a great plan, but you've got four years of high school ahead of you. That's four years of putting social media to work."

She nodded. She supposed it was okay that everyone wanted to thank her. And with everyone knowing about her plans, she'd probably get some great ideas for reaching her goal.

"Abby," Nicole said, standing behind Charles, both of her hands on his shoulders, "Charles and I want to help you make the most of your journey as a social media influencer. Jed and Valerie do too, as well as Frank and Cheryl, and Betsy."

Abby didn't even really know Betsy. Why would she want to

help? Maybe because Tatum helped her and Cheryl get reunited? It hit her then. Wow. Tatum really had helped everyone he'd traveled with on his journey home. "You don't have to—"

"We want to," Jed said. "Val and I have been talking, trying to figure out what we can do and . . . I'll let Val tell you the rest."

"As soon as you're able, I want you to come work for me. I know it will be a couple of years, and even if I retire before then, you'll have a place at Warren Veterinary. I figure you might only be able to make it over on weekends during the school year, but maybe during the summer you can fit in a couple of weekdays. If it's okay with your parents."

"It is absolutely okay with her parents," Abby's mom said from somewhere behind her. She hadn't known she was there, and hearing tears in her mother's voice made her own eyes well up and her throat tighten.

"Thank you," she said to Dr. Warren. "That is the best news ever. And the perfect part-time job. You don't even have to pay me—"

"Oh, we'll pay you," Jed said with a boisterous laugh. "We've talked about that too. It's a gift from both of us. Val just happens to have the clinic."

"And any book you need for school is on me," Frank said before Abby could respond. "Any book you need for personal research reasons. Animal husbandry, social media, anything. Any book at all. And bookcases to hold them all."

"And a desk," Cheryl added. "Mom and I will set you up with a desk and a chair. And if you want to paint the bookcases, make them fit your personality, we'll make sure you have everything you need. Our gift. Our thank-you."

Abby's head was spinning. She was overwhelmed. Her dreams were all coming true. There was just one big problem. "I don't have room for all of that."

"You do now," her dad said, coming around the end of the

table so she could see him and her mom, who came along and hooked her arm through his. "Mom and I have decided to turn one of the guest rooms into your office, since you'll be doing more than schoolwork at home."

Abby couldn't even think of anything to say. She was afraid if she did she'd wake up. That none of this was really happening. That she was imagining it all. But then at her side, Doug nudged her shoulder with his and whistled before saying, "Nice!"

Charles then pushed the box toward her. "This is for you. From me and Nicole and Tatum."

Abby wanted to take the box up to her room and look inside without an audience. Her hands were shaking as she pocketed her phone and stood up, stepping to the end of the table to lift away the top of the box. She looked inside. She looked at Charles. She looked at her dad.

Then she buried her face against the box top and cried.

"Oh, Abs! This is amazing!" Sarah said.

"No kidding," Doug added, having moved closer and crowding her.

Nicole came to her side and wrapped an arm around her shoulder. "I hope, we hope, this gives you every advantage you need."

"Oh, it will," she said, looking down again at the brand-new MacBook still in its original packaging, along with all the camera equipment she would ever need. "Thank you so much. Thank you both. I can't say thank you enough. Thank you. Thank you. Thank you."

"You're so very welcome," Nicole said, giving her a hug.

Then Abby's mother was there, giving her a hug. Then her dad and Cheryl and Jed, and then Tatum sat at her feet and barked.

Everyone laughed at that, and Abby dropped to her knees and wrapped her arms around him. He stood on his hind legs and put his front paws on her shoulders, hugging her back. He was warm and he smelled like grass and hot dog skin, and his breath was warm on her neck as he panted against her. She loved this dog so much. He was her good luck charm.

And in that moment Abby knew there had never been a better day in the history of her life.

And in that moment Abby knew there had never been a better day in the history of her life.

Jed and Dr. Warren left shortly after that. Abby had shown Jed how to find her on Instagram since he said he was more a fan of photos than vids. Hard on his eyes to follow, he'd told her. Perils of getting old. She promised to post every day so they could keep in touch on social media. He promised to post pictures of the animals he met during his volunteer work. Maybe he'd be able to help get some of them home.

Cheryl, Betsy, and Frank followed soon, though not until Frank had finished eating another plate of Abby's mom's roasted vegetables. Abby had to admit they were delicious. Especially the squash. Her mom had sent him home with a bag of fresh ones to enjoy later. They had squash coming out of their ears. Since he wasn't much of a cook, Betsy had taken them off his hands and promised to serve them up right.

Nicole had helped her mom feed the dogs before they'd gone upstairs to see the guest room. Sarah and Abby had done most of the food cleanup. Charles had helped her dad and Doug return the tables, plywood, and sawhorses to where they belonged.

Now Abby was sitting on the back steps thinking about having an office of her own. A desk and a chair and bookcases full of books. And the ability to edit her videos like a pro. She was a pro, and like her dad had said, she had four years to make social media work to fund her college education. With all this help, how could she fail?

Of course that question started all the doubt butterflies fluttering again. Even with all of Frank's books to teach her, and the MacBook to turn her videos into works of art, there was so much she didn't know how to do with her accounts. Or where to find that kind of help.

The sound of footsteps had her turning her gaze away from the chickens to the barn. Charles was walking toward her, Tatum at his side. He raised his hand, and she waved in return. It was so good to see him with Tatum, who hadn't stopped smiling all day.

"Mind if I join you?"

She shook her head. "I don't mind."

She didn't know how old he was. She thought older than Frank but younger than her dad. She'd watched a lot of TikToks, and it was so strange that Tatum didn't talk in real life.

"Can I ask you a question?"

"Anything," he said as he sat beside her.

"How did you come up with Tatum's voice?"

Charles laughed softly. "It just came out. I don't even know how or why. When we brought him home, Nicole would talk to him, and I would have him talk back."

"So you didn't make it up for social media?" she asked, and he shook his head.

"It was already a part of him, but it worked great for TikTok. Dog lovers get it, you know? The silly things we do with our pets. Things just took off, and a TikTok star was born."

She'd spent hours on Tatum's TikTok over the summer. She'd had no idea how famous Tatum was. It was wild to realize she'd played a part, even a small one, in reuniting a celebrity with his family. They were all so nice, and so normal, just real people, not at all what she'd expected once she'd found out how popular Tatum was.

"That's pretty amazing," she said, filled with questions but unable to put any of them into words. They all tumbled together and she couldn't find a place to start. "I love his TikTok."

"You've got a great start on yours. Nicole and I both love it."

She'd been so embarrassed at first to know Charles and Nicole followed her. It was easier to be anonymous. She kinda liked being anonymous, but she supposed she needed to get used to being known since her social media was no longer just a hobby. "Thanks for commenting on it. And all the tagging. I think it's helped grow my followers over the summer."

"Maybe, but you've been posting some great content."

"I'm afraid I won't be able to keep it up now that school's starting again."

Charles leaned forward, motioning for Tatum. He came up to sit on the step between Charles's feet, and he rubbed a hand over his head while he talked. "When I started Tatum Talks, I just posted whenever and whatever. It's turned out okay, but I wonder if we might've been even more successful if I'd gone into it with a plan."

"So I need a plan."

"I think since you have a specific goal you want to accomplish, that it might be a good idea. I mean, there are thousands of content creators who do what they do for fun. And that's great. What you've done so far is amazing. But going forward, it's probably worth thinking about."

"Maybe Frank could help me find a book," she said. "Something about best practices for content creators."

"Great idea. You'll learn quickly what type of content appeals to the most people. And you'll gain followers that way," he said, leaning to nuzzle his nose to Tatum's. "Just don't forget the most important thing about content creation: followers want authenticity and can tell immediately when you aren't your authentic self. You already do that, which resonates with your fans, so don't ever lose sight of that." He let that settle, then asked, "Want to go set up the MacBook?"

"Oh! Yes! That would be great," she said, getting to her feet.

Charles stood too. "And I'll supply all the software you need. We can talk it through when you find yourself ready. You also have my number, so please don't hesitate to text or call me with questions. I'll be happy to share any and all of what I've learned.

Remember, I had to make it up as I went along, and learn the hard way. Us content creators gotta stick together, right?"

"I don't know how to thank you," she said, stopping with her hand on the door, her voice trembling. "This is way too much. I did so little."

"You did so much more than you realize," he told her, his voice nearly breaking too. "You put our broken family back together."

CHAPTER 39

It was pretty crazy to think that a dog could leave home with his dad for a trip to the store and end up going all over the world and making bunches of new friends. People friends, like Jed and Cheryl and Abby, and animal friends like Lucy and Skipper and the goat named Wyatt. Who knew there were so many animals who had great mums and dads like he did?

Tatum was happy to know Jed had a new dog named Guy. He hoped Cheryl got her own dog soon. Abby had more animals than most people he'd met in his life, and he thought that was pretty great. They all made her super happy. And he knew she made them happy too. Because she made him happy.

It was also great that he'd seen so many fences everywhere he'd gone. Fences kept animals safe at home with their families. He would never go out of his fence alone. Not ever.

Tatum lay on his back staring up at the sky, his paws in the air as he twisted side to side and scratched. Not because he had fleas but it just felt so good to scratch on his own grass. He could hear his dad and mum talking. He could hear all the sounds of his house. He could hear the other dogs who lived close barking, and the birds he knew chirping in the trees.

There wasn't any wind. There wasn't any rain. There was no

storm attacking him with sharp, stabbing lightning and thunder bombs. There were just all the things he loved right there making life perfect. And there was . . .

He stopped twisting and rolled up to sit, shaking off the left-over grass, lifting his nose to sniff the air.

Was that . . . gravy?

"Tatum! Time to eat!"

Yes! It had to be gravy! Gravy made everything in the world so much better.

And that was the truth.

Look for the next book in the Dog Agency series, featuring
Ducky the Yorkie!

Follow Ducky @duckytheyorkie on Instagram, TikTok,
Facebook and YouTube to learn more.

Photo courtesty of Christine Hsu

Coming soon!

Visit our website at
KensingtonBooks.com
to sign up for our newsletters, read
more from your favorite authors, see
books by series, view reading group
guides, and more!

BOOK CLUB
BETWEEN THE CHAPTERS

Become a Part of Our
Between the Chapters Book Club
Community and Join the Conversation

Betweenthechapters.net

Submit your book review for a chance to win exclusive
Between the Chapters swag you can't get anywhere else!
https://www.kensingtonbooks.com/pages/review/